A Kiss for Christmas

ROD FLEMING

Published in 2015 by PlashMill Press, Friockheim, Scotland.

ISBN:978-0-9572612-0-4

Also by Rod Fleming:

Poaching the River	978-0-9554535-0-2
The Spring Run	978-0-9572612-5-9
French Onion Soup!	978-0-9565007-3-1
Croutons and Cheese!	978-0-9572612-4-2
The Children of Aldebaran	978-0-9572612-1-1
A Little Shop of Horrors	978-0-9565007-8-6
The Warm Pink Jelly Express Train	978-0-9572612-3-5
Fifty-Two of the Best	978-0-9572612-6-6
Why Men Made God	978-0-9572612-2-8

Follow me at Rod Fleming's World
http://rodfleming.com

Visit my Amazon Author Page at:
https://www.amazon.com/author/rodfleming

Contents

One

Decenber 24th, 1981. Christmas Eve; Paris, France.

Don't you want me baby? Don't you want me oh?

At least this Christmas, the chart-topping hit was a decent tune, I reflected. 1981. It had been a strange year. Here in France, dissatisfaction with the catastrophic economic situation and Giscard d'Estaing's patrician condescension, had swung the voters. In May, they had elected Francois Mitterand as President of the Republic, the first Socialist to hold the post. Giscard blamed Chirac, who had refused to back him. The French Right was headed for internecine warfare. The French were jubilant; they believed it was the dawn of a new tomorrow.

Back in the UK, Margaret Thatcher's government, elected two years before, had hit a banana-skin and her austerity measures had sent her poll ratings through the floor. But in a weird mirror-image of the situation in France, the Left in UK politics, aka the Labour Party, had fallen apart and looked incapable of forming a government.

In the USA, Ronald Reagan had become the 40th President and within weeks of taking office, had already survived an assassination attempt. He had seriously alarmed the military-industrial establishment with public criticism of the nuclear defence policy called Mutually Assured Destruction, or MAD for short. It was one of the most apt acronyms in history. Building nukes was big business, though. And those with their snouts in the trough expected it to be kept full.

In the USSR, the Eleventh Five-Year Plan had been launched, to public fanfare. Personally, I thought it had about as much chance of success as the first ten, but then, no-one was asking me, not any more, anyway. Many others saw things differently: perhaps control economies really could deliver the goods…and we might just overlook all that stuff about the Gulags. Meanwhile the West's relations with China continued a painfully slow, but inexorable, thaw.

In Europe, the Union was years away, still a dream. The European Economic Community had, however, established itself as the only serious player on the continent. Germany remained divided, The Berlin

Wall was intact and the Cold War was, very much, still sub-zero. Huge numbers of NATO troops were stationed along the Rhine. That was our line in the sand; if the Red Army ever got that far, we would go nuclear. Which made even West Germany a sacrificial lamb.

I was working as a waitress in a cocktail bar,
That much is true

Life had changed. The carefree days of the '70s, which had their birth in that incredible summer of '68, were but a fond memory. For a whole decade, inflation was allowed to run rampant, interest rates were suppressed and employment levels held up, by governments everywhere. Now came the hangover as the rates skyrocketed and unemployment devastated cities and even whole regions, while inflation remained resolutely high. The West lurched into economic recession.

I nodded. Working in a cocktail bar? Many were lucky to have that, these days.

A miserable Christmas it may have been; it certainly was a cold and wet one. I really wished that Harry Jonsun could for once have been on time, so I could go home and see my wife and children. The kids at least I did actually want to see. But it was pissing down stair-rods and Harry was Harry. He was probably parked up somewhere getting his dick sucked by some under-age tart only too happy to get out of the rain.

Don't, don't you want me?
You know I can't believe it
When you say that you won't see me

The jukebox was crackly and the needle needed changing, but at least inside this little bar it was warm and cosy and since the owner was a Jew, not excessively festive. I liked that.

I rubbed a clear spot on the condensation-hazed window. My God what a filthy night for Christmas Eve! No wonder there was no-one around. Clichy at this season is usually bustling but this wasn't a night for a dog to be out. Everybody must be home or indoors, I reflected. This certainly wasn't going to help the takings.

Harry is – was – a show-off. He just can't do anything the way reasonable people do. So, while every other criminal of elevated status in Paris ponced around in a Merc or a DS like a normal crook, he had to drive a fucking ZiL. Which, in case you don't know, is the favoured transport of senior Soviet apparatchiks and other Politburo types. Like everything Russian, they're built like tanks, massively unreliable and utterly drop-dead gorgeous. A paean to glamorous inefficiency, all silk purse and no knickers. What a system.

Then I saw it, sweeping into the square outside the bar, its tyres splashing spray under the streetlights, like a Zeppelin on wheels. All jet black paint and chrome, there was not another vehicle in Paris like it. It pulled up across the street and the lights flashed off, on and off again. Even without that I knew it was Harry. No one else west of the Urals has a car like that. How he got his sweaty Dutch hands on it was a mystery.

I nodded to the bartender, who was polishing glasses with a bored expression. I tried to convey that I wasn't doing a runner and would be back to pay my tab, but he, who was about twenty, didn't look as if he cared. Probably fed up working on Christmas Eve, looking forward to getting off shift and going for a drink himself. He made a completely non-committal shrug back and I ran out into the street. Jesus the rain! It was only twenty yards but I was soaked half-way there. I flung open the ZiL's door and sat down in the passenger seat beside Harry. It reminded me of the opulent leather armchairs in the Services Club.

They do make a nice motor, those Russkis, you have to admit. Apparently the ZiL was originally based on the American Packard, but something was definitely gained in translation, if only sheer scale. The damn thing was huge; the basso-profundo rumble of its V8 let you know there was some real muscle under the bonnet. Mark you, it would need it; Harry's was the armoured version and weighed nearly four tonnes.

Harry Jonsun was short, fat, balding and wore a goatee beard that made him look like Mephistopheles. I kid you not. Maybe it explained the car and the ludicrously expensive Italian suits. I kept telling him to buy French cut, 'cause at least they leave room for lunch. He needed it.

He called himself a general businessman, which is just another way of saying if you wanted it badly enough, he would sell it to you: girls, boys, guns, gemstones, cars, tanks, politicians, anything really.

Only one rule: no questions. Well, two: cash up front.

Of course, the flipside of that coin was that Harry was also the biggest fence in town. Lorry-load of VCRs to sell? He was your man. Oh, he was careful all right. He only bought the best and you needed a personal introduction to meet him. No one knew where he lived, or even if he had a wife, although there was plenty speculation. All they ever saw was that car. Jonsun didn't deal with the low-lifes who burgled apartments for drug-money. He liked a classier kind of crook, a more discreet one. But I already knew that what I had would interest him. That was why he was here.

He smiled at me and I could smell the garlic even at that range. For some bizarre reason, Harry actually seemed to like me. Lord knows I didn't encourage this, but he did.

"You could have parked closer," I complained.

"Sorry, Johnny. You know I have to be careful. Anyway, what's a little rain between friends?" He chuckled. "You'll dry out. Here. You like guns, don't you? What do you think of this?"

He reached into a glove-box and pulled out a pistol. My reflexes came on razor edge instantly. Harry was smiling though. He passed it to me, butt first. Sensible.

I examined the piece. It was a Luger, 9mm. Gold plated, with ivory grips. Inlaid into one was an insignia I recognised at once: Deutsche Luftstreitkräfte. I worked the action and popped the clip. It was full. The breech was smooth and slick, not worn at all; but it had been looked after, by someone who knew how to.

The design of the Luger's breech is very unusual. It's based on the human knee; strong enough to take a huge load, like the weight of someone running, or the pressure of a shot being fired, while straight, but flexing easily once bent. Elegant and complicated at the same time; but then, maybe I like my guns the way I like my women. But that elegant complexity makes it expensive and harder to maintain than the simpler Browning pattern. Like women.

I hefted the pistol. It felt comfortable. You know sometimes a gun just speaks to you. This one was positively affable. It felt like it had been tailor-made to fit. "Nice. Unusual, gold Lugers."

"Heh, more than you think. That was Hermann Goering's pistol."

I let out a low whistle. The personal sidearms of senior Nazis had become rather desirable. This particular gun, if it wasn't a fake, was the most famous of all. But there are many fakes.

"Hmm." I passed it back. It certainly had all the hallmarks of a pistol that had once belonged to a WW1 fighter ace. "Serials check out?"

"Of course. Goering received it in 1918 when he was awarded the Blue Max. The Germans being German, they recorded everything. And I have an affidavit from his batman. Goering gave him the gun before he surrendered to the Americans in '45. The poor man has cancer." Harry shrugged. He didn't give a shit about the batman, or his cancer.

"Anyway," I said, changing the subject. "Much as I enjoy your company, Harry, I don't have all night." I slipped my wallet out of my jacket pocket and took out a small paper packet. Harry reached out a pudgy hand.

"Uncut diamonds," I said.

"Provenance?"

"My arse? It's all right, they were in a condom."

"I didn't need to know that, Johnny." He wasn't being delicate – he didn't know how. He just didn't like to hear potentially incriminating details, which is why I told him. He pulled a jeweller's loupe from his waistcoat pocket, adjusted the ZiL's map-light and began examining the stones. When he'd done, he looked at me, sucked a tooth and nodded. "What can you tell me?"

"Bought them from a Syrian jewel trader while I was waiting to be paid." I shrugged, "He was light on background."

Harry nodded again. "Probably blood diamonds. They're getting more common these days." He gestured. "It's all right, I can have them laundered. Once they're cut and certified, well, that's that. A diamond's a diamond. But it lessens the value."

Like I didn't know. "How much?"

"Ten briques."

I shook my head. "Give me them back."

"Okay, okay. Twelve."

I still held out my hand. "Johnny, times are hard, you know…Tell you what. Twelve and the Luger, that's the best I can do."

I relaxed and cursed myself for it. The piece was worth ten thousand, maybe fifteen. Still light. I nodded. "Twelve and a half, the Luger, the letters and the Blue Max."

Harry looked hurt. When he complained, "Who said anything about the Blue Max?" I knew right away that he had it.

"Don't give me that. I don't know what pittance you paid the poor old sod, but you got both and cheap." Military history is an interest of mine; in fact I used the cover of War Correspondent regularly. I'd interviewed General Stack, the American who captured Goering, years before. Of course the famous gold Luger had come up, since we were both gun collectors.

"Goering was taken with a standard service Walther and his Iron Cross; no Max and no fancy Luger. Christ, do you think the Yanks would have kept quiet about it? Everyone thought he'd ditched them, but now it seems he passed them along to his loyal batman. And if I'm going for this I want both. You might be the biggest fence in Paris, but you're not the only one. Levy will always take diamonds and I have plenty of guns."

"Levy?" Harry raised his eyebrows. "That kike?" His tone was reproachful.

"I like Jews. And money."

Suddenly Harry chuckled and I knew I'd been had, but I would still get the asking. The diamonds were worth at least twenty-five briques: that's two hundred and fifty thousand new francs, twenty-five million old ones. The piece along with the medal and the letters made Harry's offer worth around twenty, give or take. He was getting a bargain, especially as he'd have picked up the Goering stuff for sweeties. But then, I got the diamonds cheap too. He knew that.

"Ah, Johnny, you were always so much smarter than me." He reached under his seat and I stiffened again; I could have broken his neck without twisting in my seat. He knew that too. He pulled out a slim, walnut box and turned a tiny key in the lock. Inside the plush lining there was a hollow, perfectly formed to take a Luger, some papers, a couple of spare clips and the gong, all azure blue and gold. The case had that old smell but wasn't moth-eaten or worn. Harry slipped the piece into its place and held it so I could see, then closed the lid with a faint smile. "Deal?"

The difference between me and Harry is I have a weakness for beauty, even if my idea of it is a bit unusual; his only weakness is for cash. He was already computing what he could get for the diamonds once he'd laundered them, while I was visualising that Luger in my display cabinet. We both knew I wanted it.

"Deal," I agreed. What the hell? I'd worn a Frenchie full of diamonds up my arse from Damascus to Paris, but so what? Anyway it was Christmas, I was still turning a healthy profit just on the cash. Besides, I really couldn't be annoyed tracking Levy down in that weather. I've done worse.

Harry nodded and reached into the recesses of the dash.

I waited while he counted out thousand-franc notes from a huge roll; I had often wondered how it was that he could have been so blasé, carrying so much cash, even if his armoured ZiL was bullet-proof. He never travelled with a bodyguard either. But the answer was obvious; Harry was protected. Touch him, you die. Someone much, much bigger, was standing behind him.

In fact, several someones. Harry was a kind of lubricant, the oil that allowed the gears of the criminal underworld to mesh smoothly. He owned everything from property to politicians and would buy and sell anything imaginable. Without him the gang bosses who ran Paris would have been at daggers drawn, forever fighting over who had the right to buy and sell what and whom.

What you have to understand about gangland is that somewhere, there must always be a point of connection, a bridge between it and the legitimate world of tax-paying punters and everyday commerce. Without it, criminals can only deal with other criminals. At the end of the day, there's only so much you can sell to someone who's quite happy to go out and steal his own. Harry was that bridge. He made it easy to get on with the everyday businesses that actually made money.

So, no turf wars, no pissing contests, no internecine fighting. Harry was kind of like a UN peacekeeping force with a goatee beard and bad breath.

That was why the flics left him alone too; whoever protected Harry also paid them off. And in any case, they knew fine well that Harry dead meant lots of other dead, including, without shadow of doubt, a significant number of their own. Far better to quietly let live and rake in the percentages due to every hardworking copper.

Harry was under no risk at all, since only the dumbest, most naïve, amateur low-life would even have thought about turning him over; and of course, he had nothing to do with types like that. They were so far beneath him on the criminal scale of evolution it was like comparing monkeys to amoeba.

I guess I should have felt privileged, but I'm only a part-time criminal, really. I just do it for fun and extra cash and to stop myself getting bored.

I ran back across the street with the box under my arm. I paused in the doorway of the café just long enough to see the ZiL rumble off into the night. It was still pissing like God had just cracked his seal after drinking beer all night with the angels. I pushed through the door into the warmth of the bar and went back to my seat.

While I had been out, two guys had come in and were sitting at a table playing cards. Swarthy, stocky, black hair and stubble, but not Arab and not Italian either. Portuguese maybe? There were a lot of Portuguese casual workers in Paris. They weren't paying me the blindest bit of notice. After a while my attention began to drift away.

The thing is, it had been a long three months. It began when I'd been contacted by a 'friend of a friend' to organise delivery of a consignment of new Mercedes limos to an Arab buyer in Damascus. I don't usually do that sort of work these days but I was in a dry patch and it was certainly lucrative, with expenses up front. I put in a few calls and quickly rounded up a crew of reliable drivers I'd used before. There were six cars in total, each with a driver and a co-driver.

The journey would be non-stop; there's just too much can go wrong when you have a dozen testosterone-charged professional drivers, all ex-military and most ex-rally drivers, stopping over in hotels and hitting the booze and the whores. The last thing I needed was for one – or more – of them to get thrown in the slammer or worse. So the deal was four on, four off and enough amphetamines to make up the difference.

Our route took us from Bonn, where we picked up the limos, down through Austria and Italy and across to Greece, then through Turkey and into Syria. There's a much straighter route, of course, but the Cold War and the Iron Curtain that divided Europe in two made that impossible. Furthermore, there were bonds to be posted at several borders, equivalent to the local purchase taxes on the cars; this was returned, at least after the appropriate cuts for the various police and customs officials had been taken, on exit. In theory, anyway, to be fair, although the baksheesh was significant, it was acceptable.

All this bureaucracy took time though, so, together with the circuitous route imposed by the political situation, a trip that should really have taken around forty-eight hours of steady driving took nearly a week. But in the end, we arrived, undamaged and relatively un-ripped-off, in Damascus. The Syrian border guards had already been bribed by the client, which at least made that crossing easy.

I paid the guys and waited for my end. That was where the trouble began. For some reason, I wasn't getting it. Now I know this sounds daft, but the fact is the client was one I'd worked for many times before and I trusted him; you have to trust people in business. And sometimes there are delays. Naturally, I wasn't handing over the cars until I had the cash, so I ended up sitting in a hotel in Damascus (client paying) with the cars stashed (client also paying) while he sorted it out.

That was when I bought the diamonds. I was spending a lot more time than I'd planned on this gig and I needed to make up the financial ground. In the end, though, it got too close to Christmas and I had promised the children I'd be home; besides which, Damascus is a dump and I wouldn't touch the whores there with someone else's. So I told my client either he coughed or I took the cars back to Europe as default payment.

Those were some very high-end Mercs and my client had worked with me long enough to know when I'm serious. The next day, after weeks kicking my heels in an Arab shit-hole, I was to hell and gone, the dosh in my account and my bum bunged full of uncut diamonds.

So by the time I ended up in my preferred watering-hole in Clichy that night I was pretty whacked. Add to that the heat in the bar and the brandy; I suddenly realised I was dozing. Well that was no good. I had twelve and a half briques, a few uncut diamonds I'd held on to (insurance,) an unlicensed and supposedly non-existent gold Luger and a very fancy medal, both of which once belonged to the man who personally ordered the Blitz of London. This was not a night to be getting mugged. Anyway, I was desperate to see the kids.

I went to the bar and paid the tab, then moved to the john to freshen up.

I had pissed, flushed and was just splashing water on my face when it started. The door opened and one of the swarthy men came in. I knew right away what was happening. I twisted, tripping the little knife in its spring-sheath above my right wrist so that it slipped into my palm, but I was too late. There was a noise like a whip being cracked and something plucked at my left arm. But in a stride I had crossed to the door and kicked it hard so that it smacked into the gunman, sending his second shot wide.

He didn't get a chance for a third, as my knife described an arc, the apex of which was his windpipe. His eyes wide like a calf in a slaughterhouse he dropped the piece and his hands came to his throat. The sound of a man dying like that is not one you forget. But I had no time to savour it, because I knew there were two of them; since they were clearly not pros, the other one was going to come barging in, guns blazing, like he was Doc fucking Holliday.

Except he didn't. Oh, he came barging in all right, but even with one arm hanging uselessly by my side I was more than a match. Three rapid punches to his face made him reel and he dropped the gun. Then he was mine. I kicked his knee and heard it give. Then he was on the ground and I was on his back, my knee pressing down on his neck and my little knife at his carotid. Amateurs. Really.

"Who sent you?" I barked and then cursed as I heard something crunch. Fucking cyanide tooth, that's all. The man's face turned blue and his agony was clear; but with cyanide, it's quick. "Fuck you!" I snarled and picked myself up. "Fuck you." I kicked his body, not that it would do any good. He was dead all right.

Breathing hard, I stooped to pick up his weapon. It was immediately recognisable: a suppressed Ruger Mark 1. Not exactly your weapon of choice for an everyday knock-off artist, or even a mob hitter. Standard issue for US Navy SEALs and CIA black-ops though. Despite its size – the integral suppressor made it a long weapon – I slipped it into my coat pocket.

Gritting my teeth against the pain I quickly checked the pockets of the two men. No ID, no car keys, nothing. Some spare change and several full clips for the Rugers. I had a feeling I'd need them.

I made my way out into the bar. There was no movement. A quick look behind the bar showed why. The bartender was lying there in a crumpled heap. They'd shot him in the face. They must have waited until I flushed the toilet, because even a suppressed Ruger isn't that quiet. Just quieter. This was no casual robbery, but a deliberate hit. That could mean only one thing: Julie and the kids were in danger.

I moved to the payphone. It was a gamble, since if anyone had come in, I'd have had some explaining to do, or some shooting. But I needed to check. My home phone rang three times and then went straight to answering machine. My stomach twisted into a knot.

My attackers' clothes had been quite dry. In this weather you couldn't have walked a hundred yards without being soaked to the skin. It looked to me like they'd been in a car, but no car keys? They must have been dropped off. Someone else was involved, but where was that someone now? I didn't need more than one guess. I had to get back to the flat, like yesterday.

The adrenalin was beginning to wear off now and while shock was still dulling my senses. I could feel the pain from the wound in my arm begin to mount. Shit who was I kidding? I looked down at myself. The left arm of my coat was soaked dark with blood and a steady drip was falling from my fingertips.

See, those Rugers used a standard .22 Long Rifle cartridge, the usual rim fire type, available anywhere. So they don't have a lot of stopping power, but that doesn't mean they can't kill you as dead as a .45. It's just less immediate. As Bobby Kennedy demonstrated. The bullet is solid lead, not jacketed, so it deforms on hitting the body and will bounce around in there until it's spent. And do a lot of damage in the process.

It wasn't the first time I'd been shot, of course, but it's not something you get used to. My arm was, at the same time, completely numb and felt like someone was playing a blow-torch on it. I needed medical attention, quickly, but I had to get back to the flat. I collected my wits. My clothes were actually working as a bandage, slowing the flow of blood. As long as I didn't try to move the arm, the bleeding had slowed to a regular drip. The blood itself was dark: a good sign, since it probably meant no major arteries had been compromised.

That didn't help the fact that it was completely paralysed from the shoulder down, of course. And I tried hard not to think that this might mean a nerve had been severed. But even if it had been, that in itself wouldn't kill me, whereas I had good reason to fear that someone was doing exactly that to my family.

The trouble was, the bar I was standing in, surrounded with corpses and bleeding profusely, was in Clichy; my apartment was in St Germain, over five miles away. Where, I was pretty certain, the third party, the driver of the car that dropped off my two would-be assassins, was performing the same service for my wife and two children. I was probably far too late already, but I had to get there. Yet how? I could hardly just hail a cab: "Mais oui, monsieur, pas de probleme. Et votre bras? Il me parait que vous allez saigner a mort...." Or maybe the Metro? Yeah right, I'd get two stops before the police arrived. In desperation, I lurched back over to the bar and went through the dead boy's pockets. Damn, no car keys. But then, Paris isn't a car city. I'd been clutching at straws.

Who was there in all Paris who could help? I desperately needed some, but it's not like I've spent my life cultivating friends I could call on at times like this. Harry? Get real. One look at me in this state and he'd be pedal to the metal and gone in a cloud of petrol fumes.

Don't you want me baby?

Fuck I hadn't even noticed the jukebox was still playing that damn tune. But instead of a cute English girl walking through the rain towards me, I saw another image, one I would rather not have, but it was indelible: a beautiful young woman, tears streaming down her face, saying "Any time, Johnny, any time. You call, I'll be there. Any time."

And the worst damn thing was, she meant it.

Don't you want me oh-oh?

Fucking Phil Oakey. I shoved a franc into the payphone, dialled and waited. That bullet was nothing compared to what I felt when she answered.

"Oui, allo?'

"It's Johnny."

(Pause)

"Johnny? Is that you? Are you okay? It's been over a year."

I had tried to keep my voice level, but honestly, that girl is a mind reader and anyway...Well let's just say that she knew things would have to be bad for me to call. I have done more shitty things in my life than I will ever admit to, but right there and then I knew I was doing the shittiest thing yet. "I…I need your help. Right away. I've been shot."

(Pause, longer this time.)

"Okay; sure. Where are you? I'll be as quick as I can."

After she hung up I slumped against the wall by the payphone. It was only partly the shock and the pain. The girl I'd dumped to save my marriage was coming to help me save the woman I'd dumped her for. And there was worse – helping me would put her in danger. One thing was for sure: I didn't deserve her.

Don't you want me baby?

From slick pop soap-opera, the song had turned into mockery of me.

Two

Irene. For those who didn't pay attention at school, that's Ee-reh-na. It doesn't rhyme with 'icecream'.

She said hardly a word when she arrived outside the bar in her red Peugeot 205, the ultimate Parisian chick car. I'd been waiting in a doorway across the street – I couldn't stay in the bar and run the risk of discovery – and just jumped in the car before she'd even fully stopped. She drove about a mile towards the centre of town and then pulled into a side street. That was when she got talkative.

"Johnny, what the hell's going on?"

"I told you, I got shot."

"You got mugged? Well then we have to get you to a hospital. Julie will understand." She paused. "Why didn't you call the police?"

"Irene, I don't know if Julie's still alive. So before we do anything else, we have to go to my apartment. And I've stopped bleeding." This last was only partly true; I'd stuffed my sleeve with a bar-towel, so at least I wasn't actually dripping. "Please trust me. The police would only slow things up." Yeah, especially with three corpses to explain...

Silence. Then, more quietly: "Oh, so I'm just a taxi?" She sounded hurt. She was right to be.

"I'm sorry. Really I am sorry. I couldn't think of anyone else who would even consider helping. Just drop me off near the apartment, you shouldn't get involved."

She banged her hand off the steering wheel and cursed. "Not get involved? I spend a year trying – unsuccessfully – to forget you, then you call me up on Christmas fucking Eve and tell me you've been shot and you don't know if Julie's alive and you think I'm not already involved? Jesus, Johnny, you can be a heartless bastard." She started the car and angrily reversed down the side-street and out into the main drag at high speed. "Right. I'll take you to your apartment, you go in, check everything's okay and when you find it is and it's just that paranoia of yours working overtime, you come back and you tell me what the fuck you think is going on. Okay?" She looked at me that way French girls do when they're driving that scares the shit out of you. It

14

focuses the mind. "And I don't mean just about what the hell's going on tonight. I mean why you thought it was okay to call me. You owe me that much."

I nodded with what I hoped was appropriate sincerity. I mean, ending up wrapped round a lamp-post didn't seem an attractive outcome. "Yes. Yes, of course, Irene. I'll tell you. I promise." She nodded and thankfully, her eyes turned back to the road ahead, as she neatly avoided a bus. Poor kid! She may have thought I was a wheeler-dealer, a professional traveller and a bastard, but she didn't know the half. Not the half.

St Germain was no more festive than Clichy. There were precious few revellers out and about. I usually hate the rain, but blessed it tonight. Torrential downpours blattering down so hard the drops soak you coming back up are perhaps the best weather conditions of all, for those who would rather not be observed.

I left Irene in the car. I put the walnut case with the Luger in it under my seat; I still had the silenced .22. "There's a gun in there," I said. I debated with myself whether to tell her she might need it, but decided not to. Time to freak her out later, as if she weren't already.

The apartment block was reassuringly normal. The entry-phone system was working. I tapped in my code and took the lift to the top floor. We have a great view of the Eiffel. Or rather we had. Amazing. Not a thing out of order. Not that I expected there would be. I had that cold, leaden-ice-cube feeling in my gut; the two hitters in the bar may have been amateurs, but this one was a pro.

No sign of forced entry. I slipped my key into the lock and gently turned it. The tumblers fell with satisfying snicks. I opened the door a crack and ran my fingers lightly up and down the space in the jamb. Where was it? Ah. My skin brushed a nylon monofilament.

From that gentle graze I knew that Julie, Sam and Michael were already dead. Under any other circumstances I would have got the fuck out of there. But I had to see them one last time. I had to bear witness. I had to give them that, that I had come, albeit late.I had seen their Calvary. I slipped my Ronson Variflame through the crack and burned through the nylon. I put the lighter back in my pocket and picked up the .22 Ruger I'd laid down beside me. Then I gently pushed the door open.

No withering hail of gunfire. I paused to examine the bomb that had been attached to the cat-gut. Enough C4 there to blow me to hell and gone. I thought I recognised the workmanship.

I moved into the dimly-lit apartment. I stopped first at Sam and Mike's room. It had been quick. They had been asleep when the killer entered. It looked like Sam was the first, because he had died as he lay sleeping. Indeed, apart from the horrific bullet-wounds and the blood, you'd have thought he still was. The shots, however, must have wakened Mike, because he'd jumped out of bed and run for the wardrobe. It had always been his Safe Place.

Not that night. The killer got him half-way there. His little body lay crumpled in a black pool of blood.

Like a man already dead, I turned. There was no hope whatsoever that Julie remained alive. For all her faults, the drinking, the moods, she was a wonderful mother. She would never have allowed this to happen and not die first, or with them.

She was in our bedroom. There was a glass of wine on the bedside table and she was dressed in a negligée. Maybe she'd been planning to give me a pleasant surprise. She was kneeling by the bed, her shoulders slumped over it. She might have been praying. She looked peaceful, apart from the bullet-wound in the back of her head. Her grey eyes were open and calm, making the gaping hole above them even more ghastly. This was not a .22. The shot had blown her forehead out and the pillow was covered in dark blood, bits of bone and brains. I moved forward and as I did so my foot caught on something. I stooped to pick it up; it was one of our bathroom towels, but it was blackened and burned.

The killer must have used it as a silencer…but why? I moved to the side of the room, to the safe where I kept my collection of guns. It was open. At first I couldn't see anything out of place, but then I realised: my father's Webley .455 service revolver was missing.

Yeah, well, that was certainly enough gun to have done the damage I could see.

The Webley was gone, but it didn't matter. That pistol was a registered firearm with a police licence in my name. Guns that use the old .455 calibre ammunition are few and far between, especially in

France. I mean it was an antique: I would never have been so open about a weapon I might actually have used to kill someone. Despite this, it was an accusing finger pointing straight at me. I came home, calmly executed my family with one of my own weapons, then disappeared. That was why Julie had been shot in the back of the head; it's a bit difficult to shoot yourself that way. Scotched the depressed-mother-murders-kids-then-commits-suicide line of defence right away. Doubtless the plan had been for me to become part of some new building being constructed, or perhaps the extension to the Peripherique. Or maybe just lead wellies and a dive in the Seine. Then my history would have been leaked and there would we be: British secret agent on furlough finally twisted off, could be anywhere, on the run, after a horrific slaughter of the innocents.

Except the two guys in the bar had fucked it up royally. Instead of me being dead and about to be permanently vanished, I was alive, well, kinda and kicking, sort of and they were both history. But then, that worked too: this killer was a pro. Using Dad's gun made sure that I would be wanted for a horrific triple murder on Christmas Eve. Every cop in France would be after me. As an insurance policy it wasn't bad.

Maybe that was why the killer had left. The guys in the bar would have been told to call to check in, either to say I'd left the bar unharmed or was successfully snuffed. If it had been the first, I'd have got a pace through the front door and then been delivered a lead aperitif. If the latter, job done, time to collect the refuse.

When they hadn't called in the killer had known: they were dead and I still alive. Which told me something. This killer didn't want to face me down. That meant he – or maybe she – knew exactly who and what I was. No. This one didn't want a fair fight, but one where the dice were loaded against me.

It was exactly what I would have done, were I organising a hit. If you think I found that thought comforting, you haven't been paying attention. This killer was, unquestionably, another spook. Shit.

Suddenly I felt very tired and sat down on the edge of the bed.

"Sorry, Julie," I mumbled, half-expecting the terse response I'd become used to any time I attempted communication. Right then I'd have loved it. But it didn't come, because Julie's brains were all over the quilt beside me. Paisley is so very good at concealing the contents of one's skull, should one be careless enough as to have them blown out in the bedroom, isn't it? I almost laughed. And then I wondered and a chill spread through me, that stifled the mounting hysteria and lifted some of the heaviness I could feeling pinning me down. A spook? Certainly. So why the bomb? And why so easy to spot? Another spook must have known that I would have checked. Which could only mean that...

"DECOY!" My mind screamed at me as I made for the door.

You know those dreams, where you're running, where you're trying to get to keeps getting further and further away? That was what it was like as I legged it full-pelt down the corridor towards the front door. Except I wasn't running at all, but staggering, bouncing off the walls and my head felt like it was about to explode. Fucker! The bomb at the door was put there to make me think I had time; that once it was deactivated, I would be safe. But the killer had planted a gas-cylinder somewhere, which had been slowly poisoning the air ever since I entered. Oh, you clever bastard and stupid, stupid me.

I fell to my knees at the door. It had swung closed, but I knew it wasn't locked; I had been very careful to snib all the catches in case quick exit were required. I reached for the handle and pulled, but I was as weak as a baby and getting weaker every second. Oh no, please, don't let the bastard win!

Suddenly the door burst open towards me and I looked up, helpless as a lamb at an abattoir, to see the face of my gloating assassin.

But it wasn't the killer. It was Irene. She was holding Goering's damn Luger in both hands, which were so tiny they made the gun look huge. She was shaking.

"Johnny? Jesus Christ, what happened?"

"NO! NO! Stay out!" I croaked. "Gas!"

I must have made sense, even though my own words sounded like gobbledygook to me, because Irene blanched, bent down and dragged me bodily over the threshold, before reaching in and slamming the door behind us.

I hyperventilated, still crumpled on the floor. If the killer had poisoned the communal warm-air system, then we were both fucked anyway; if not, then this might be clean air. The fact that Irene seemed quite normal – well, given the circumstances – pointed that way too.

Within a few dozen breaths I began to feel some steadiness return to the world around me. I struggled to my knees. Irene was crouching beside me with a thousand questions on her face.

"Come on, we have to get out of here, now." I gasped.

She nodded, then looked back at the door. "Julie? The children?"

"All dead. Nothing we can do here. The killer might come back any minute, so let's get the fuck out."

"But Johnny...the police!"

"Forget the damn police," I snapped. "Don't you see? The killer set it up to look like I did it. In fact the police are probably already on their way."

I slumped against the wall. "I'm sorry, darling." I don't know why I said that, it just slipped out. Funny thing was it felt right. "I didn't mean to sound short. But the police can't help and I have to get somewhere I can rest for a while. I know a hotel that's good for this sort of thing. Will you take me?"

Irene did something really surprising. She reached up and kissed me on the cheek, then said, "Fuck the hotel, Johnny. Come on, let's get back to the car."

Somehow, together, we made it to the lift, then out through the hall – the concierge only worked days – and out into the night, where the sharp cold air was a blessing. It probably looked, I reflected in one of those bizarre moments of lucidity, like a young girl helping a drunken man across the road, as Irene guided my back to the Peugeot. She shoved me into the passenger seat and then got behind the wheel.

"Drive," I said, then passed out.

"Monsieur!"

I was in my parents' bed, on a Sunday morning. Outside the window I could see faces made in the tracery of branches in the rowan-trees on the lawn. There were no leaves. Of course, it was spring. I was fascinated by the faces. I liked Sunday mornings, when I could spend time lying between my father and mother. I turned back to the window and ignored the voice.

"Monsieur!"

But it wasn't time to get up for church yet; mum and dad were still in bed and we hadn't even had breakfast. But the voice called again.

It was insistent. And then came another, one I recognised. "Johnny! Johnny!"

I knew that voice from somewhere…but how could that be? I was only three years old…I looked towards the voice and a face, out-of-focus and blurred, appeared. My mother's face, of course…maybe it was time for church after all. I looked into her deep brown eyes, flecked with gold, as they became sharper. But then I realised: my mother's eyes were the palest ice blue…I felt confusion mount in me and then suddenly, Irene's face snapped into sharp focus and in the same instant, every detail of the last few hours did so too…The men in the bar…Julie, Sam and Mike…the gas.

"You are awake, monsieur?" I recognised the first voice and moved my eyes towards it. I saw a middle-aged man, heavily built. He had a beard and wore glasses. I realised that he was holding my wrist, which at first confused me but then I understood that he was feeling my pulse. He smiled mirthlessly. "I am a doctor. Irene brought you to me."

He let go my wrist and looked away, towards Irene. "I think it's all right." His voice, with her, was warmer, gentler, like an uncle's. One of her clients? He looked down at me again. "You are rather a lucky man. The bullet nicked a vein but not any arteries. It has chipped your humerus. Tell me, do you know what you were shot with?"

"Suppressed Ruger .22," I replied.

"Ah yes. That explains it. The .22 is a low-energy charge and of course the sound suppression robs even more velocity. Still deadly, of course, but that is why the bullet came to a halt so quickly." He nodded. "The bone is not fractured, but the chip will be painful. There is a lot of bruising. Your arm will be partially paralysed for some time. And of course, you lost a lot of blood. It takes time to build up again."

"How long?"

He shrugged. "It will certainly be a week or more before you can attend to the finishing of this matter." His gaze, which had not been particularly friendly, hardened. "And monsieur, I can tell that you will indeed be attending to it, just from looking at you." He reached over and, using a pair of forceps, picked a small object from a steel bowl. "This is the bullet. As you can see, it is intact, just a little deformed by the impact. It was relatively easy to remove. Irene tells me that she has a safe place for you to stay, so I am going to give you a sedative. I strongly advise you to rest your arm for at least a week. The stitches should have taken by then. I have repaired as much of the damage as I can, but you must give it time to heal. Otherwise…" His voice trailed off and he shrugged, as if to say, that otherwise, he would not be responsible.

"Do you think we can get you on your feet?" he went on. " I do not wish to appear harsh, but my grandchildren are wondering why their papi is not with them on Christmas Eve."

I nodded and, with help from the doctor and Irene, got into a sitting position on the examination couch. My head was still spinning, but my arm was pleasantly numb. "It will be a little while before the local anaesthetic wears off,' said the doctor, as he adjusted a sling for my arm. "I expect your arm will be very painful after that. But pain, you know, is the body's way of telling us not to abuse it. You should listen." He and Irene draped an overcoat on my shoulders.

"How much do I owe you?" I asked, tugging the lapel of the coat with my good hand, half in jest.

To my surprise he shook his head. "Oh, the coat is an old one. I can do without it and yours…is in rags, I am afraid. You are welcome to it. And as for the bill, it has been taken care of, monsieur. But…When you go about the business of settling whatever this matter is, I would rather you went elsewhere, should you need further medical care. My clinic has…a rather exclusive clientele. I am not seeking to add to my list. Do we understand each other?"

I nodded as I got to my feet. "Yes, we do." I felt like my legs were made of jelly, but at least I could walk. Irene moved to my side and I my hand on her shoulder as we headed for the door.

"Merry Christmas, monsieur," said the doctor as we left his surgery.

Three

So it looked like I had a partner. Not that I was complaining, mind you; and anyway I wasn't in a position to do much about it. I had to hole up for a while, at least until I could recover some of my strength and fitness. The bullet-wound in my arm had seriously weakened me. I didn't need to think about it too long to see that going up against whoever had planned the events of the night before in anything less than top condition would be tantamount to suicide.

I couldn't stay where I was, no matter how pleasant Irene's flat in a quaint block near l'Odeon was, or how many sweet memories it evoked. Just at the moment, the whole of Paris was too hot. And it wasn't just that I was quite sure that whoever the other side were, they would still be after me; as soon as the police got hold of what had happened, they'd jam up Paris solid so that no-one could move.

My only chance was to move fast, in the hope that the law was hampered by the fact that it was a public holiday. I suppose you might reasonably ask why I didn't just lift the phone and put a call through to Glover at the Firm's headquarters and ask him to get me out in a hurry; but you see, I'm the suspicious type and I hadn't ruled out the possibility that they'd got dirt on their noses over this one. Mind you, the Firm is usually pretty good that way. People who retire from the KGB don't generally live long. But still I wasn't satisfied that my ex-employers were entirely innocent. After all, they did know where to find me.

I could hear the splash and hiss as Irene showered. I managed to force myself into a sitting position on the edge of the bed, though the pain in my arm was intense.

Irene came out of the shower, briskly towelling her hair. "Johnny! What are you doing? Are you crazy? You must rest!"

"No. I mustn't let myself get stiff. If I don't move around, it'll be ten times worse by tonight." I struggled to my feet and crossed to the window where the dim daylight was filtering into the room. I took a look outside, taking care not to get too close to the window. Everywhere else in the world it was Christmas and here it was the worst nightmare

I'd ever known. I let the curtain drop. "I have to get out, Irene."

She was sitting at her dresser, putting on her make-up. She could see me in the mirror. She didn't look round. "What's the matter? You don't like it here?"

"It's not safe. Look, you must realise that those people...The people who...They won't stop until they get me. Or I get them. Christ, they even might have followed us here last night. They could be out there, now, preparing to attack."

"Why haven't they done anything yet?"

"Oh, I don't know. They blew it last night. They may be waiting for instructions, I don't know." A thought struck me. A faint hope, but a straw worth clutching at. "Irene...Do you have a radio? Get it and switch it on. I'd like to hear the news. She nodded, left her seat and went to the kitchen. When she returned she had a little transistor set in her hand. I took it and switched it on. I turned the volume up loud; aside of letting me hear the news, that would screw up anyone who happened to be listening.

"Do you know anywhere," I asked Irene quietly, "Outside the city? Somewhere where we can hide, until I'm fit?"

Irene had returned to applying her make-up. It was still the only thing she had on, except the towel she'd wrapped around her wet hair. Then she said, cool, as you like, "Sure, I've got a place." I must have looked a little incredulous, because she laughed and turned her swivel stool so that she was facing me again. "I do, Johnny. It's out by Versailles."

That was even more incredible. Property prices in that area are, well, outside my pocket by a long way. I looked at her; she'd returned to the job in hand. There were times when I thought I'd spent my life in the wrong business, but this was one of the times when I knew it.

"Don't look so astonished, Johnny; don't you know me by now? I'm careful with my money. And, you know, raising the mortgage is easy when your bank manager is a client." She frowned. "Was a client. He had a heart attack; fortunately he was not with me at the time." I had to hand it to her; she had it all worked out. She finished with the make-up and turned to me. "But how are we going to get there? If you're right and they – whoever they are – know you're here, then they'll just follow us again."

That one had occurred to me. Before I could reply, however, I heard the familiar tones of the radio news signature. It was the usual, Bonne Noele, commiserations to all those still working, like the newsreader. Then the news. Big pile-up on the Boulevard Peripherique, Paris' ring road, between Porte Maillot and Porte de la Muette; I raised an eyebrow, that was just south of our route to Versailles, if we were to go there directly. There would be hold-ups. That was the only local news; all the rest was national or world affairs.

"What's wrong, Johnny?" asked Irene.

"No mention of the murders." I shook my head. "You're not going to tell me that a juicy story like that, woman and two children murdered in their beds wouldn't make the headlines. No. They must have gone back, after those two guys in the bar didn't show up and got rid of the bodies."

"Maybe nobody told the police yet." Irene shrugged her shoulders. "Looks that way, doesn't it?"

If that were true, then the faint hope I'd perceived might just be enough. We might still be one jump ahead of the game, enough to get out before the police closed the city. As for the other side, I knew that there was a good chance that they'd seen us the night before; they probably even got the number of Irene's car. But if that was all they'd done, if they hadn't followed us, if they'd relied on being able to trace the car through the number, then the fact that it was Christmas might save us yet. It was a window that I couldn't afford to let slip by.

"We have to move now," I said.

"Where are you going to go like that?"

"Where are my clothes?"

"Mostly in the bin. The doctor had to cut your shirt and jacket off you and your trousers were soaked with blood. But never mind, I think I may be able to help."

I raised my eyebrows. She gave me a cheeky smile and pulled a suitcase out from under her wardrobe. You know how some guys keep mementos of their conquests? Well Irene had a collection like that; only it wasn't made up of frilly knickers and bras, but shirts, ties, jackets – even a couple of pairs of trousers. That really made the mind boggle. It took a while to sort out clothes that were a decent fit and didn't make me look like something the Salvation Army had turned out, but we got there.

Then I had Irene shave my face and try to make me look respectable before I dressed. The last thing I wanted to look like was a wanted man, after all. There's nothing more certain to make an interfering policeman give you a hard time than looking rough. You have to remember that they're trained like that. If you look the part and speak in a well-bred voice, they'll leave you alone. So I hoped. I don't think Irene really realised just how bad things were. She was wondering why I was being so picky, but I knew what I was doing.

It took a while to get me dressed, because I was weak as a kitten. Even the slightest effort made me want to throw up. Then, while I finally sorted myself out, just the easy bits that I could cope with on my own, Irene got ready. I must have got through to her about the need for haste, because she was standing before me, dressed in a woollen and tweed country outfit, with an enormous fawn woollen coat over the top, arid a pair of brown riding-boots, in ten minutes flat. She looked like she was going to a photo-session at Vogue.

"You packed?" I asked her. She nodded, pointing to a maroon make-up case. "That's all?" I was a little surprised; you have to remember that the only woman I really knew well enough to take away like this was Julie, who couldn't go to the beach for a picnic without a full suitcase.

"Sure; and my handbag. I keep clothes at my other place. In fact the only clothes I have here are evening dresses. For work."

"Okay; what about my wallet..."

"And the two guns and the money. I thought you might get around to that. It's all in the top drawer of my dresser. Oh, sorry, I forgot; I'll get the stuff." I didn't bother to count the money; Irene isn't like that. I slipped the Luger into the waistband of the trousers I was wearing and nestled the .22 into the sling we'd improvised for my arm. It was safe there, invisible and ready.

"Let's go," I said. I took one last look out of the window and we went.

Four

When we left the city it was by Porte d'Italie, mainly because no one in their right minds would try to get to Versailles from there. Unless they thought they might be being followed. We drove southeast for about fifty kilometres, then turned off the main road towards Fontainebleau and took to the back roads.

Two hours later we pulled up in a side street in Joigny. There's a pension there, where I'd stayed before. The landlady knew better than to ask any questions. The Nazis had got a hold of her during the War, when she'd been involved in the Resistance. She hadn't told them anything, so I thought she could probably keep a secret. She gave us a room that overlooked the street; the hotel is an old coach-inn and has a courtyard at the back.

I got Irene to stash her car. Little red Peugeots may be the height of fashion, but they stick out a mile in a quiet street. It was about four in the afternoon by the time we were settled. I was done in. I had to get some rest.

"Could you use this?" I asked Irene, holding up the .22. She sucked in her cheeks, sighed and nodded. I showed her where the safety was. "Don't try anything fancy if you have to use it. Aim for the middle of the body and keep pulling the trigger until he goes down." I lay down on the bed, on my back, with the Luger still in my right hand. I left the safety off. A light tap on the door woke me up. I swung the gun to point at the door. Irene's eyes widened; milliseconds before I'd been fully asleep. "Qui est la?"

"C'est moi, Françoise." It was the landlady. She'd brought us some food. I bade her come in and then almost laughed; she was bearing a tray laden with all the best Christmas cuisine that rural France can offer. I'd forgotten what day it was. The rest and the food did me a lot of good. Outside, it was pitch dark and raining. I told Irene to get some shuteye after we'd finished the meal. It was only eight in the evening then; but she did as she was told. I took up station in the chair by the door. She was a good sleeper, Irene. I had to rouse her quite energetically when it was time to go.

"Get ready. We're leaving." She rubbed the sleep out of her eyes and yawned.

"Johnny…Now? What time is it?"

"Late. Gone midnight. No, don't switch on the light. Get your things." There was a little servant's passageway that ran parallel to the main one, that ended in a stair down to the courtyard. To get into it we first had to go through the landlady's bedroom. Raising no light, we crept along the hall. I tapped on her door. She was expecting us. Ushering us into the room, she gave me a torch. "Use this. Follow me."

The passage led out through a little cupboard. Although they called it a servant's passage, it is one of those little idiosyncrasies of eighteenth century French buildings; it only has a door into the master bedroom, which was once that of the husband of the family. It bypasses the lady of the house's bedroom altogether, so that the husband could come and go in the night unnoticed. Françoise' husband was dead,and anyway, she wasn't the kind of woman you could have banished so easily. The door moved so easily on its hinges that I was suspicious that she'd been using it to let her own lovers in without causing gossip amongst the staff.

"Here, take this," said Françoise when we stood at the top of the little staircase that led to the courtyard. "It belonged to Pierre; I don't need it. I am getting to the time of life when I would welcome an intruder in the night, you know?"

The gift was a twelve-bore shotgun and a bandolier of shells. It was a nice thought.

The streets were deserted as we drove out of the town, taking the back road towards Étampes. From there we would cut across country to Rambouillet and on to Versailles. I made Irene leave the car lights off until we were away from the streetlights. We stopped after six kilometres to see if we were being followed. It was all clear.

The rest of the drive was smooth and uneventful. By the time we drove into Versailles at a little after five a.m. I was beginning to feel a little more relaxed. So far we'd been very lucky. By that time I had an idea how the whole thing had been set up. It was all so neat. It was that business with the Webley that made me so sure.

Julie must have known the man who had killed her; someone whom she would trust to allow into the house, someone who knew about the gun-case in the living-room, who had contrived that cold-blooded, deadly plan. Whoever it was knew that I was coming home and when to strike. They had either picked me up at the airport or else…Or else Harry Jonsun had a tale to tell.

I wondered about Harry. Somehow I was sure that he knew something, though I doubted whether he'd have had quite the moral courage – or the acting ability – to sit in the back of that car of his with me, doing business and joking about his whoring exploits if he'd known that he was sending me into a trap in that café.

Five

Irene's 'other place' turned out to be a modern villa on the Paris side of the town. We put the car in the garage and I scouted around. There was no sign of anyone outside; so far so good, I took a good look around the inside of the place before we settled down to rest, to get the lie of the land, understand the layout of the house. It was built on two floors, set into the side of a steep hill, so that whilst the front door opened onto the upper storey, the lower floor opened through the back door.

The whole place was tiled, which I liked; a man can give himself away with a footfall very easily on one of those floors. The bedrooms were downstairs, too, facing away from the road. I thought we could risk taking a few hours sleep. Irene was looking as shattered as I was feeling.

She led me in to her bedroom. I had been unconscious the night before when she'd got me into the bed at her flat; somehow waking up in someone's bed isn't the same as getting there. It had been a long time since we'd been involved. Even though I was dog-tired, the sight of her undressing in the soft light of the bedside lamp brought back memories.

She noticed that I was having trouble getting my clothes off with one arm in a sling. She laughed and came to help. I remembered that sweet perfume of her body. She kissed me and we went to bed. Irene fell asleep almost as soon as her head hit the pillow, but I couldn't; my head was still buzzing.

The next morning we woke late. It was still raining outside; the whole world was sodden. Both Irene and I were still tired. We hadn't got used to being fugitives, but there was nothing else for it until I could recoup my resources.

The news about the killings didn't break until two days after we'd arrived at Versailles and for every moment of those two days, my stomach was tied into a knot. The thought of Julie and the kids, just lying there…It was almost more than I could bear. Many times I thought of giving it up, of turning myself in, of telling someone so at least those three pathetic corpses could be looked after; but always my training and, yes, my naked desire for revenge, stopped me from doing anything so stupid.

When the shit finally did hit the fan, I was relieved, even though it meant that the hue and cry was well raised after me. We caught the news on television at lunchtime. It seemed that our elderly Polish daily help, Mrs. Gribowski, had gone to the flat for the first time since Christmas. She had found the bodies.

Poor Mrs. Gribowski was deeply attached to my darling wife. She had lost no time in pointing the finger at me as the likely perpetrator of the outrage. I guess, having survived the Nazi occupation of Warsaw she thought that such sights as she had seen when she'd walked innocently into the house were safely part of her past.

The police hadn't needed any encouragement, anyway. As soon as they got the forensic report that confirmed that it was my gun that had fired the fatal bullets, I was guilty, as far as they were concerned. We were lucky to have got out of the city when we did; I couldn't have moved a hundred yards without being caught, or perhaps even summarily dealt with by an angry mob, after that news report.

It was also just as well that the picture they had shown of me was old, the one from my Resident's Application; that was about the end of the good luck, though.

I thought a lot about my marriage and my family, after the report was finished; mostly sad recriminations. I wished I could have been there, to make sure that they had the best treatment, but what could I do? I had other fish to fry. I had to stay loose, to avenge them.

Irene was pretty upset by the report. Up till then, she'd rather regarded the whole affair as a bit of a game. Actually seeing the pictures of the bodies being carried out on stretchers made it really sink in. The poor girl began to shiver. I couldn't blame her.

There was no mention of the two guys I'd hit in the men's room of that bar in Clichy, where the nightmare had begun, or of the bartender, whom they'd taken out just because he was there. Someone must have gone there and cleaned up; no bodies, no suspicions. The bartender was probably wherever they'd planned to put me. Irene got up and poured herself a brandy.

"You want one?" she asked me. I nodded.

"Why not. Cheers," I said, grimly. "Look. I think this is going to get very, very nasty. I think you ought to go back to Paris. I'll contact you when I need you."

She smiled and shook her head. "You wouldn't phone me, be honest. No. You need me; you have no-one else, now. When you don't need me any more, then you can tell me. Then maybe I'll go. But right now, you can't help yourself. You saw that picture; step outside this house and you'll be caught. And anyway, that arm; you must rest."

I looked at her. "Thanks, Irene." My voice caught a bit as I said the words. We were silent and I thought about her. She didn't deserve me, that was for sure. I'd taken her when I wanted her and then, when I'd found myself getting in too deep, I dropped her. The fact that she made her living with her body had nothing to do with it, because it had never been that way between us, never. The fact of her lifestyle was just something that was, like the fact of my marriage, my family.

I'd met her two years before, when I was in a bad patch. I'd just got used to the fact that I had a duff marriage on my hands and I needed someone. I met Irene one night in a nightclub, where I was drinking rather than go home to face Julie and the reality of a failure. The Firm never showed me how to deal with failure. I'd been in a bit of a mess.

Irene found me a taxi and got me home; if she hadn't, I'd have spent the night in the police cells. Of course, I went back to the club to thank her and we got to talking. We had a lot to talk about, it turned out, being, I suppose, in similarly shady lines of business. It went from there. It was good because we'd been honest from the start.

Then Julie had decided that we should really give our marriage another chance, for the sake of the kids. We came to a simple agreement; she'd stop screwing around if I would. So Irene got the heave one day and my God I hated doing it. I could see the hurt in her eyes, the way they'd glazed over as if I'd been another trick and I cursed myself for my heartlessness. The thing was, I knew then, without her ever saying a word, that if ever I needed her, she would be there; and when the time came, she'd kept her word.

"Johnny," She interrupted my train of thought in a soft voice. "What are you going to do?"

There was a question. "I'm not sure," I replied, thinking about it. "I want to get in touch with Harry Jonsun first, just in case he knows anything." At the mention of his name, Irene cracked a broad grin.

"You know him?" I asked.

"Sure. You know he has a thing about that car of his? Always wants to make it in the car. But I don't see so much of him; he's mean, he doesn't like my prices. I tell him if he wants to catch a dose, it's his choice, go and cruise Pigalle."

"Could you find him?"

"Easy."

"I may get you to do just that," I mused. "But not quite yet. First of all, we're going to have to do something about the way I look. And there are other things I'm going to need. So, in the morning, you take the car and go into town. You'll have to buy me some clothes and some hair dye. Can you get a pair of spectacles? Get a few pairs, if you can. And I'll need lots of paper and some pens."

"I've got that here," she put in.

"Good." I always find it helps to clarify the facts, if you write it all down. Helps you to see the pattern. "And you'll have to lay in a good stock of food."

"Sure."

"How many people know about this place?"

She cast down her eyes. "Only you. And the bank manager, but then he's dead. Silly old fool."

"That's even better. What about the neighbours? Are they the nosey type?"

"No. The house behind us is empty. On the other side it's an old couple. They're both a bit deaf."

"Then I think we may be okay here, for a while." I thought about my shopping list. For the time being, that would do. "Do you have a hacksaw?"

Irene looked puzzled. "What? I don't know; there's a box of tools that the last owner left. Would you like to look?"

I nodded.

There was, indeed a hacksaw; in fact the tool case was interestingly replete. "Who did you say you bought this house from?"

"I didn't say. Someone who had to leave in rather a hurry. But it's all legal; I just got it for a good price."

One look at that tool case and I had a good idea what the last owner did for a living and why he had to leave. Still, it might come in useful.

That shotgun was a real asset, but it was too cumbersome in its present state. Half an hour with the saw and I'd taken fifteen inches off the barrel and six off the stock. Shortened and lightened, a very good friend in a close quarters fire fight. After I'd altered the gun, I stripped it right down and thoroughly cleaned and oiled it. Then I did the same with the pistols. It was to become: a nightly routine.

Irene sighed and left me to it while she went to fix dinner.

Six

The next week was spent recuperating and trying to draw a line on the events of Christmas Eve. Irene and I hardly noticed New Year as it came and went. She had gone into town and got the things I'd asked for; then we'd dyed my hair a deep brown and fitted me up with a pair of glasses.

We bleached the hair at my temples again to add a few years. I practised wearing pads between my lower teeth and my cheek to change the shape of my face. That was as much as we could do, but on passing glance I wouldn't have been recognised. We worked out a cover story for me in case anyone happened to stop by; and with the addition of some rather unfashionable tweedy suits I began to look as innocent as we hoped to make out.

I began to analyse the 'events' in the way that I'd been trained. Every detail written down, then every detail that each of those jogged back into the clear focus of memory; then you put it all together and try to make out the pattern. It took me two days of carefully checking over my facts and putting the whole thing together every way I could think of. In the end I was happy I'd got the story as far as I could.

It went like this; somebody wanted me out of the way. It wasn't someone who'd taken casual offence, either; it was somebody who thought that I was enough of a threat for them to take really radical, decisive action, to set the trap and then have the patience to wait for the perfect moment to spring it. You see, whoever organised the job had given themselves a very high profile by doing it at all. They'd built in the failsafe of framing me, but there was always the possibility that the police wouldn't have been fooled. And I was, in every way, committed to vengeance myself now; you don't fool with a bee's nest unless you really want the honey. They knew they might get stung, but they were prepared to take the risk.

Everything pointed to it being a house job; but why would the Firm take action against me? And wouldn't there have been other, simpler ways? It could have been one of the other companies, of course; the Russians were known to bear a grudge, as were the East Germans, not

34

to mention my old friends the IRA. Not their style, though, too subtly handled. They were more the hammer and anvil types, all of them, you know, the bomb under the car routine, the quiet bullet in the back of the neck; all this extra flak the killers had thrown in, that had a distinctive flavour all its own.

Whoever it was, they'd spent a lot of time researching the job, getting the feel for it, planning, setting it up so, so carefully. The only place they'd slipped up was in sending those two goons after me. And somehow I knew that they were important. They were like a slightly non-authentic part, something that sat uneasily with all the other parts of the jigsaw.

No real pro would have bothered with the boy in the bar; the streets had been deserted, it was one of the wettest Christmases in memory. They could have taken me outside, nice, neat, silent, but no, they chose to come into the bar. It was nice and quiet, there were no other customers, no chance of a passing stranger on his belated way home from an evening' carousing seeing anything and raising the alarm. So they hit the boy and then came for me. That was clumsy, almost amateur. It struck me as odd that someone who had the ability to plan the hit on my flat would be involved with guys like that.

Of course, the other side to this story is that while the two men were trying to kill me, their pal was busy terminating Julie and the kids. That thought didn't make me feel any better, I couldn't help myself asking, what if I'd only had one drink and then gone home, what if, what if…But I knew I was not being rational. The planner had set up the evening entirely in accordance with my movements; if I'd gone home instead of to the bar, no doubt they'd have had another scheme in hand.

While I was giving myself a headache working things out, I had also begun a crash fitness programme. There wasn't a great deal I could do with my left arm, although it was healing quickly enough; the Doc had done a good job. It was only a flesh wound, even if it had been a messy one. I set myself a strict routine. Four times a day I sprinted up and down the stairs twenty times, then did bunny hops and stomach-curls until my muscles were screaming.

Irene was at first perplexed by all this; it only highlighted how little she really knew about me. I could see her, sometimes, just watching, wondering. I knew that she was itching to ask, but couldn't; probably for the same reason as I, when I lay next to her at night and couldn't make love to her. I think I had an idea of what was wrong; and it was coming from me.

They used to call it post-combative shock. I don't know what the Firm's shrinks call it now, but I'll bet the guys are still getting it. It sort of ties you up, like a paralysis. If you're good, then your training will show through and you can still function, still plan, still fight; but you don't really work properly until that tension coiled up inside you like an over-wound spring can be released. I knew I had a bad case and Irene didn't need to be told that there was something way wrong.

The thing is, that this state of mind, this awful limbo, gets worse when the action is quiet; when you're out there, you just don't notice, but when you're back at base, planning, resting, training, it can sap the strength from you like a bad case of hepatitis. I was doing all the right things, I knew, to get my body back in shape, but I could tell that my head wasn't going to be in the right place until I could break the block. I was too close in; a planner needs to be able to draw back, to coolly appraise all the angles, all the approaches, all the risks.

It was Irene who did it for me, in the end; it must have been a week after we'd arrived at her house, just a couple of days after New Year, maybe. We were sitting together, watching the evening news on television. I was taking notes, of everything, anything that might in some way, however remotely, be connected with the nightmare I was living in. When it finished, Irene got up from her seat and switched off the set. She delved into a drawer in her sideboard and produced an unopened pack of caporal cigarettes. She took one of them out, without looking at me and lit it. She inhaled deeply. I looked at her. "I thought you'd given up?"

"I had." She sighed. "I guess that this seems as good a time as any to start." The way she looked at me left me in no doubt as to the real reason. "Do you know, Johnny, that in the time we've been here, you've hardly spoken a word to me? You act as if I just wasn't here. You're not the man I knew. I want to help, Johnny; help with whatever you're going to do, but it's very difficult, you know, with this barrier between us."

I reached out and took her hand. It was cold and she didn't return the friendly squeeze I gave her.

"I'm sorry. I know what it is; I've had it before, when there's been... Trouble."

"What sort of trouble, Johnny? I don't know, when you and I... When we first knew each other, I just thought you were a lonely guy whose wife didn't care; I knew you travelled a lot, you were away so much, but all this...The killings? And the guns and the things you do. Where did you learn all that? And where did you learn to push yourself until the veins are sticking out of your forehead? Johnny, you frighten me! God knows this thing is weird enough, bad enough, without that." She stubbed the cigarette out angrily. "I suffered agonies giving those up!"

"And I'm driving you to them again."

She flicked her hair away from her face and sat down again, on the sofa by my side. She was making sure I couldn't see her face, but I knew she was crying. I looked at her. How old was she? Twenty-three? Twenty-four? Oh, no-one would ever say she was an innocent; she was a tough kid who'd pulled herself out of the gutter by hard work, using the only blessings she had; her good looks and the fact that she knew how to please a man. But that was her job; otherwise she was just like any other girl her age, from time to time needing support.

I got up arid fixed us each a large cognac and then sat down beside her. I put my arm round her shoulders. "Drink this. You know there are things about my past that I've never told you. And one of those things is that I used to work for the British Government. As a spy, though that's not the word we use."

"A spy?" She looked at me, her eyes wide with astonishment.

"Yes, sort of. The Firm and I parted company some time ago now, of course, long before I met you. I gave it up to try to sort out my family life...And you know how much of a success that was."

"Oh, you must stop blaming yourself for all of that; and it's too late now." She paused and swirled the brandy round the bottom of her glass. "Tell me, what did you do...When you were a spy?"

"I worked all over the world; Vietnam, then Rhodesia, you know, when there was that trouble with the Smith government. It was in Vietnam that I learned about the Martial Arts. Made the combat we were taught look like child's play. But all that was before I joined the real pros...The Firm."

"What's that?"

"Her Majesty's dirty tricks department," I chuckled. "The boys who look after all the jobs that MI6 wouldn't dirty their precious public-schoolboy fingers on. They really had me running around the globe. I was with them for over ten years, in the end. I have to admit it was with mixed feelings that I finally handed in my ticket. But at the time it seemed the right thing to do – the only thing."

I fell silent for a few minutes, smiling at the memory of those days. Danger? It had been all part of the job. "Yes," I went on. "I saw a lot of service with them, in Northern Ireland, South America, Africa, the Middle East, you name it. Anywhere there was a crisis and the British interest was concerned, then we were in there."

"Doing what?"

"That depended. Sometimes we just had to watch, to wait, to observe and report...Other times more than that, much more."

"And do you think that they did this to you?"

"I don't know. They may have decided to terminate me; but I don't know why they would. I'm still valuable to them, even if I'm off the active service register. It might have been one of the other companies; but there's something funny about the way it was done."

"What do you mean?"

"Well, the Firm and most of the other regular outfits, only use one man on a job; especially a hit on a trained operative. One field agent and a control. In this case, they'd have used one field man to hit me and one to hit the flat...But that would be all. Unless..."

"Yes?"

"Unless they wanted me to think that it wasn't one of the companies; but I don't know. I have a feeling about this, a bad feeling, but I can't say what it is; not yet, anyway."

The girl beside me on the sofa reached out and touched my hand. "This doesn't change anything," she said, quietly. "Not as far as I'm concerned. I still want to help, if I can." She sighed. "What is different is that, well, at first I thought that you were overwrought, that it might have been a burglary attempt which had gone wrong; but it isn't that, is it?"

"No. It couldn't be that. Believe me, I know what it was." I paused.

"Still sure you want to be with me? This is going to be the most dangerous thing you've ever done. They're two steps ahead already, maybe more; and they'll try to hit me again, I know that."

Irene had the knack of just ignoring anything she didn't want to hear, but I knew it was useless to repeat myself. She smiled, sadly and, as if to change the subject and ease the moment, asked me how I'd got involved with the Firm.

I smiled. "That's easy. Third generation Navy, I am. Father was a Rear-Admiral. I wanted to prove myself, not just go along on the strength, you know, so I joined the Marines. More fool me, you might say. After a while, though, I was asked to join the SBS, the Naval Special Forces team. They're really under deep cover; hardly anyone has heard about them, even in Britain. I served with them for three years and they sent me to Vietnam, attached to a U.N. unit, to observe on guerrilla warfare. We had been caught with our pants down in Cyprus and a few other places. The SBS had no intention of getting egg on their own face if ever they were thrown into a war like that.

"That was in 'sixty-seven, when it was really beginning to get out of control. I saw a lot that made me think about the way we fought wars. When I came back, I made a report that recommended training for our guys along the lines of guerrilla outfits. You know, really train them in the Martial Arts, because it could make them deadly, so that they could move in silence and kill instantly with their hands. The V.C. cadres we brought in were the most committed fighting men I'd ever seen and I believed that it had to do with their training, the way that they could empty their minds of everything except the job they had to do. And I couldn't see how you could stick to a rulebook in a war like that; it was dog eat dog. Somebody in the Admiralty got a hold of the report and must have been impressed, because the next thing I knew, I was attached to Naval Intelligence, with the rank of Commander.

"I was with them for two years. I was bored stiff; I was a field man, I needed the action, the danger. It was one thing to do a job and then come back and do a study and a report on it, but two years sitting reading other people's field reports and working on them had just made me fat and soft. I got an offer from a friend who was organising a mercenary operation in West Africa and I was on the point of accepting it when the Firm got in touch.

"It was very discreet; I was in the Services Club, having a drink one evening, when I was approached by a man. He told me something about the Firm, how it was independent of the other Services; it was even further underground than MI6. I had an interview and then I joined them. I had to resign my Commission, of course, but I didn't mind that; at last I was doing what I wanted to do.

"That's how I was recruited, anyway; it's the normal procedure for field men. Research agents, like Julie, were usually recruited from University."

"You mean your wife was…"

"Yes. She was in it too. She was the control for several of my European jobs."

"I see. And then you left."

I frowned and scratched my head. "Like I say, my superiors didn't get along with some of my ideas. I changed and the climate changed. The British Government had less faith in us that they once did and, to be honest, I had a lot less faith in them. You have to believe you superiors have got your back, that they won't just hang you out to dry for political convenience. I guess the Firm made me cynical that way. It's not uncommon. They weren't happy, but they let me go dormant. I'd given them over ten years of my life, then; Julie, she had just had our second son, had been dormant for a while by that time, too. I just thought that I owed it to them, her, the boys, to have a crack at a normal life…"

My voice trailed off. "But that didn't work either. I couldn't keep a regular job, so I got into the line I'm in now and I started to drink. Then I met you and. I think you know the rest."

There was silence in the room for a long moment and then I felt the soft pressure of an arm slipping round my neck, the wetness of a long, deep kiss, then she was pulling me back onto her. I was willing, willing.

I can't remember how often we fucked that night; I do remember that each time was like a desperate prayer, like a plea for releas. Each time we climaxed together, a tiny part of the pain was eased away. We made love there, on the sofa, then we went through to the bedroom and we made love there, again and again, until we were quite, quite spent.

Afterwards, as I lay and listened to the splish-splash of rain outside the window, I knew, I knew that I'd come through; that my emotions were intact, that I could function again. Who was it said that laughing and crying were the same release? Or was it the sane release? I don't know, but I do know that in that evening of passion, my hurts, the deep hurts, began to be healed. I knew it would be a long upward struggle before I could really find my centre again, but still I was on the way.

I'd been frightened, before, with Irene; that was why I'd ditched her so easily. I knew she could open doors in my soul I'd been fighting to keep shut. But that night, for the first time, I realised that those doors led to the only freedom I would ever know.

As for Irene, she just curled up with her head on my chest, a smile on her face as I ran my fingers through her hair. I could tell that she was happier than she'd ever been. It made me feel very good. I had things to do, important, dangerous things; but now there was something to come back for, to stay alive for.

Seven

January the tenth. I'd set up a meet with Harry Jonsun. I didn't really think he had had anything to do with the hit, but I did think that if there was anyone in town who might know something, it would be he. We were to meet at the corner of the Avenue Kleber on the Place du Trocadero, opposite the imposing frontage of the Palais Chaillot. It was a cold, wintry day and the vicious little wind made me huddle into my coat as I waited for his car to arrive.

I could see, across the square, Irene sitting behind the wheel of the nondescript Volvo we'd hired. She looked frightened, but I could tell, even from that distance that her jaw was set in the jutting angle of defiance that was so characteristic of her. It was gloomy. I looked at my watch. Three-thirty five. The bastard was late, but that was typical. I huddled lower in the collar of my coat, shivering.

Then I saw it sweeping into the traffic, that long black vehicle, the zeppelin on wheels. I smiled. At least Irene would have no trouble following that one. The car pulled up alongside me. Harry was driving, as usual. He gestured me to get in beside him, but I got in the back instead. I felt safer that way. He shrugged and pulled away in a silent hiss of well-muffled automatic transmission.

"Hello, Johnny," he said, full of that tiring cheeriness of his. "You look different."

"Wouldn't you?"

"I suppose so; but then, the Sûreté isn't after me, not yet, anyway, not as long as I keep paying my dues."

"Yeah. Drive towards the Arc de Triomphe."

"You're hot property, my friend. I would be careful how you speak; I might just be stopped by the police."

"Then you'd get a very bad headache," I hissed, viciously. "I'm not in the mood for games, so don't push your luck." I could see his face in the driving mirror and it paled as I stuck the muzzle of the silenced .22 in his ear.

"Now you're going to answer some questions. And you'd better have the right answers, Harry my old friend."

42

"Okay, okay, you don't need to get mad, Johnny," he said, trying to soothe me.

We were coming up on the Place Charles de Gaulle, where the Arc de Triomphe stands. It also happens to be the craziest traffic circle in Paris, with cars cutting in from every direction. This part of the route we'd agreed, so Irene would be okay, but it might help to fox anyone else who just happened to want to follow the black limousine.

"Okay, turn into the Avenue Hoche, just by the Metro, there." He did. Soon we were heading away from the mad rush of the traffic. I kept a weather eye out behind, but I could see no trouble there. Irene had fallen a long way back. The Avenue Hoche leads, at the end, through the charming park of Monceau. I ordered Harry to turn off the road again. We parked under some trees.

"Okay, that'll do. Now get out." I leaned forward and removed the keys from the ignition. Then I followed Harry out into the gloom. "Walk over towards the open ground."

"Okay, Johnny, okay."

"Just keep walking."

"You sure are a very worried man, my friend."

"You bet your fat Dutch arse. But if I were you, I wouldn't be too cocky about the future."

"What do you mean?"

"Don't come it, Harry. Christmas Eve, remember? Don't tell me you forgot already. Remember the little present someone so thoughtfully arranged for me?"

He swallowed. "What about it?"

"I want to know what you know." We were out on a stretch of open grassland. I made sure that I kept Harry between me and the trees; but from that range, we would have merged into the murky gloom anyway.

"I don't know anything, Johnny," he protested. Then he grunted as my foot caught his personal equipment with polished accuracy.

"Next one like that and I shoot your prick right off, Harry. Then where will those clap-ridden whores you like be?"

"Johnny, Johnny, I..." He could see I meant business and the act fell apart. "Look. I didn't know they were going to hit you. I swear. I didn't even know they were there that night."

"Go on."

"I just sold them the guns, that's all, Johnny."

Jesus. I might have known. "My name come up in conversation?"

"No, no; I don't need the business so bad I'd set up a friend!" I looked at him and was sickened. The slug really thought I was a friend. Jesus. Still, it was better than having him as an enemy. "Okay, what else. Who were they? Who were they working for, where did they come from?"

"I don't know; they paid good money, over the odds for the hardware, because they weren't connected. Nobody knows who they were."

"Language, accent; where were they from? Come on, Harry, don't try to string me along."

"I'm not sure, but I think they were from Spain."

"Spain!" Now that really upset the apple-cart, "I've never had anything to do with the place. What were they, brought in pros? They didn't act like pros."

"Not pros, Johnny; I don't know, they were like crazy men; like they didn't know the rules." Sure. That figured.

"Okay. What about the buzz on the street? What do the ears say?" I meant the Mob's information-gathering system, the most effective in the city.

"Look, Johnny, I got nothing to do with – "

"Cut the crap, Harry, for Christ's sake! Don't you realise I know more about you than you think? Now you know exactly what the buzz is and you're going to tell me. What happened to the three bodies in that café?"

"They were collected. Shortly after you left the place, a van drew up. Two people got out; they were in the café for a while. Then they brought out the bodies and drove away, after they'd locked up the café so no-one got suspicious."

I whistled. "What about the van – registration, that sort of thing?"

He shook his head. "It was stolen for the job."

"Anyone know where it went?"

Harry sighed. "You know what's going to happen to me if anyone finds out I told you all this?"

I chuckled. "Just worry about what's going to happen to you if you don't."

"It was seen crossing the Seine at La Grande Jatte, about ten minutes after it left Clichy. So, I guess – "

"They still had the bodies with them."

"Sure. We don't know where it went after that, except that it disappeared somewhere in Courbevoie. The next thing we know is that it was dumped in the Car Park of the RER station at La Defense."

I thought about that a while. Courbevoie is a large modern suburb to the northwest of the city; there are a lot of immigrant homes out there; it could fit in with the Spanish connection. "The Police have no ideas, I suppose?"

"Why don't you ask them? Sorry, Johnny. They're treating it as just another vehicle theft. It was clean when they found it."

"And the Boys? What are they going to do?"

"Nothing. They were a bit upset about someone ruining a nice safe café, but they don't want to know any more."

I nodded. "Thanks, Harry."

"Is that it?"

We had walked in a large circle and we were now close to the place we'd started from. I took Harry's car keys from my pocket with my left hand and smiled. "That's it, Harry. For now. Only, you haven't met me."

He nodded. "Would I shop you, Johnny?"

"If the price was right." I pulled a couple of hundred franc bills from the inside pocket of my coat and wrapped the keys up in them. "Payment for your time, Harry," I said. I threw the keys and the notes into the distance. His face fell.

"Happy hunting!"

I split, running along the avenue of bare trees. I saw the lights come on in the Volvo and Irene roared towards me.

Eight

Moments later we were on our way. Irene was frightened, badly; I could tell by the nervous edge on her voice. It's always worst when the ordeal is over, when you think you can relax.

"Are you all right, Johnny?"

"I'm okay." I told her what Harry had said, as we drove, keeping watch behind all the time for anyone who might be following. I chuckled a little at the thought of the podgy Dutchman scrambling around on his hands and knees in the rain and the mud looking for those keys. Served him right.

I wondered, idly, whether the Boys knew that he'd sold those goons the guns. Somehow I doubted that; they wouldn't have liked it. And they had a way of letting you know when they weren't happy which usually left an impression.

I told Irene to drive out of Paris via the route that the killers had taken on that fateful night. It was almost dark and the traffic was beginning to build up into the nightmare of the rush hour in Paris; I didn't think there was too much danger of being followed, We crossed the Seine via La Grande Jatte, an island leisure park cum picnic ground for the citizens of Paris during the long hot summer. A memory of a painting of the place jumped into my mind's eye, a painting all full of soft sunlight and warmth. It didn't look so very inviting in the flesh, that day in January as we passed the broad lawns of the island.

We cut through the suburbs towards the towering glass and concrete fortress of La Defense. It was quite pretty, then, in the dark of a winter's evening, with the glow-worm soft lights illuminating it. A massive structure, shopping mall, railway intersection, offices, homes, the lot; a great French tribute to modern architecture. Personally, it made me shiver.

Then we were heading out of town, towards the villa which had become our sanctuary. As always, I gave the place a thorough once-over before we relaxed. I checked each room, carefully examining the little strips of tape I'd stuck between the doors and their jambs. It was okay; none of the doors had been opened.

Irene lit up a caporal and switched on the television to watch the news. I took a seat beside her, but I wasn't really paying attention to the newsreader; I was thinking about the things Harry had told me. All that stuff about the van and the bodies being got rid of, that was no surprise; and I suppose that if I'd thought about it long enough I'd have come up with the notion that Harry himself might have supplied the weapons.

I mean, Harry would sell you anything, if you paid him enough. There weren't many suppliers who could get you hardware like those .22s, not at any price. The real spanner in the works was the nationality of the killers. Harry was no fool, though he might like to give the impression that he was slower on the uptake than he actually was. If he said they were Spanish, then I believed him. But what the hell were a couple of Spanish thugs doing trying to hit me in a lonely bar in Clichy?

They were a long way from home, that was for sure. And I was convinced that they hadn't been real pros; all those little things, those small anomalies, were a dead giveaway. Furthermore, I'd been pissed, I was knackered after my flight back from Istanbul and as I said, getting there in the first place hadn't been a holiday; my reactions were slow, at least by pro standards.

A witness to that was the fact that they had succeeded in wounding me. But if they'd really been on the ball and found me in that state, it would have been bye-bye Johnny and no messing. So who brings a couple of amateur hoodlums from hundreds of miles away to hit someone like me? And when you then think that someone else was wiping out Julie and the kids in the most cold-bloodedly professional manner, it's a recipe for a brain-storm.

"Merde alors, another one!" Irene's voice broke into my stream of thought. "Another what?" I asked, more out of politeness than real interest."

"Another bomb; haven't you been listening?"

"What bomb?"

"Outside the British Embassy."

The report was over by the time my attention had been caught. All Irene could tell me was that it seemed that no-one had been injured. I frowned. There was something about that tiny snippet of information that was making the little hairs on the back of my neck stand on end, as if my subconscious had just seen something which my waking mind was ignorant of. Believe me, it's not a pleasant sensation.

"You said 'Another one.'"

"Sure," replied Irene. "Of course, I keep forgetting that you've been away from Paris for a while. There have been several bombs in the last month, six weeks perhaps."

I'd left Paris to lead that convoy of new Citroëns to Damascus on the twenty-first of November; I'd been two weeks getting there, a week waiting to be paid, then I'd been in the east of Turkey picking up the stones, before coming home. In all that time I hadn't seen a French newspaper once and though my Arabic is good enough to understand the Syrian newsreaders on the radio, they'd been too interested in the Israelis to pay any attention to the European situation. So for all I knew, there might have been mass riots in the streets of Paris; I just wouldn't have known.

This business of the bombs; I pursued it with Irene. Unfortunately, like most people, she didn't have much of a memory for news; unless something affects you personally it's quickly forgotten. Or unless it is your business to be interested in such things. She couldn't even remember how many there had been, or when they had happened, exactly, or where, just that everyone in the city had been very nervous.

It had been unusually quiet on Christmas Eve; at the time I'd just put it down to the awful weather, but if I thought about it, I'd never known the weather get in the way of a Frenchman when he was in the mood for a good time. But this explained it much more clearly; there's nothing like a series of bomb scares to make people righteously stay at home with their families where they belong. I couldn't tell why, or how, or anything, yet, but that prickly sensation of warning I'd had was slowly becoming a very convincing hunch.

The more I thought about it, the more likely it seemed that there must be a connection between the bombings and the attack on me; and if you think I was relieved to have that feeling, you'd be way wrong. That would put the whole thing into a different league, a different level, a far far more frightening level than a simple revenge killing. The more I thought about it the more the hunch grew and the more I could understand why my hackles were up in a premonition of fearful danger.

I could hardly eat, even though I'd been feeling hungry enough earlier; I waited on the edge of my chair for the re-run of the news at nine o'clock. Poor Irene must have been getting used to me by then, because she just sighed and cleared away the plates. She poured me a drink. It helped a little.

At last the news came on. The bombing was the third item; it seemed that TF1 rated a speech by the US President on 'Fortress Europe' and an item on the steelworkers pay claim hotter news than a bomb attack on the British Embassy. I listened avidly.

At five fifteen that afternoon, a car bomb had exploded outside the compound gate in Rue Saint Honoré, only a few yards from the main entrance of the Embassy. It seemed that the Ambassador, who was a creature of habit, normally passed through that gate in his chauffeur-driven Rolls at exactly the time the bomb exploded, yet by chance and good fortune, on this day of all days the Rolls had been taken to a garage to be serviced. He was late, so the chauffeur picked up the Ambassador from the main entrance of the Embassy, some twenty-five yards from the car-bomb.

The Ambassador had already stepped into the Rolls when it went off. His only injury was a knock on the back of the head he'd received when his chauffeur had floored the throttle and got out of there like he'd been trained to.

The French Government was doing its level best to play the affair down and avoid an international incident. The security boys at the Embassy would be going nuts, the FO would be taking a very dim view of the whole affair and heads were going to roll, for sure.

No one had taken responsibility for the attack, at least at that time, though this meant little. Although most terrorist groups seek publicity, some of them will only own up to successful ventures.

"Do you think it's important?" asked Irene. I bit my lip and nodded, but I didn't tell her about the way my stomach was churning. I'd already discovered how stubborn she was. There was no hope of me persuading her to be sensible and get lost for a while, so there seemed little point in frightening her. I was frightened enough for both of us.

Nine

Iknew what kind of people did these things; ruthless killers who had no thought but the end they were trying to achieve. They had no compunction about killing innocent bystanders. They wouldn't think twice about being killed themselves in the pursuit of their aims and they wouldn't even consider showing mercy to their enemies. Of course, the precise nature of the 'enemy' would depend upon which particular group of psychopaths you were dealing with, whether it was the IRA or the Angry Brigade, or the Red Army Faction, or the Viet Cong or Islamist fanatics. I'd seen enough of those people in action to know how dangerous they were.

I know there are those who, perhaps from some kind of misguided idealism, say that these people are fighting legitimate wars against oppressors. I suppose you can't expect them to know what it's like to find a fourteen year old girl up an alleyway with her kneecaps drilled through with a Black and Decker, treatment doled out by her own people just because she happened to be seen chatting to a soldier. They've never walked into a village that had dared to refuse help to the VC and had had three of their young men taken out, hacked into little pieces and then a piece delivered to every house just to let the families know whose side they were on; no, you can't expect those cosseted middle class liberals to know, but I've seen it, at first hand, in the jungles and towns of Vietnam, in the fields and streets of Ireland and other places sick with the stench of violence and their streets slippery with blood.

I'd been wrong all along about this little nightmare, when I'd thought that someone, somewhere, had arranged all the savagery to get rid of me, when I'd thought that doing so was the only object; when I'd been racking my brains day and night to try to remember who it was that hated me so much and who fitted the other facts. I'd been so wrong. This was much, much bigger. I was just a peripheral affair, a skirmish.

I wondered if Irene had sensed my growing apprehension. I hoped not. All through that night I couldn't sleep as my mind kept making connections, trying to find a pattern, a solution that would fit the facts.

It seemed like an eternity since I'd stepped off the plane from Istanbul and into this nightmare. I wanted more information about the bombings; not just the most recent one, at the British Embassy, but all the others too. I needed to know what the buzz was, if there was any going.

To my surprise it was Irene who came to my assistance. "I could look around for you, if it would help." She turned around. She was sitting in front of the mirror on the dresser in the bedroom, putting on her make-up, with all her usual patient attention to detail. "Sure," she chirped, brightly. "I'm a working girl, remember? The girls, they see things, they hear things. I'll ask around."

She returned to the task in hand, watching me through the mirror. "And I do have friends, Johnny; maybe you don't know about them."

I looked hard at her. It was beginning to be painfully obvious to me that there was a lot I didn't know about her. She cocked her head on one side and flashed one of those huge grins of hers at my reflection. Christ, I thought, five foot four, slender as a two day old foal and as innocent looking and every ounce of her full of surprises.

I was nevertheless reluctant to let her go out on her own, but she pooh-poohed my fears with disdain. "Stop being so protective. I can look after myself, Johnny; I may not have all your fancy training, but I was around for a long time before I met you."

I sighed.

She finished putting on her face, got up from her seat and crossed to where I was standing. She kissed me.

"Okay," I said. "You take your own car, go into town. Find out everything you can about the bombs and about any Spanish terrorist groups who might be in the city. They probably have a safe house in the La Defense area."

"Sure."

I checked my watch. It was after ten. "I'll leave half an hour after you. We'll meet up here at, say, nine tonight?"

She nodded.

I hesitated and then lifted the Luger from the bed. "Want this?"

She shook her head. Then she brightened. "But I'll take the shotgun, if you don't mind. I'll put it in the car." The thought of the petite girl standing in front of me cutting loose with that cannon was so startling that the surprise must have registered on my face, because she laughed.

"I once had a boyfriend who taught me how to shoot with a shotgun." She went out into the hall, where we kept the gun in the umbrella stand. When she returned, she quickly demonstrated that she did indeed know how to use the thing. I shrugged. I'd feel better knowing she had it with her. She had also brought a large golf umbrella and she slipped the weapon, which was less than two feet long, into its folds and then buttoned the strap at the top. No one would have known there was anything suspicious. Unless it began to rain.

Things like that made me wonder who the boyfriend was, but Irene was giving nothing away. She just smiled one of those irrepressible smiles of hers and breezed out.

I left the house after half an hour; though I had a lot to do, I didn't want to crowd Irene.

Outside the house, the weather was its usual, depressing, January grey. I turned up the collar of my coat and thrust my hands deep into ray pockets, where I could feel the comforting bulk of Goering's Luger. I walked down the path to where the Volvo was parked.

I was nervous about going into the city but I had to do it sometime or another. It had been a while since I'd seen my face on the cover of one of the papers. I was dressed in clothes that I ordinarily wouldn't have been seen dead in and my cheeks were puffed out by the cotton-wool pads. Irene had been convinced that I was unrecognisable, but somehow I didn't quite share her easy confidence.

My first stop was the central library, where I wanted to check the back references to the other bombings that Irene had mentioned. At least it was warm in there. The girl who brought the papers I'd asked for was very helpful. In fact she was so helpful that I thought I was going to have trouble getting rid of her, but in the end she took the hint and left me in peace.

It didn't take long to find what I was looking for. Twenty-third of November; that was just after I'd left for Damascus. Someone had set a bomb outside, of all places, the Russian Embassy. Several of the staff were killed and a couple of civilians injured by flying glass. No one had claimed responsibility, arid the Police had made a statement to the effect that in their opinion, it was an isolated incident, engineered by a lunatic element; in the meantime there was nothing to worry about.

The Russians hadn't thought so, however. On the twenty-fourth, the French Ambassador to Moscow was summoned to the Kremlin and given a severe dressing-down.

I've never taken any of those Official Police Statements seriously; I haven't known them to be right often enough to justify it. And this was a case in point, because on the sixth of December, wouldn't you just know it, off went another one, this time set in a briefcase left in the foyer of the Continental Hotel.

They'd had to scrape the bellhop off the ceiling,and the leader of a German trade delegation had been very put out.

And then, ten days later, another, on a Sunday, outside a Lutheran Church on the Left Bank. This time the target was a Dutch Cabinet Minister and this time the bombers hit. Not only was the Minister blown to smithereens, but so were his wife, his body-guard and chauffeur, when a bomb went off under his limousine as he was preparing to leave.

The French had protested that they had asked him to stick to the itinerary they'd set, but you can bet that didn't do their reputation any good.

Then another, in the week before Christmas. This one was very public; it had devastated part of the Gare de l'Est. At first it did seem as if the bomb was set to kill civilians. It did that very successfully, with seven known killed and thirty-eight injured; closer scrutiny, however, revealed, that, in fact, there had been a delegation from the Ministry of Finance due to leave for Strasbourg to attend a summit on the possibility of links between the currencies of the member states of the Economic Community. At the very last moment they'd changed their plans and flown out instead.

Four bombings. Five, if you include the most recent, at the British Embassy. And I was convinced that they were all carried out by the same group. There were so many similarities, too many, like the nature of the targets. All public figures, true, but not the most public; yet the bombings had all been acutely embarrassing both for the French security services and the Government itself. It was a signature, but whose?

By the standards of the world's most indiscriminate murderers, five bombs in two months would be mere peanuts; but in the capital of

France, Paris itself, such a thing was unheard-of. This was calculated, refined. And then there was the business of claims. Not a single authentic claim had been made for any of the attacks. That was very, very peculiar. Usually these bloodthirsty bastards can't wait to hoist their colours over the scene of each new carnage. These bombings were different.

For two hours I researched, cross-referenced and made notes. Soon the little black notebook I'd brought was crammed with pages and pages of the tiny, spidery shorthand writing that is used only by those trained by the Firm. I thought I had all I was going to get.

I thanked the pretty assistant librarian who'd been so helpful. She smiled, fluttering her long dark eyelashes over the frames of her highly fashionable glasses. I thought I heard her sigh as I pushed through the swing doors, but it may have been an effect of the wind.

The sleet that had begun earlier had turned to real snow by the time I stood outside again. The street was almost deserted. I turned up my collar and began to walk back towards a café.

I sipped my third cup of coffee and looked around me again. There was no-one even faintly suspicious-looking in the bar or paying any attention to the bespectacled, rather dull looking man in the corner by the window, his overcoat damp from the melted snow, writing notes in his little black book; I smiled.

I checked over my notes again. There was something niggling at the back of my brain, some thought that hadn't quite fully formed, some thought that, perhaps, I didn't want to face. When I was working for the Firm, I had to do the full range of a field man's work; but as well as that, I was in charge of certain operations myself. In fact, it was on one of those that Julie and I had first been thrown together.

Ever since I'd been in 'Nam, I'd become increasingly aware of the necessity to identify terrorist groups when they were at work. I regarded it as imperative that we, as a security agency, should be able to tell exactly who was involved in any job we might be asked to tackle, anywhere in the world. I also regarded it as important that we should study these groups so that we could, if ever we had to, imitate accurately any group in the world, whether that group was official or freelance.

Julie devised a computer programme that could tell, just by looking at the regular news material that was fed into it every day, who was working, where in the world. It was a beaut, if I say so myself. It could even pinpoint individual agents.

If we could tell who was doing what, then we were in with a sporting chance of being able to tell what they would do next. And the programme that we had devised did that. Julie was one bright kid.

I wished to hell I could get my hands on the damned thing again, just for a few minutes; that's all it would have taken. But there was no way.

I'm a suspicious sort of a character; I know that it's not a very pleasant characteristic, but at least it's kept me alive. And I wasn't even sure about the Firm itself. I mean, they were in the perfect position to hit me; they, more than any other agency, could have found someone whom Julie would have trusted enough to let into the flat. And as for motive, well, I guess you could say that somebody might get round to the idea that we knew too much.

It's a sick world; and until I was quite sure that the Firm was in the clear, I wasn't going near them. And by 'in the clear' I meant really in the clear. Even if they'd not been behind it, then most of the official companies would have tipped them the wink if they were going to hit me; it's a sort of professional etiquette.

Field men are too valuable and often too exposed; it's one thing for a man to be hit when he's on a job, but it doesn't often happen when he's on leave, or retired, or ill. It could lead to a wave of revenge killings as each company hit back at whoever it thought was up to no good. There would be no time to get any work done. So the companies have a protocol. They clear an op like that first. So even if the Firm hadn't been behind the hit, they might have sanctioned it.

I once hit a pensioned-off KGB colonel, living quietly in a dacha on the shores of the Black Sea. Even though the Russians are supposed to be the other side, we cleared it through Moscow first. He was no more use to them; they extorted something they had wanted from us. I went in quietly and slipped him a little pill that made it look like a massive heart attack and then came out the way I'd gone in, by canoe back to Turkey.

What the KGB hadn't known was that that particular colonel had been a double agent all of his life. He wouldn't defect, in the end, for fear of what might have happened to his family. So he was a threat to our network of operatives permanently stationed in the USSR.

So I think I had cause to doubt the Firm. Until I knew they were kosher on this, I couldn't trust them.

There were a few companies that I could write off straight away, although they were known to bear a grudge against me. I was convinced that there was a link between the bombings that had been shaking Paris and the attempt on my life. So it couldn't possibly have been any of the Irish organisations; too subtle by half. And the targets were all wrong for any of the Muslim groups.

There were some European home-grown murderers who were known to pull stunts like these, from both the extreme right and the extreme left, but many could be ignored. The Red Army Faction, for instance, was committed to a fund-raiser; they were at the time systematically robbing the northern Italian banks. Baader-Meinhof was out the window; they'd paid dearly in their last shoot-out with the police in Germany and were, for the moment, a spent force. The loony right in Germany was concentrating its efforts on recruiting from Germany's growing, disaffected unemployed youth, while the British contributions, like the Angry Brigade, were a joke.

In France, they didn't have too many indigenous violent political groups. Mostly they'd been smoked out after sixty-eight. Their recruiting-grounds in the Universities arid Colleges had been cleaned up and the extreme left and right had returned to being little more than discussion groups. This was the way I liked it and one of the reasons I liked France.

They did, however, have two provincial groups who were quite good at killing innocent people. By far the more important was ETTA, the Basque separatist movement. Up until then, they'd concentrated their activities in Spain because the Spanish were less skilled in dealing with their sort than the French, but also because they have support in France which they were always reluctant to compromise. Still, it tied with what Harry had said about the men he'd sold those .22s to.

The only thing that stopped me from being sure that ETTA was behind the bombings was the extra flak. Like trying to hit me. I'd never crossed swords with them in the past; why should they attack me now?

And why move their campaign to the French capital? What was the underlying strategy behind that? Their support in the country would melt away like snow on a warm morning if it became known that they were operating within the boundaries of La Belle France. Perhaps that was the reason that no-one had claimed responsibility for the attacks.

Ten

I was just writing down the names of possible candidates when it hit me. As if I'd been trying not to think it so long that in the end my subconscious took control and made me write it anyway. It sort of flowed off the end of my pen and, when I saw it, my eyes fixed on it in astonishment.

Bald Eagle. I shook my head and looked again, but it was still there: it hadn't gone away. Bald Eagle! Shit.

I skimmed through the list of other names I'd written down, the Bulgarians, the Vietnamese, the Libyans, but when I really thought about it, none of them came close. None of them had the ability to plan such a campaign. Or to add the little details, like using my own gun to terminate my family; that sort of thing took a special kind of operator.

But Bald Eagle...In Europe? In the very heartland of the Western Alliance? That was nuts. But there was no-one else.

Chile, Nicaragua, El Salvador, Iran, Lebanon, these were all the well known operating grounds of the notorious division of Uncle Sam's finest, the Central Intelligence Agency, that specialised in the disruption of 'hostile' regimes. The CIA itself was the biggest, the most active, secret service of them all, with more agents in the field at any one time than the KGB and the East Germans put together. And believe me, that's quite a comparison of giants.

Bald Eagle. It was so secret that half of the Directors of the CIA didn't know about it. And they only played one game. Disruption.

No routine surveillance, regular intelligence gathering, that sort of thing; none of it. They provided one service alone: to make it impossible for a government, or even a multinational interest, to go on doing something that the White House didn't want them to. Including the business of governing itself.

Governments of the wrong political hue are toppled, individuals are persuaded to take a back seat, or stand down from office, or just disappear; big multinational companies are encouraged to do certain things – and not to do certain others. The techniques? Everything, from simple blackmail and murder, through kidnapping and ransoming, to the active involvement in and encouragement of, insurrection, riot and revolution.

Disruption. All the countries that cut any ice in the world have got divisions within their secret services for it; and Uncle Sam's is the biggest and best equipped of the lot. And mean to match.

Bald Eagle. The codename for 'Active: Deep Penetration'. Like all the CIA's divisions, it has a title composed of pure jargonese. The British equivalent is known only as 'the Firm'.

The more I thought, the less I liked the way things looked. I was sure, now, who was operating in Paris, who'd planned the bombs, who'd planned the hit on me; and I was shivering and the hairs were up on the back of my neck just thinking about it. How I was going to fight them? And what the hell they were up to; why were they in Paris? That's unheard-of. It's like the Firm taking up a campaign in Washington. It's against the rules of the Western Alliance.

There's nothing to stop companies operating against the interests of nominally friendly nations when those interests are overseas; interests in the Third World, particularly. It's open day out there. But back home is different. Taboo. Off limits.

I looked out of the window of the café again. It had grown dark; it was time I set out for Versailles, or else Irene would be home, worried. I paid my bill and left the place, once more walking out into the swirling snow.

As I drove out of Paris, all those details that had lain dormant for so long flipped up before my mind's eye. It was Kennedy who really pumped the money into Bald Eagle. He was so upset by the debacle the CIA had suffered at The Bay of Pigs that he determined that the agency should become the best in the world. Bald Eagle was accountable only to the President, through a completely separate chain of command. In effect, an agency within an agency.

They'd gone on to great things; they'd been the spearhead of Operation Tomahawk in 'Nam, which had been almost one hundred per cent effective, until it was shelved because of humanitarian pressure. That showed up Bald Eagle's great weakness. It could not stand publicity. There was none of that when it was involved in Chile, though; not till way after the event. And there it had a field day. Things didn't go quite as planned in Iran, but set against that were successes elsewhere in the Middle East. All in all, Bald Eagle had a pretty convincing track record. And that didn't make me feel any better.

I didn't take the direct route back from the city out of natural paranoia, helped along by having discovered the identity of my attacker, but instead cut northward towards St. Germain. I figured that if the road to Versailles were being watched, then this way I'd miss them; and if they were already on my tail I could ambush them in the quiet back roads. That was what I thought, anyway.

It turned out to be a big mistake.

I got through St. Germain with no trouble and turned off to the south along the back road, as I'd planned. Visibility was very low and the snow was coming in flurries. I had to drive dead slow because of the conditions, even though I was itching to get a move on. I had a sort of premonition that there was something going wrong, somewhere.

I stopped just outside St. Germain to see if I was being followed, but I couldn't see a damned thing for the snow. I told myself that at least it would make life difficult for anyone on my tail and set off again. Less than two kilometres further on, I swung round a bend in the road and, dead ahead of me, I saw the lights of a line of stationary cars. I braked as firmly as I could and thankfully managed to stop before I cannoned into the rearmost one. I swallowed. I didn't like the look of this.

The snow whipped and swirled around the car, so that I could hardly see anything. Then, out of the gloom, I saw two figures with torches approach, swinging their capes around their shoulders. Gendarmes! For a horrible instant that seemed to stretch forever, I thought that I was caught in a roadblock. What if someone had, after all, recognised me in town? In the library, in the café? What if they knew about Versailles; and all the roads were blocked? What if they had Irene?

My mouth went dry as parchment. I looked over my shoulder, ready, in that moment, to stuff the car into reverse and make a run for it; but too late. A lorry was already rounding the bend and slowing up behind me. There was no escape that way. Almost without my conscious mind willing it, my gloved right hand found the catch of the courtesy locker in the dash and withdrew the silenced .22 that lay there.

I was aware of the friendly bulk of the Luger in my coat pocket, but I knew it would make too much noise. I slipped the .22 under my thigh and looked to the front again. The two black-caped figures were almost upon me, now, shining their torches into the car; I was sure that they were looking to see my face. The one on the left tapped on my window and I rolled it down.

"Switch off your engine, monsieur." I nodded slowly and reached forward. There was something awfully final in the sound of the engine dying. I looked up at the gendarme. He was behind the light, so I couldn't see his face. What was he thinking? The other stood a little way back. Could I get them both in one move? Two shots, clean, neat? Could I get out, away?

The gendarme shone his torch on my face and I felt my hand slip onto the cold butt of the .22. He let the light rest there a moment, then it slipped away. He swung it around the rest of the car, following it with his eyes, which were now illuminated in the reflected backwash. "You are alone?"

"Yes." I forced the word out, my throat tight with anticipation.

"Where are you going?"

"Rambouillet," I lied. It was close to St Germain. "Look, officer, I'm in a little of a hurry. What is going on here?"

The gendarme swung his light back onto my face and for a moment I thought I'd gone over the score. "You are not, by any chance, monsieur, a doctor, are you?" His question came in a less terse, more relaxed voice. I saw a ray of hope.

"No." I shook my head. "Why do you ask?"

"There has been a bad accident, monsieur. A truck skidded into a car and crushed it. Very bad. It is a pity that you are not a doctor. The ambulance has not arrived yet."

"How long will we be delayed? Only...my wife will worry. You know how it is."

"Of course, monsieur. I cannot say; forty-five minutes, a little more, perhaps. We will be as quick as we can."

I nodded. "Thank you, officer." The two gendarmes withdrew, fading into the all-enveloping snow, I wondered, later, what they'd have thought, if they'd turned again and looked back, to see me rest my head on the steering wheel, shaking with relief, soaked in a cold sweat.

As it turned out, it was near half past nine before they waved me on my way, saluting and shouting ”Vas-y. Vas-y!” I was late and I knew that Irene would worry, but I dared not go quickly on that deadly road surface. I counted off the kilometres as they passed, until at last the lights of Versailles loomed like ghosts through the snow.

I had almost forgotten my earlier panic as I swung the car into the street where that familiar villa stood. The snow itself had slowed to a gentle sprinkling and was more pretty than threatening, now. I stopped the car some way from the house and began to walk up the hill.

Eleven

I don't know what sixth sense it was that made me leave the car and walk those last few yards; but I had cause to be grateful. I noted the blurred outline of Irene's petite footprints in the snow; she had not attempted to drive her little car up the snow-covered slope either. And then I saw the other prints, coming out of the rhododendron bush at the side of the path. My mouth dried up like a crisp. There were clear signs of a struggle and I could make out two pairs of distinct prints amongst those of the newcomers. They had overpowered her almost at once but there was no sign of blood. I was thankful.

I slipped silently into the shadows of the garage. I could hear no sound and there was no sign of a guard. The .22 nestling in my hand, I made a recce of the house. I prayed I wasn't already too late. I cursed the faint squeak of the fresh snow compressing beneath my weight at every step, but I knew that it wouldn't be heard over the gentle sighing of the wind that had blown away the snow-clouds. The house, remember, spanned two ground levels. From the front of the house, looking into the upper floor, I could see nothing except a thin sliver of light escaping through the little gap in the living-room curtains. It was a fair guess that someone was in there; someone who meant no good.

I moved slowly round the house into the gloom of the garden at the rear. The ground sloped steeply away here and I could look inside There was a light in the master bedroom and, my heart in my mouth, I made my way forward. As I drew nearer, I began to hear voices, voices full of aggression and anger.

One of them was unmistakeably Irene's, spitting out, "Cochon, cochon! Leave me alone! Cochon!"

The other was the voice of a man, a rasping, brutal voice, shouting, "Putain! Whore!"

I moved slightly into the light in time to see Irene spit in her attacker's face. The man, dark and thick-set, drew back his fist and punched her in the mouth so that she was thrown across the bed, then then leapt on top of her. God only knows how I stopped myself from smashing through that window there and then; I can only assume that it was my training that blocked my desperate urge.

I knew that there must be at least one other, somewhere. I had to deal with him, first, otherwise saving Irene from her rapist would be to no avail when his accomplice came in with guns blazing. I doubted if they'd give me the same leeway as they had on Christmas Eve. It's funny, how the fear flees when there's work to be done; now I was into my stride and the years between then and my last operational mission melted away. Even the slight residual pain in my left forearm vanished as I retraced my steps to the front of the house.

There was a door that led directly from the garage into the little pantry at the back of the kitchen. I had a key for it. I knew it didn't squeak. Within moments I was inside the house. I slipped off my shoes and began to make my way towards the sliver of light that betrayed the men in the sitting-room. I realised that I was grinning like a hyena.

There was the sound quiet conversation, in a foreign language I didn't recognise. I could tell what they were talking about, though, because Irene's muffled yells and the rhythmic panting coming from the bedroom below signalled that the man there had overpowered her resistance. I wondered if the men in the sitting-room were awaiting their turn or whether they'd already raped her and were comparing notes.

I listened carefully at the door, trying to place the men inside. One voice was a little more muffled than the other. I guessed that the speaker was sitting on the sofa with his back to the door. Suddenly I heard footsteps as the other man moved across the room, then the unmistakable clink of Irene's fine crystal brandy decanter being knocked against a glass.

That was all I'd been waiting for. I swung open the door and the .22 in my hand jumped and made its dull thud twice. The man with the glass in his hand dropped it and it fell to the floor in an explosion of shards. His face registered shock as the blood welled from his obliterated left eye and he slumped to the floor.

His companion was good; he sprang from his seat as if he'd been electrocuted and let go a burst with his Uzi at the vacant space by the door where I'd been standing less than a second before. But I had not forgotten the training that had kept me alive on nearly two dozen missions as a field man; fire and move, they told me, fire and move.

And by the time the second man got off his shots, I was already over by the piano. His burst of gunfire ended as my bullets smashed into his body.

Blast him, though, the racket he'd made would have wakened the dead. I had to get to Irene fast. I flew down the stairs with my feet barely touching the ground and threw myself at the bedroom door. It was locked. Evidently somebody didn't want his buddies to come and spoil the party.

I could hear the struggling going on inside. I drew back and kicked the door just below the handle, a full-blooded kick that sent the door splintering open.

After God made Irene, he surely broke the mould. Her attacker had obviously been in mid-stride when he heard the shots. She had scissored her legs around his body and hung on like a limpet, whilst he desperately tried to reach the gun he'd left on a chair by the door. He had succeeded in dragging their combined bodies off the bedand half way across the floor; but Irene had a good grip on the bedstead and she was determined.

Just as I entered the room he drew back his hand to strike her again. I saw her eyes flutter shut, her face brace itself against the blow; but it never fell, for I stepped forward, stuck the muzzle of my pistol hard into the back of the man's neck,and said, in Spanish, "You hit her and I shoot out your throat and leave you to die."

He froze like a rabbit in front of a fox. Irene was looking at me with an expression on her face the like of which I never want to see again. The blood was trickling from a cut at the corner of her mouth and she was going to have a splendid black eye. Her bottom lip was quivering and her chest was heaving. She pulled herself away from the man and retched. She looked at me again in that awful, wild way, got to her feet and began to stagger towards the shower-room, one hand clasped to her mouth, the other feebly pulling the tatters of her skirt down over her injured sex.

I watched her leave; right at that moment she needed to be alone. I heard the ghastly sound as she puked.

I was slowly, almost unconsciously, running the thick barrel of the .22 along the back of the man's neck. I could feel a revulsion toward him such as I'd never known before. Oh, I'd killed other unsavoury types in the past, quite a number, in fact, but they had all been jobs, done as neatly and professionally as possible, no mess, no fuss. This was different; I was personally involved.

I suddenly knew, for the first time in my life, how sweet was the taste of revenge.

"You are going to die anyway," I told him. "You can choose which way it's going to be; slowly, or quickly."

He began to shiver, kneeling there on the floor and muttered a prayer. "You see," I went on, "I was in Vietnam. I learned a lot there. Including how to hurt a man so that he pleads for death, begs for it, but never letting it come to him, never letting the pain be washed away by the sweet release of death. Oh, yes, I learned these things and tonight, my friend, you are going to learn them too. But you are not going to walk away; in the end I will kill you, but it will be in my own time, when I have grown bored with you and your pain. You will thank me when I bring you death." My voice was a whisper, caressing the words.

"On the other hand, it could be quick, clean; the decision is yours."

The man was shaking so much now that he could barely speak; he turned round to face me and raised his hands to beg. "Let me go, senor; I will tell you everything I know."

"And what do you know, scum? Who are you?"

"We are ETTA," he whimpered. "Basques. We are fighting to liberate our homeland from the oppression –"

"Shut it! Since when does your noble cause justify rape?"

"Senor, but she is a whore, she –"

The fury flared up in me. I brought the barrel of the gun crashing into the man's face, raking it into the flesh, my eyes narrow with hate. "Be very careful, my friend; you are going to die for what you did to that girl." The terror in the man's eyes shone. "Who sent you?"

"I...I do not know. Serge, he knows. He is upstairs."

"He can tell me nothing. Who sent you?"

"I swear I do not know! They contact Serge by telephone. We are never allowed..."

"You must have picked up the phone by accident, once, at least; tell me about it, tell me about the voice that spoke." I grabbed a handful of the man's hair and jerked his head back. "Speak!"

"No, no; they always phoned at a certain time. Only Serge knew the time. He always answered the phone."

I could tell he wasn't lying; he was too terrified. "Okay. Now tell me where your safe-house is."

"Senor. I –"

My gun slashed into his face again. "This is only the beginning, my friend. Where is it?"

"A flat. Flat thirty two, at number four, Rue Michelet."

"In Courbevoie."

"Si, Senor."

"Why were you sent?"

"To avenge our comrades. Serge said that the man who killed them was here, living with a whore."

This time, he lost two teeth when the gun smashed into him.

"Stick to the facts," The man's breath was bubbling through the blood welling from his shattered lips and he spat out the fragments of his teeth. "To avenge your comrades," I went on. "The ones who died on Christmas Eve?"

"Si."

"And the bodies?"

"They are buried in the basement there."

"How many more of you are there?"

"Three." The man was hanging his head, quite cowed. Blood was dripping onto his knees. "You planted the bombs – like the one at the British Embassy? Your group, I mean."

"Si."

"They told Serge, as well? Why? Why pick those targets?"

"Senor, I do not know. I know that they supply us with weapons and money and that from time to time they ask us to do things for them."

"Who? Who asks you?"

"I don't know, I don't know, I don't know." He began to weep in earnest now. There was little more he could tell me. I watched him as his body shook with his weeping; I could almost feel sorry for him. How old was he? Twenty-three, twenty-four? I wondered if he'd ever seen any of his victims, those he'd condemned to death, or maimed, with his bombs and his guns.

Just then I became aware of a presence by my side. It was Irene.

She was ghastly white. She had washed the blood from her face. Her skirt was wet where it had dragged carelessly in the bidet, as she had tried to wash the stain of the man from her body. There was something frightening about her, as of one not quite sane. Something shiny in her hand caught the light. Her voice was expressionless, calm, as she spoke. "Has he told you everything?"

"Everything he can."

"Good." She moved forward. "Stand up, cochon. Filth! Stand up!"

The man looked at her and then at me. "Senor, please, she is crazy, please..."

"You should have thought of that," I said, quietly. "Stand up."

The man stood. His singlet and his socks were the only clothes on his body. His penis hung free. Irene smiled and I wondered what she had in mind. The man's eyes rested on mine, as terrified as a calf in an abattoir, brown eyes, Mediterranean eyes. Irene stooped in front of him and stroked his penis.

"Such a pretty little thing, now; isn't it a pity?" Her voice was sweet, sweet and deadly. Suddenly I knew what she would do and I could tell that the man did, too. As if that were what she'd been waiting for, Irene sliced swiftly with the razor-blade, the glinting razor blade. The horror and pain were writ large in those terrified calf's eyes, as his mouth opened in a scream. It was a scream that never sounded, for Irene stifled it by popping the severed penis delicately into his mouth. Then she spat in his face again. The man doubled, the blood pouring from the stump where his manhood had once been, clasping the wound with his hands, choking and trying to spit out the still-warm flesh of his own body which, through the taste of the blood, must still have tasted of his own Irene's juices.

"You have finished with him?" she asked me.

I knew what she meant and I gave her the gun. I didn't think I needed to remind her how to use it. The man was still doubled over. Irene swiftly went round behind him. She viciously shoved the muzzle of the gun between the cleft of his buttocks and into his anus. A look of sheer, wild terror appeared on his face as he tried to twist away, but he was too late.

"Now I rape you, bastard," hissed Irene and pulled the trigger. The man collapsed forward onto the floor, writhing in agony, like a worm that has been cut in two by the gardener's spade. Irene looked into my eyes and I could see the baleful, mad fever begin to die, as she drew back from the edge.

"Oh my God," she cried. "Finish it, will you?" she pleaded, her voice vibrant with hysteria, "Will you finish it for me?"

I took the gun and put it to the man's temple, pulled the trigger and ended his pain. When I looked round again, it was in time to see Irene stagger and fall, unconscious, to the floor. My heart leapt into my mouth as I saw the deadly trickle of blood that had been running down the inside of her thigh.

Twelve

"That's right. Flat thirty-two, number four, Rue Michelet. Be careful; there are at least three still in action and they're armed. You'll find the bodies of two others and a boy buried in the basement. You'll also find the bodies of another three of them in the car park of the RER station at La Defense. Yes, they're the ones responsible for the bombings. You owe me one. Goodbye."

I hung up and made my way from the telephone box back to the car. It had been one hell of a night, one hell of a night. I thought of Irene and my stomach churned. If she died, then I would be to blame, for I had brought those terrible things into her life. I realised that if she died, then a light would go out in my life, a light that I'd only just realised could shine at all. No. They couldn't take Irene: they had taken too much already.

I drove back to the Doc's place, every second of the way desperate to hear the news and yet not so; I turned over the events of the night in my mind. It was then a little after five in the morning; dawn was still hours away.

After Irene had collapsed on the floor, I wasted no time. I didn't wait to phone; I just carried her out to the Volvo and drove straight into the city, to the home of the doctor who'd treated my gunshot wound. He didn't take too kindly to being awakened so late at night, especially by me.

After I told him why I'd come, he loosened up a little. Irene hadn't regained consciousness. I was worried sick; he could see that. I left her with him. I knew that there was other work to be done.

I drove back out to the house and thoroughly cleaned up. They must have come in a car, those animals, but I'd no way of knowing which one. It was probably booby-trapped anyway.

Fortunately the house had tiled floors so I didn't have to hide huge bloodstains in a fitted carpet. Still, it took me a while to clean up the gore; the guy with the Uzi, whom I thought had been the one called Serge, certainly had a lot of blood in him.

Nice thing about big cars; you can get three bodies in the back seat.

Once I'd got the corpses out to it, cleaned the place up and gone over it for dabs, I sorted out a suitcase full of clothes for Ireneand picked up her travelling make-up case. As for myself, well, I didn't have so many clothes, but I took the time and trouble to remove every trace of my presence in the flat.

Then I found all the shell-cases that had scattered over the floor. There hadn't been a lot I could do with the bullet holes around the door of the living-room. Once again I cursed Serge for his quick reactions. We'd been lucky that the next-door neighbours were out.

As for the weapons themselves, by the time I'd finished, the boot of the Volvo looked like an armoury.

Then I locked up the house and made my way back towards the city. I dumped the bodies in the car-park. At the time I allowed myself a grim smile at the thought of what the law would make of the state of the guy whom Irene had so colourfully terminated.

Then I called my journalist friend and told him the story. He'd make sure that the gendarmerie flushed out the last of the terrorists from their hiding place in Courbevoie; and it also meant that I had an ally in the Press, which might be useful.

The doctor took his time about answering the door; poor guy, it wasn't his night. He was pale with anger and shaking. He glowered at me as I brushed past him into the flat.

"Are you responsible for this?" he demanded.

"If you mean 'Did I rape her,' the answer is no. And you know it." If I was short with him, I think I had an excuse. "You can take comfort from the knowledge that the man who did do it won't ever do it again."

The doctor paled.

"How is she, anyway," I went on. "I'm in no mood for idle chatter."

"She'll be all right; she had a little tear, but it had closed by the time you got here."

"I can live with that," I muttered. "Do you have any alcohol in the house? Brandy, schnapps, whisky?" The doctor nodded, reluctantly.

I watched him as he led the way into his lounge and poured us each a drink. It occurred to me that I didn't even know his given name; the note in Irene's address-book just had him as 'Doctor Maybach.' He was about forty and had the pot belly and baggy eyes of early dissipation.

Still he had a feeling for Irene; and that made him useful.

I don't know why, but I had the strangest suspicion that he was not practising his trade legally. What the hell. I had another brandy. "What about the rest of her?" I asked, when he didn't volunteer anything.

"As well as you'd expect for someone who's been raped and beaten up," was the reply, in none too friendly a tone.

I glanced at his eyes; they slid away from my gaze. "I never got round to thanking you for the job you did on my arm," I said, to lighten the atmosphere. It didn't work.

"Sure. Any time. I told her you were bad news then. I said, 'Turn this guy over to the flics, do yourself a favour,' but no, no, little Irene went right on ahead with you and look where it got her." He moved closer. I could see the red lines around his watery eyes. "I don't know who you are, mister, or what you do, but I don't want you here. You're bad news."

I shrugged my shoulders. I wasn't going to let myself be riled by a backstreet abortionist and I didn't care how useful he might be. "Okay," I said. "Where is she? We'll leave." I began to make for the door, but he jumped into my path with surprising agility.

"You're not taking her!"

"You're going to stop me?" He was a big boy, for all that his body had gone to seed. He was probably fool enough to fancy himself. A few people have made that mistake; I mean, you may have gathered that I'm not that imposing to look at. I wondered if he'd try. Very gently I pushed him to one side. He resisted at first and then made a grab for my shoulder. The back of my clenched fist hit his solar plexus and his knees buckled. Really. These amateurs.

"Don't play with fire," I cautioned. "You might get burned." I pulled my wallet from my pocket and counted out five hundred francs. "We were never here."

I threw the notes down at his feet; he was still choking and holding on to the back of a chair. I put my face close to his; not for long, because his breath soon made me move, but long enough to say, "And if it ever comes to my notice that you forgot, that we weren't here," I drew my finger in a line across my throat. "Okay?"

Generally I don't go for such theatrics, but I could tell he was the type to be impressed. "Don't bother to get up; I'm sure I can find her on my own."

She was asleep on a little folding bed in the dining-room.. Her eye was already puffy and blue. I could tell that in two days it was going to be every colour of the rainbow. She sighed as I slipped my arms under her and lifted her up, blankets and all; once again, as when I'd picked her up from the tiled floor of the bedroom in Versailles, I was struck by how little she weighed. She woke and opened her eyes. "Johnny?"

"Yes. It's okay. We're going somewhere safe."

"Johnny, I..."

"What is it?"

"I had such a terrible dream, Johnny. I'm glad you're here now."

Poor kid! She was doped up to the eyeballs, well away with the fairies. She sighed again and submitted to the effort of keeping her eyes open. I realised that my face was wet and I could taste salt; but I didn't care a damn.

The doctor had recovered his composure. He at least had the good grace to open the door for me. I sincerely hoped that our paths wouldn't have to cross again and I could tell that the feeling was mutual.

Outside, the first weak glimmer of dawn was beginning to think about lighting the new day. It didn't seem too keen on the idea.

I took a circuitous route, as always, but my destination was the only safe place I could leave Irene; Françoise' hotel in Joigny. I hated the thought of getting her involved, but what could I do? This time it was Irene who needed sanctuary. How could I deny her?

Between Paris and Joigny, my only stop was to pick up a tank of petrol; I used the pay-phone in the service station to call ahead and warn Françoise that we were coming.

The sun had been up for a full two hours by the time we got there, though it was one of those weakly, half-hearted suns of mid-winter, shiining pink on the snow-covered fields. It was almost pretty, or would have been if it hadn't been marred by the memory of the ugliness.

Françoise was ready for us when we arrived, ushering us off the street and into the courtyard. She closed the wooden gate behind the car and came towards me. There was a man with her, in his late fifties perhaps, with white hair and an impossibly thick moustache. He said nothing, but helped me to get Irene from the car and up the stairs to a roo.

He saw my look as we deposited Irene on the bed. He lifted a hand and waved it, deprecatingly. "It's okay, I am an old friend. I am also a doctor."

I felt the pressure of Françoise' hand on my shoulder and heard her whisper, "It will be all right. She is safe with Joseph. You must come with me now. I think a cup of strong coffee would do you no harm."

I grinned. "Where would I be without you, Françoise?" and followed her from the room; I heard the snick of the clasps on Joseph's medical bag just as I drew the door to.

Françoise led me down into the kitchen. It was one of those enormous old fashioned hotel ones, with an open range The beams overhead were crowded with suspended sausages, hams and cheeses. There was a wonderful smell and the warm glow from the logs on the range was most welcoming thing I'd seen for a long time. Françoise helped me to take off my coat and then made me sit while she prepared coffee.

She didn't say anything much until she was finished, when she handed me a cup of coffee and sat down by my side. Christ that coffee tasted good!

"I'm sorry, Françoise," I began. "I never wanted to get you involved in this; even coming here the last time was bad, but now it's worse, much worse."

She reached over and took my hand. "Johnny, how long have we known each other? Twelve years? Fifteen years? When have I ever turned you away from my door, even when I knew you were in trouble, in danger? And you have always repaid me, in some way or another, in your way, in whatever way you could; this time is no different. I can see that you are badly in trouble. You need my help, now; don't question it."

I smiled. "Look. I just want you to take care of her," I nodded over my shoulder towards the room where Irene was lying. "I won't stay here. No," I said, forestalling her objection, "Hear me out. I have things I must do; I will go back to the city. But first I must speak to Irene, to make sure that she's all right."

Françoise was looking at me quizzically. "I heard about you on the television, Johnny. They're still looking for you. They think you killed them, you know that, don't you?"

I nodded. "I was set up. I didn't tell you the whole story before, because I thought it would be better for you if you didn't know."

"Sure. I'm not a nosey woman," She paused and looked closely at me again. "You care about that girl, don't you?"

"Yes. Very much."

"It's funny; in all the time I've known you, I've never seen that light in your eyes when you spoke of a woman before." She smiled gently. "It is good. You are lucky; I have known men have their hearts burned out by less than you've been through, so that they could only feel hatred and bitterness, so that they had lost their capacity to love, to have compassion for another. Yes," she said, rising to pour more coffee. "I think you will come through this all right."

"If I come through it at all, Françoise, if I come through it at."

I stared into the glowing embers awhile and then told Françoise my story. She listened patiently, asking a little question here and there, to clarify a point. She laughed when I told her what I'd done to her shotgun.

Presently Joseph, the doctor, joined us in the kitchen, helping himself to coffee. "She will be okay. She's still in shock though; it is a terrible thing."

He sat down on another of the wooden chairs close to the warmth of the fire. He pulled a packet of Gitanes from his waistcoat pocket and offered me one. I declined.

"I suppose," he said, lighting up, "That I should not smoke. No doubt you think something like that; but I am at the stage of my life now when I no longer care what the rest of the world thinks of my actions. I have few pleasures and they are all dear to me."

He looked up into my eyes. "My friend, I have been a country doctor for most of my life. I have seen some dreadful things; but I would never wish to see again what I just have. Who would do that? What kind of man, what kind of animal," the old sawbones threw up his hands in a gesture of despair. "Who did this?"

There was a light in his eyes which made me think that he would have gone after Irene's rapist and killed him with his own hands, Hippocratic Oath or no. I warmed to him. "The man himself is dead," I said.

"Did you kill him?"

I hesitated, then nodded.

"Of course," he said.

"He was a terrorist; one of those who have been setting bombs in Paris. He was sent, with two friends, to kill me. But they found her first and they decided to have some fun with her while they were waiting."

"The others?"

"All dead."

Joseph gave me a long look. "You are more than you appear to be. You know, I was in action in Algeria during the troubles there, before they had their independence. There were some men, they brought them in to my field hospital for treatment once, men who had been sent far into the rebel territory; you remind me of them, my friend. There is something in those eyes of yours, something very deadly. I would not care to have you as my enemy."

I looked into the fire. "That's not likely."

The doctor turned to Françoise and murmured something to her. She nodded and withdrew. I smiled. Something about the way they were together, the things they shared, the way they were so comfortable about each other's space, told me that they were lovers.

"Times are hard," mused the doctor. "Françoise has had to let the staff go. There is no trade in the winter. So I have asked her to I go down to the pharmacy for me, to get some medicine for your young friend. Some tranquillisers, that is all. I have a nice arrangement with the pharmacist; there are so many of these drugs now and he is a young man, very keen. He keeps up to date. I just tell him what I want to treat and he sends me the right drug; then, at the end of the month, I write out the prescriptions." He grunted. "The art of the healer, my friend, does not come out of a little bottle, but through these." He held up his long-fingered hands.

I knew that Irene would be safe in his care. It was a good feeling.

It was late in the afternoon before Irene recovered enough to speak. I was at the side of her bed, holding her hand, when her eyes opened.

Joseph put a hand softly on my shoulder. "One moment, my friend and then you shall have her to yourself." He stepped forward and took Irene's wrist, feeling her pulse, timing it against a gold fob-watch that he drew from his waistcoat pocket. He nodded, then produced a little torch and looked into her eyes. "Hmf. Young lady, if I may say so, you have the constitution of an ox. Quite belies your petite frame."

Irene smiled at him, then winced. "Yes," the doctor went on, "That cut will hurt. There's nothing I can do about that. But otherwise, how do you feel?"

"Very, very sore."

"Yes. I'm afraid you are going to be...sore, for a little while. The man who assaulted you was quite brutal."

"I know." The memory flashed up in her mind and her face contorted in pain. "Johnny, I..."

"Ssh. It's all over."

"Yes but..."

"No buts," I said. "You must try to forget all of that."

"There is something you are not revealing," murmured Joseph in my ear. "But I daresay you have your reasons. Your friend here is quite right, miss, may I call you Irene?" he asked, in a clearer voice. "You must do your best to forget. Now that eye of yours, can you see quite clearly?"

"Yes."

"Not a pretty sight, my dear, but I think I can do something with it. However, first of all I will leave you with John here."

Irene looked at me. "Did I really do it...to that man? It wasn't a dream?"

I nodded. "You responded according to your instincts. He had hurt you very badly."

"Yes, but...Oh, God." She thought about it for a few moments, then sighed. "Well. Mine are not the only problems."

"Irene...I'm very sorry that it happened. I blame myself."

"Don't be silly. How could it be your fault? You tried time and time again to warn me. I knew the risks."

"Hmm."

"There is something I want you to know; the worst thing was not that he...raped me, or that he beat me up; I've been beaten up before, by other men, who were just as brutal. No, the worst thing was...That *you* saw!"

"Irene, please..."

"No, let me explain. It is different with you, Johnny. So different. I knew it was different the very first time I met you, in that night club, when you were drunk. That was why I took you back to your own home, not to my place and let you pay for a trick in the morning. It has always been different. And if we, if we ever get through this thing, then I will never go back...To that way of life, not if you don't want me to. Even if I have to work as a cleaner in a bar."

"Irene, I –"

"Johnny, please!" There were hot tears in her eyes. "Don't patronise me! Do you understand what I'm saying?"

I swallowed and nodded.

"Hold me!" I cradled her head in my arms for a few minutes.Then she lifted herself,and made an attempt at a smile. "When this is over, I'm going to, I, I don't know..." A look of puzzlement crossed her face. "But I do know you'll like it."

She sighed, as thought crossed her mind. "You know about Harry?"

My eyes narrowed. "What about him?"

"He's dead. Murdered."

"Jesus! When?"

"After you left him, the same evening. He was garrotted." She squeezed my arm. "Oh God, when will it all end?"

"When I finish it," I sighed. "And not before. Unless they finish me first."

"You must be very careful."

"Do you know anything more about it? About Harry or the bombs?"

She didn't. Or, at least, nothing I didn't know already. Then I told her the things I'd found out. All the time her one good eye widened with astonishment. The revelations were clearly more than she could cope with in her weakened state. She kept drifting away and her eyes would glaze over; then, the next moment, she would be alert, listening intently again.

When I had finished, she sighed. "So what are you going to do now?"

"I'm going back to Paris. You're going to stay here with Françoise until you're better. No, I've made up my mind," I said, forestalling her protest. "I must get back there before the trail cools completely. I have to try to pick it up, to see if it will lead me to whoever is organising this."

Irene leaned back on the pillow, her eyelids drooping.

"Before I go, please try to remember; is there anything at all that you heard that might help, anything? Like something about Harry, for example."

Irene screwed up her eyes in concentration. "Harry...There was something. They found him in his car. There was something else, something one of the girls said to me. I'm sorry, I can't remember now."

"Okay; you rest now; but as soon as you remember, tell Françoise; she'll know where I'll be."

"Oh, Johnny, I'm sorry; I just can't seem to concentrate."

"Don't worry about it. That was a pretty heavy sedative Maybach gave you. It will take a while for it to pass completely."

"Yes, she said, squeezing my hand.

At that moment, there was a light tap on the door. It swung open and Joseph walked in, bearing a tray, on which were set several bowls draped in white cloths. "That is quite enough for today," he said, smiling through his moustache. "I don't want you to exhaust my patient."

"Sure. We were about through, anyway."

Joseph sat down on the edge of the bed by Irene's side, setting the tray on a bedside table. "Now, my dear," he said, "Let's have a look at your eye, shall we?" He took his torch out again and examined the eye itself very closely. Then he gently touched the swollen flesh with his fingers. Irene winced.

"That hurts, does it? That is good, you know, it means that we are still in time to do something." Joseph leaned over to the tray and picked up a little mirror. He held it up in front of Irene, so that she could see the damage for herself.

"Oh la la!"

"Yes. It's not a pretty sight, my dear. Now we can do something to help, if you trust me, or else you will have that mark for weeks to come."

"Will it hurt? What you will do?"

I was wondering myself about what the doctor had in mind.

"This is a remedy that country people in this area have known for centuries. It doesn't hurt, but it may feel a little odd. First I must close that eye."

He gently pulled together the eyelids and set a strip of Elastoplast to keep them that way; then he returned to the tray and brought over one of the bowls. He drew off the cloth and looked at me. In a small amount of water at the bottom of the bowl were several black, worm-like objects, each about an inch long and very much alive.

"Leeches," said Joseph. "My friend, the mortician, has a passion for tropical fruit. He keeps a large greenhouse, so we have a supply of these all year round. They are very effective; not only do their mouths contain an anaesthetic, but also an agent to help the puncture to heal afterwards. We put them on like this," he said, picking one of the leeches up with tweezers and applying it to Irene's skin, taking care to keep it out of her sight as he did so. "And in half an hour or so, they will fall off, having drunk their fill. There will be no bruising, no black eye. One of nature's little remedies."

I decided it was time to go and speak to Françoise, so I made my farewell to the semi-conscious Irene. I kissed her gently, trying not to look at the animals festooned on her face. I'd had enough of leeches in Vietnam to last a lifetime. Joseph was chuckling as I closed the bedroom door on the macabre scene.

Françoise was in the kitchen when I returned there, feeling, I must admit, just a little squeamish. "He showed you?"

I nodded.

"It really does work, you know. He did it for me, once, when I walked into the edge of the door, there. I thought I wouldn't be able to show my face in public for a month, but two days later, once Joseph had performed his little trick, no-one would have known."

She poured me some coffee and then pointed to the evening paper, which was lying on the large oak table. "You should read that."

I picked up the paper. The banner headlines on the front page told the story; "Three Killed in Shoot-out." It seemed that the remaining three rats in the nest at Courbevoie had decided to make a stand. The police, taking no chances, had called in the Squadron Bleu, the crack anti-terrorist unit. They'd made pretty short work of the bombers.

However it was clear that I'd achieved a degree of notoriety, if anonymously; the discovery of the three bodies in the car-park must have raised an eyebrow or two. The newspaper even postulated that it was the work of a vigilante group who'd ritually mutilated one of the men as a warning to others. I laughed, bitterly; if there was a warning, it wasn't about setting bombs, but then, who was ever going to know?

I could see that Françoise was looking at me strangely. "He was the one, wasn't he? Who did it...To her?"

I nodded but said nothing. "Did you do that, to him?" she went on.

I didn't need to ask what she was referring to.

"No, he didn't do it," came a voice from behind me, the slow and soft voice of Joseph. "She did it herself. Isn't that so, my friend?"

I nodded. I hadn't wanted to tell them, but I should have known that Joseph would have seen the truth.

Françoise gasped and put her knuckle to her mouth. "Oh!"

Joseph nodded. "Your young friend will need to be cared for, when this is over. The emotional scars will not be removed so easily as the physical ones. Now. I must get back there and see how my little helpers are getting along." He helped himself to coffee and left.

"I must return to the city," I said to Françoise. "I'm going to leave the car here; don't worry, it's on a long hire. I'm going to take the train up to town."

She nodded. "I have a timetable."

"Good." I sipped my coffee reflectively. "I'll stay in a little pension near to the Gare de Lyon. I used it once before, it's a good place. I have the number here," I pulled my little black pocket-book out and found the page. "Yes." I gave Françoise the telephone number. "I want you to call if anything happens, or if Irene remembers anything more about the attack, or about Harry, or about anything else."

Françoise nodded. "When will you leave?"

"Tonight. There's work to be done. Finishing that terrorist cell changes everything. The people behind this, they must now find another way to work. They probably already have someone waiting, either more of the ETTA people, or another group. But first they must eliminate me and this time they'll do it themselves."

"You know they're going to come after you and yet you...You're crazy."

"No. They'll get to me sooner or later, whatever I do. Their last two attempts got innocent people killed or hurt, though I escaped. And anyway, I wasn't ready for them. This time I will be and I'll be working alone. And this time it will be someone who can tell me something who comes, not just a hired hand."

"Johnny..." Françoise threw up her hands in despair. "All right. Do it your own way. But I think you ought to call us, every day, just to let us know; just to let her know, if no-one else."

It was hard to deny the logic. Anyway, I had a responsibility towards Irene. I'd got her into this mess, after all. And she would be worried sick about me, to the point that she wouldn't stay here, out of harm's way, but would almost certainly come looking for me. I was beginning to understand something about Irene and I knew that I had to make allowances.

"Okay," I agreed. "I'll call you every day. We'll set the time for each call as we go along."

In a way, this would be better: I could choose a different call-box every day, to avoid the possibility that the enemy could be listening in to calls to the hotel I would be staying at.

Thirteen

Françoise drove me to the station in her car. Leaving Irene was a wrench, but Joseph still had her under heavy sedation. I don't think she really knew what was going on around her.

With me I had a suitcase packed with a change of clothes,and a few other personal items. I'd left the silenced .22 behind; too bulky. The Luger was slipped into the waistband of my trousers. A nine-millimetre handgun packs one hell of a punch and the soft tipped bullets the Luger was loaded with made it one very efficient man-stopper.

The action on a Luger, though it requires to be looked after carefully, is virtually jam-proof. It also contributes to the high level of steadiness and accuracy of the weapon. I suppose the armourer at the Firm would have thought it a little old fashioned, but I'm like that.

My train pulled into the Gare d'Austerlitz at a quarter past ten; from there it was only a short ride on the Metro to Quai de la Rapée and a walk around the block to the pension which I proposed to make my base. As I'd expected, there were rooms to spare. I got one that overlooked the Rue de Bercy. It was small, but clean and well aired. There was a double bed, a little table, a wardrobe and a shower cabinet and toilet in the corner. By the bed was a little night-table.

I looked around, nodded and asked the boy who'd accompanied me to bring me a bottle of cognac and a glass. He did; I tipped him and then locked the door. I hung up my clothes in the wardrobe and washed. Then I kicked off my shoes and lay on the bed, with the bottle of cognac at my side.

For starters I stripped the Luger, then cleaned and reassembled it. Not that it needed it, perhaps, but it reassured me to do it. I pulled back the breech and released it slowly, several times. Sweet as a nut. Don't ever believe that crap you see in films about people clicking the hammer down on an empty chamber just to try it; ruins the firing-pin and that's one of the bits you want to be able to rely on.

Then I pourec a large cognac and settled down. It was a long time since I'd had a proper night's sleep and I badly needed the rest. There would be time for fighting in the morning. Before I submitted to the drowsiness, however, I performed one last ritual; I leaned a chair against the door and removed the bulb from the overhead light fitting. Now the only light in the room would be the bedside lamp and the switch for that was at my side.

I undressed, but held on to the Luger; insurance.

In the morning I woke late, about ten. I felt refreshed by the rest and as I shaved, I surveyed my plans for the day. Somehow I had to find out more about the operation the CIA had mounted. I didn't think they'd break cover unless there was a tasty prize to be won. And that prize would have to be me. I was going to have to set the trap and be its bait at the same time.

I bought a coffee and a croissant for breakfast. I took a seat by the window of the pension's bar to enjoy my repast with a copy of the morning paper. That was when I saw it. I must admit I'd been looking for something of the kind ever since Irene had told me about Harry Jonsun and there it was, in the announcements; the funeral was to be held at the Cimetiere du Nord that very afternoon. I suppose that Harry's influential friends had jollied along the usual procedures of post-mortem examinations and the like, so that their friend and servant wouldn't have the indignity of lying on a slab under a sheet with a plastic tag on his ankle for too long,

I made up my mind to go; after all, Harry had considered me as his friend, even if my own view of the situation had been less intimate. And in any case, it was a sure way of advertising my presence in town; if the 'ears' hadn't already twigged, that was.

I sipped my coffee and turned to the main news pages of the paper. There wasn't much happening; another scathing statement by the American C-in-C Europe on the growth of Europe's anti-nuclear movements, in which he attempted to show that the peace movement was only a front for KGB propaganda. I thought about the hordes of nice middle class people he was actually talking about, interspersed with a few derelict hangers-on from the sixties hippy movements and I had to laugh. There was one thing for sure, the American high command wasn't getting any more politically sophisticated; of course, that was CIA business, not that of an ordinary military man.

On the European front, it seemed that the nations of the Common Market had staged a naughty little attack upon the dollar and had succeeded in taking the wind out of the White House's sails. The concerted action which made this possible was regarded by many as bolstering the arguments in favour of a united European currency.

Another item caught my eye, too. There was to be a summit meeting of all the Common Market countries, in Paris, beginning only a few days later. Now that was interesting. It would be a juicy target for anyone wanting to stir a lot of shit up; the Prime Ministers and Presidents of half Europe would be there and numerous others whose names were never far from the headlines. The security services had moved in force to the city; but I knew that they couldn't stop real pros from hitting the mark if they wanted to. Mind, the planners would have to use operators just a little more sophisticated than the Spaniards who'd been operating from Courbevoie. It was very interesting, but just then it was only an idea.

I went back to reading the paper. I idled the rest of the morning away, drinking vast quantities of coffee, until it was time to go out for lunch. I put on my coat and stuffed my hands into the pockets, the right one firmly grasping the butt of the Luger.

I went to a little restaurant not far away. It was well frequented by the sort of people who remember a face and are prepared to sell the information. Not that I was inquiring, so much as advertising my presence.

I enjoyed my meal; they do nice fish in that place. When I came out again I felt the steely edge of fear. That was where I was at my most vulnerable, out in the open. A fast car, a motorbike with a shooter on the back and I could have been blown away there and then. But I wasn't.

I made it to a little Jewish tailor's shop to buy a black tie and an armband. After all, I had to be respectful of dear old Harry Jonsun's memory.

Fourteen

The funeral was as grey and as grim as I'd expected. What is it about Christians, I wondered, that makes them so depressing when it comes to death? It happens to us all and the misery does no good for the dear departed. It only makes everyone else glum. I've always preferred the way of the Scots, who just have a party, as if the dead were still amongst them. I think that's the way I'd like my friends to behave when they finally put me away.

I got the taxi driver to let me off by the line of long black cars which lined the high wall outside the cemetery, which is huge. The continual motorcades that accompanied funerals had been causing many of the fine Victorian sculptures to subside, so they'd been limited to three cars.

I was impressed, I had to admit, by the very high turnout for a man who had been little more than a lecherous old black marketeer.

The Boys were represented in force, of course. Under normal circumstances I try my best not to associate with hoodlums; I don't like their methods or their attitude. But this was going to be very interesting. The priest had said his piece by the time I'd arrived on the edge of the small crowd by the graveside. A man stepped forward to deliver a eulogy. I raised an eyebrow. Making Harry sound saintly in death was going to be quite a feat.

I didn't at first recognise the speaker; he was about forty-five, I'd have guessed, with jet-black greased hair which receded about his temples into a widow's peak and heavy black eyebrows over his deep, brown, Mediterranean eyes. He was rather short and quite overweight; I once knew a Royal Marines drill-sergeant who would have knocked three stones off him in six weeks. For all his bulk he did not appear flabby; I guessed that his mental and physical reactions were very good.

He had that kind of aura about him, anyway, such that you didn't really notice his body. His whole personality seemed to be projected through that magnificent, cruel face of his, with its slab cheeks and fleshy mouth.

He was well chosen as a eulogist, as well, with a commanding voice, which rang effortlessly around the cemetery. I racked my brains to try to get a fix on why it should have been that I found his face so familiar. Then it struck me; this was Auguste Delauney, the most influential baron of the underworld in Paris, a leader of leaders in the Mob, a man whose name was practically synonymous with high-level organised crime. I was shocked.

I had had no idea at all that the man I'd treated with such a lack of respect, Harry Jonsun, was so well connected in the underworld. It quite took me aback. With friends like that, Harry should have been assured of dying peacefully of old age.

Delauney didn't go on too long, just long enough to impress the gravity of the situation on everyone's mind by the very fact that he was actually standing there, delivering the speech. I was left in no doubt that he took a very dim view of the whole affair. I didn't reckon he was a good man to make an enemy out of, either. When he'd finished with praising the dear departed Dutchman, he stepped forward and picked up a shovel. I was quite sure that wasn't something he'd done since the last funeral.

He cast the first earth onto the coffin with a gesture of frightening intensity and fell back as the first of a line of others followed suit. He folded his hands before him and raised his eyes. Then he saw me, as the crowd opened a little. He turned to one side.

I thought about leaving, but there would have been no point. Anyway, I thought it might be useful to talk to him, even though I really didn't fancy the idea. I've never had much time for hoods like Delauney and I knew I wouldn't be able to trust him an inch; but I'd far rather have him on my side than the other.

Even though I do like to work alone, I was feeling pretty exposed and the idea of a little bit of back-up didn't seem so bad; maybe, just maybe, I could get along with these hoodlums long enough.

I felt the pressure of a hand none too gently gripping my arm above the elbow. I began to move, but stopped when I felt the ominous hard shove of a gun-muzzle in my kidneys. I turned to look at my new companions, as best I could, that is. They were short and dark, dressed in the uniform grey coat. Men with forgettable, invisible faces, the faces of soldiers, only these were the soldiers of the Mob.

I sighed, "You only had to ask, boys."

"Quiet, you. The man wants to see you."

"Okay. But you don't need the piece."

"Why not? Who's going to complain? Only family here, pal." I nodded philosophically. There was no point in making a production out of the affair.

I felt a hand begin to frisk me. "Knock it off. The gun's in my coat pocket."

The man who was doing all the talking grunted and fished the Luger from its resting place. He chuckled. "Where d'you get this antique?"

"Be careful; that gun happens to be a collector's item."

"Yeah? Move. The man don't like to wait for zeros like you." I began to walk towards the car, where I could see the unsmiling face of Delauney looking in my direction. The two apes fell back a pace or two, just far enough to be out of my way should I have had a brainstorm and tried anything.

We got to the limo and the ape who talked opened the door. He motioned me to enter with the barrel of his gun. I got in the car.

"Here he is. He was carrying this." The ape passed Goering's Luger across my body to Delaunay's waiting hand. "You want anything else?"

"No. Tell the drivers to get going." The door clicked shut. I could tell without trying it that I couldn't open it from inside. Delauney reached forward and tapped on the glass which separated the driver from us. I had no doubt that it and all the other glass in the car, was bulletproof. Delauney looked at me a long time before he said a word, looking slow and deep and all the time hefting my Luger in his hand.

I was aware that I was in the presence of a powerful, ruthless intelligence, a man who commanded respect, who could strike terror into a weaker heart with only a glance, a man used to absolute power of life and death over all those around him.

It's difficult to fully describe the sensation sitting beside him produced; perhaps like being in the presence of a lion, or standing on a sea wall in a gale while the waves crash all around you; as if with the tiniest effort you could be swallowed up, disappear without a trace. His presence, his aura, was truly elemental. I could see how it was that he'd come to be the man he was, achieved the power he had. It was like sitting next to some dynamo of concealed but fantastic power.

"I see you are a man of some taste, Mr. Macfarlane. At least in some matters." He gave me back the Luger and sucked his lip.

"Thank you." I took the gun and slipped it into my pocket. At no time did it cross either of our minds that I would have used it.

"I apologise if my people treated you discourteously. They are not used to dealing with such as you." His voice was breathy and deep, like that of a Shakespearean actor offstage, reserved, with its capacity coiled, ready, yet relaxed. He spoke slowly, but not pedantically, in careful English. He chose his words at leisure, but with precision.

"I'm getting used to it," I replied.

"A man should not allow himself to get used to...that which is beneath him." I thought he was on the point of launching into a philosophical discourse. Thankfully he stopped and looked at me again. "As I was saying, you are a man of good taste, in some things. That gun. Very nice. I have always liked German guns. And you know how to behave; you have a reputation for being polite. Harry always spoke very highly of you."

"That was kind of him."

"Do you mock him, now that he is dead?"

I smiled. "No. I, well, let's just say that that I only ever saw the seamier side of his nature."

Delauney chuckled. "Touché ! I begin almost to like you. And you are such an interesting man; I have heard some things about you which are very enlightening."

"Such as?"

"You have some interesting friends. And I too, have some interesting friends. Some of whom work for the Sûreté. They know of you."

I shrugged my shoulders. I doubted that the Sûreté had any idea of who I really was or what I did – or had done, which was more to the point. I'd worked with the Deuxieme Bureau once, when they were trying to clean up their act and stop some of the leaks. But Delauney clearly liked to be enigmatic, so I played ball with him. "Monsieur Delauney, I'm sure that you didn't ask me to speak to you just for the pleasure of the conversation."

"Hm. You should not be too pressing. My interests in you are very varied. But to begin with, I could ask why it was that you were in a certain café on Christmas Eve, a café in which the garçon and two strangers were killed? Why, I wonder, were you not at home, where someone unknown was putting an end to your family...And in such away that the blame is pointed firmly at you? I am interested to know who dislikes you so much. You must have done something bad to annoy them.

"And then, you had a meeting with Harry on the day that he met his unfortunate demise."

I didn't say a word.

"In fact, on both of these occasions, you met Harry. One might almost think that you and he were up to something; but then, I have sources which tell me that this is not the case. Or one might think that you were implicated in some other way, in Harry's death."

"I didn't kill Harry. I don't think that you believe that I did, either. And as for that boy in the café...That was unprofessional. I was sickened by it."

"Ah, you may indeed be right; I never for a moment really thought that you...No. I think that they died just because of their contact with you. That, in itself, might be reason enough to do away with you, in case the disease is contagious."

That stung me. "Look," I snapped. "I came back from a business trip abroad, early, to find that someone had paid my family a visit. Rubbed them out, just like that. And they had the nerve to try to take me out. There's a blood debt there to be paid. Then there's Harry. I really do think that that man regarded me as his friend. I may not have reciprocated all that well, but he adds to the blood debt; his death is on my conscience, you know."

"Okay. You don't need to be so touchy. I know what you desire to do. I don't disagree with your right; but I am disappointed that any of this is happening at all. There has been peace in the city for many years. We have all grown used to it; everyone is happy, we are, the people are, the authorities are.

"Then there are bombs. Well, there have been bombs before. They did not hurt us, though we didn't like them. But now, these bombers are found, murdered, mutilated; the Press begins to make up ideas of vigilante groups and such like. We are not happy with this. It begins to make life...Awkward. Others may try to jump on the bandwagon and before long there will be armed men in the streets at night. And they may not all be looking for bombers.

"My old friends at the Sûreté are very unhappy about all of this too; they have told me as much. I cannot afford to let this situation go unchecked."

Pompous fool! I was amazed at the high-handed manner this gangster had adopted, but I knew that I was treading on thin ice, so I held my tongue.

"Of course," Delauney went on, "If you were able to tell me the name of the person who hit Harry, then I might let you live. On condition that you conduct your affairs somewhere else. A long way away."

That was big of him. "I don't know who killed Harry...Yet. But I do know who sent the killer."

Delauney's thick eyebrow lifted a fraction. "I may be interested in that information," he nodded.

Christ, I thought, I'd have liked to take him down a peg or two. But he could be too good an ally and too bad an enemy to cross. And I needed to have a free hand to finish my task.

"Your conditions aren't good enough. Oh, you could just kill me, but then you wouldn't get Harry's killer. And the bombs will start again, you mark my words."

"You propose to barter with me? I hold your life in my hand!" I smiled and carried on. I remembered something that had happened years before, how this same Delauney had contributed to a fund for the commissioning of a statue to edify de Gaulle. There had been much patriotic posturing at the time. It gave me an idea.

"What are your politics, Delauney?"

He looked at me as if I'd just crawled out from under a stone. "I am for France," he said.

"No sympathy for the Socialists, I don't suppose?"

"Merde! They are ruining all of us."

I'd expected something like that. For the first time the man beside me showed real emotion. The French are like that with their politics.

"How would you feel if you found out that someone outside was trying to interfere with the Government here, for their own ends?" I could see I'd caught his attention. "How would you feel if you found out that the someone was American?"

Now there's one thing that a true Gaullist hates more than a socialist politician; that is an American politician. Especially when the subject of La Belle France is on the agenda. The thought of American interference in France's domestic affairs is usually enough to induce apoplexy.

So it was with Delauney. His colour went from puce with shock to crimson with suppressed rage as I told him what I knew. I really enjoyed it, in my little way. It was something to see the beast angered. I wouldn't like to be on the receiving end of one of his tantrums.

"So, you think that the Americans are behind all this unrest."

"I know that they're behind it. I don't think." There was silence in the car for a time, apart from the steady hum of the motor. We were driving along the Boulevard de Sebastopol. It struck me that we were going in a large circle, with Montmartre at the centre. "And I'm going to find the field agent who did these things. Then I'm going to kill him."

Delauney gave me one of those looks again. "You? Alone?"

"How much do you really know about me? Is it just my name or do you really know the whole truth?"

"I know that you worked with the Deuxieme Bureau in seventy-seven."

"Ah. The Deuxieme Bureau. The leakiest secret agency of them all. I suppose you have a permanent mole there."

He shrugged. "That is for me to know."

"Sure. Anyway, I'm going after these people alone. I prefer to work that way. I don't like interference."

"You dare to say that to me?"

"I don't know how highly placed your man at the Bureau is, but he should be able to tell you that you haven't a hope in hell. They'll go right underground, go dormant, you won't even see them move, until you find yourself the target."

"And you think you can do what I, with all my power, couldn't?"

It was my turn to look at him hard. "Yes. They want me. They don't want you. They'll break cover to get me. It's the only chance there is. And if you really want to avenge dear old Harry, you'll give me the leeway I need."

Delauney thought about this and then he grunted, "Okay. You have one week. Then we smoke these people out."

I nodded. A week? That should be enough. "Okay. But I want you to help."

"So you would like me to help, now?" The sarcasm was thick.

"Yes; I want you to put the word out on the street that I'm here, where I'll be staying, that sort of thing."

"You like to live dangerously, monsieur. I salute you. Though I think you are going to get yourself killed. Which may be no great loss." Delauney leaned forward end tapped on the glass that separated us from the chauffeur. The car slowed and pulled into the kerb. From nowhere, or rather, from the car that must have been following us, the talking ape appeared and opened the door for me.

As I stepped out, Delauney spoke again, "Remember...You have one week. Then I want the business settled and you out of town."

Fifteen

I stood on the corner of the Boulevarde de la Chapelle and watched the two cars purr sway like long sleek pythons. I smiled. I wondered if the car had been wired, perhaps by the enemies of that powerful man. Men of power always have enemies. And often closer to home than they'd like to think.

It had begun to rain by the time I got back to the pension. It rains a lot in Paris in the winter. I went inside and ordered myself a coffee and a cognac at the bar. I thought I had a cold coming on. All I had to do now, I thought, was to maintain a high profile.and stay out of the hands of the law. The other side would come. I knew they'd come. They'd tried twice and failed; the pressure was on them now.

I suppose, thinking back on it, that I must have been, just a little bit crazy; I mean, there I was, alone, just waiting for them to come, not knowing how or when they'd try, but being sure that they'd try harder than before. But I was nursing my desire for vengeance, a desire which had only been strengthened by the events that had taken place at Versailles. Seeing those thugs dead wasn't enough, I wanted the person who'd sent them.

Later, I went out and called Françoise in Joigny. All was well there: and it seemed that Irene was making a remarkable recovery. She was giving Joseph a hard time, because he wanted her to rest and she wanted not to. The thought made me smile.

I asked Françoise if Irene had remembered more details about the hit on Harry. Françoise said that she would ask her again. I told her to call the concierge's desk at the pension if anything came up, no matter how slight. We arranged that otherwise I would make a routine call at the same time the following evening.

I returned to the pension and sat down in the bar for a cognac. The place was empty apart from me and the barman. We talked about the weather for a while, then I went to the magazine rack and took out the evening paper. Not that I didn't appreciate the conversation, it was just that I preferred to sit somewhere with a clearer view of the door.

The funeral had attracted attention. 'Big Turnout for Gangland Slay Victim' was the headline. There were pictures of the three black cars leaving the cemetery.

I ordered another cognac and scanned through the rest of the paper. The US Treasury was squealing about the way the European nations had put an end to the dollar's rise the previous day. Things were hotting up, I thought.

Out of the corner of my eye I saw a woman enter the bar. She was tall and fair, dressed in a way that advertised her profession. Her long blonde hair was hanging loose about her shoulders and she carried a handbag. The barman smiled as she entered and soon they began to talk.

I looked her over carefully. She seemed to have a more than passing acquaintance with the barman, so I began to lose my sense of unease and returned to the evening paper. I kept an eye on her, though; she had a sort of decadent attractiveness that appealed to me.

I wondered how old she was and settled for a guess at between twenty-five and thirty. She had set herself up on a bar-stool and was smoking a cigarette with long, extravagant puffs, drawing the smoke swiftly into her lungs with a gulp. She was drumming idly with her fingers on the counter of the bar, looking around. The barman was occupied polishing glasses and she didn't seem too concerned about pursuing conversation with him.

She caught me watching her and I swore silently. That was fatal. She was bound to come and make me an offer. Sure enough, she uncrossed her legs after a few moments and sidled over to my table.

"Hi." It was a statement. I noticed that she had a slight accent; Alsatian, maybe. I nodded my greeting, but didn't fold up my paper. "Lonely?" she went on, laying her hand on the back of the chair opposite. "Mind if I sit down for a moment?"

The hackles on the back of my neck began to twitch again. "I'm a married man, honey; I'm not buying."

"Too bad. You have nice eyes. Want to just talk?"

"That depends." She pulled out the chair and sat down. Her glass was empty and she set it on the table. I smiled and waved to the garçon. He came over and filled her glass with cognac. I motioned him to do the same for me while he was at it. He seemed a little put out by something;

I guessed that he didn't like being deserted like that.

"Cigarette?" She offered the packet in my direction. Gitanes, the same as Irene smoked. I shook my head.

"Thanks. I don't. Bad for the health." She laughed at that and looked at me through a puff of smoke as she flicked out her match. I noticed that she did it by holding the lit match between her first and second fingers and flicking the stub with her long thumbnail, dousing the flame effortlessly. She tossed the dead match into the ashtray and took the cigarette from her mouth. "I haven't seen you here before," she said, quietly. "New in town?"

"Just passing through. Business."

"Oh. What sort of business, or is that a secret?"

"That's a secret."

She shrugged her shoulders. "One shouldn't be afraid to talk of one's business. But then, that's easy for me to say; everyone knows mine."

I smiled. "This your regular patch, then?"

She nodded. "I work between the station and the Quai de la Rapée. There are some clubs, hotels like this where lonely 'business' men stay from time to time. It's a living."

"You know the barman, then? Only he doesn't seem too happy about you being over here with me."

"Oh, don't worry about him. He doesn't matter. Anyway I'm sure you can look after yourself."

I looked at her for a long moment; she had crystal blue eyes that seemed to always be veiled. She didn't flinch her gaze from mine.

"What's your name?" I asked, out of politeness. It looked as if I was stuck with her company whatever I did.

"Jeanne."

I nodded. "Mine's John...But my friends call me Johnny."

She looked askance at me. "You are not French?"

"No. Thank you for the compliment, though. I'm British."

"Oh, but you have the air of a Frenchman; you must have lived here for a long time."

"I have a gift for languages."

"Bah! I couldn't manage even English at school. How many languages do you speak?"

"That depends on whether you mean fluently or so-so. I speak all the major European languages pretty well and I can hold my own in Arabic and Russian and Vietnamese. I have a smattering of a few others."

Jeanne's eyes widened. "Merde alors! I'm impressed...Johnny."

"There's nothing to be impressed about. You either have a flair for languages or you don't. I mean, it wasn't difficult for me to learn all those languages; I just did. I suppose."

She looked glum for a moment and then brightened. "I have my own gift." She gave me one of those looks, dripping with sexuality.

I had no doubt that her gifts were abundant and sweet indeed but at the time all that smouldering look did for me was remind me of Irene. "Yes, I guess you do." I glanced at my watch. "Look, do you want another for the road? Then I really must call it a night."

She looked disappointed and I smiled at her. "I told you, I'm not buying tonight." The barman seemed to have disappeared, so I went to the bar and rang the little brass bell. He appeared from a back room and poured two more cognacs. When I got back to the table, I found Jeanne had picked up the paper. She was perusing the story about Harry's funeral with an odd look on her face, shaking her head.

"What's the matter," I asked, as I sat down. "You don't look too happy all of a sudden."

"Poor Harry," she said, by way of explanation.

"You knew him?" I asked.

"Every girl in Paris knew Harry. Harry and that long black car of his. Why? Did you know him too?"

"Only in passing. They say that he was garrotted."

She made a face. "I know. Poor man."

I sensed that there was something she wasn't telling me. "Do you know any more than that?" I quizzed her.

She bridled like a startled horse. "Are you a cop?"

I shook my head. "No; I told you, I knew him. We did some business from time to time. I just wondered I mean, who would want to kill old Harry?"

Jeanne shivered. "I don't know. I don't know anything about it."

She was so obviously lying that I could hardly let it pass. I leaned towards her. "There are people who would pay very well, for any information, you know. And I know these people." I tapped the picture of the cars with my forefinger. "You could make some money."

"No! No, I tell you, I don't know anything!" I pulled my wallet out of my pocket and began to count off one-hundred franc notes, very discreetly. I could see her watching, counting with me. I stopped when I got to ten.

She looked into my eyes, then turned away, biting her knuckles. "I don't know. I'm in it up to my neck already. I just don't know whether I should..."

I reached over the table and took her hand. "Listen to me. No one will ever know where I got the information, if you don't want. Straight deal, I'll pay you for anything you can tell me. Then you're out of it. No police, no repercussions. Think about it."

She pulled away and stood up quickly. "No. That's enough. I told you, I don't have any information." She smoothed her dress. "I must go. I am sorry,"

I looked hard at her. "Okay, But, if you change your mind, I'll be here tomorrow. I'll be looking out for you."

She shook her head violently and, picking up her bag, left, without saying goodbye, either to me or the barman. I sighed. She knew something, I was sure of that. Only I didn't know how much.

I was tired, so I left the table and asked the boy for the bill; he'd come out of his hidey-hole when he heard the door close behind Jeanne. He made a face after her.

"Friend of yours?" I asked the waiter. He gave me a narrow look, the kind that says, wise men don't ask questions like that in this end of town. I swore and pulled out my wallet. I threw a couple of hundred-franc notes across the counter and repeated my question.

He shrugged his shoulders."Non, monsieur. The first time I saw her was last night. She came in late, stayed a while."

"So she isn't a regular?"

He stopped wiping the bar top long enough to look me in the eye. "I wouldn't know, monsieur, I am new here, I only started last week. For all I know she could be a regular, yes."

"And?"

"And that would be a pity!"

"Why so?"

"I don't like people who play games." He tossed his head in an expression of disgust towards the door. I left enough to cover the bill and turned away. Smart-arsed little sod, I thought.

I made my routine call to Joigny later, from a call-box at the Gare de Bercy. Irene was much better and that was a relief. I mentioned meeting Jeanne in passing and then made my way back to the hotel.

As I went through my routine of checking the door and the gun before turning in, I wondered what it was that Jeanne knew, what it was that frightened her so much; I wondered if she'd come back to tell me.

Sixteen

I was pretty excited by my meeting with Jeanne. Until Irene could recover her memory fully, I had so little to go on that any glimmer of a clue was worth pursuing.

The next evening I went for dinner locally then returned to the familiar and very welcome warmth of the hotel bar. I nodded to the barman and he nodded, his eyes flashing across the room. I turned to look. It was Jeanne. And she was very, very upset.

She saw me and hurried to my side. The fear was shining from her pale blue eyes. I watched her narrowly. I still wasn't sure about Jeanne; I wasn't sure about anyone any more, to tell the truth. She saw my look of reserve and backed off a little.

"Oh, Johnny, I'm so glad you're here," she began and took a seat on the stool next to mine. She was shivering and her make-up was in a mess. The big fur coat she was wearing was soiled and wet, as if she had fallen. She looked into my eyes. "I don't know what I'd have done if..."

I signalled to the garçon. He sighed and filled us a glass of cognac each. Jeanne drained hers in one go, but I was more circumspect. The garçon filled up her glass again and I smiled. I was watching her curiously. Distracted, she lifted the hem of her coat and examined a long ladder in her stocking.

"What happened?" I asked, when I could stand the silence no longer.

She stuffed one of those caporal in her mouth with shaking fingers and drank down the smoke deeply. "You're in terrible danger," she hissed, at last. "They're looking for you right at this very minute!"

"Who are?"

"I don't know who they are, the people who killed Harry. For Christ's sake what have you done to them?"

"I wish I knew the answer to that one myself."

"Jesus, I wish I'd never met you! Now I'm involved!"

That was a change in the weather. "Calm down, for Christ's sake. No one's going to hurt you; it's me they're after." I paused. "Anyway, I thought you were glad to see me?"

She stubbed out her cigarette viciously. It was hardly begun. "I'm sorry. I'm very sorry, it's just, it's just that I'm not used to, to –"

I could see that she was getting hysterical and I grabbed her arm. "Knock it off!" I hissed at her.

"Johnny, they're out there!" Her eyes were big, pleading. "Look what they did to me already." She made a gesture that encompassed all of her hurts.

"Where?" I asked. "And how do I know you're not trying to set me up?"

She looked at me with eyes full of disbelief, then turned away quickly. "You smug bastard! I spend half an hour talking to you in a bar and for my pains I get jumped, asked questions. I was lucky to get away at all."

I thought about that. Maybe she was telling the truth; but she hadn't got away. They let her go, because they knew that she'd come to me. Maybe she'd told someone about meeting me and the conversation was overheard "Where?" I repeated. "Where did all this happen?"

"Rue de Bercy. They were in a car; I thought it was, you know, a trick, a job. Then they dragged me into the car and started to ask questions about you. I couldn't tell them anything. They took me to the car park at the station. I swear to God I thought they were going to kill me there. Killed and dumped, like those other, those other ones."

"What kind of car?"

"I don't know, I'm not sure."

"Come on, Jeanne, you must remember something!"

"It was a foreign car, a big one, a Mercedes, I think..."

"You think!"

"Johnny, for Christ's sake it was dark! I didn't hang around to admire their wheels!"

"Okay, okay. You stay there." I crossed to the window of the bar; it was dark over by there. I looked out, into the street. Nothing...No! Wait a bit; was that a gleam of chrome over there, by the opening of a cul-de-sac nearly opposite?

When I got back to the bar, Jeanne searched my face. "They're out there, aren't they? Aren't they? Answer me!"

I grabbed her arm again and stared angrily into her eyes. "Listen to me!" I hissed. "Don't get hysterical. Our only hope is to stay calm."

"Our only hope? Our only hope?"

"Yes. Like it or not, you're in this up to your neck now. You either help me or you get yourself killed. I've seen them at work."

She struggled to bring herself under control. "What are you going to do?" she asked.

"I'm not going out there to get cut in half, that's for damned sure. I'm going to go up to my room; you come with me. Make it look like I bought some time. They'll come after me."

She looked terrified at the prospect. "It's okay," I went on, in as soothing a voice as the adrenaline coursing through my veins would allow, "I'll be ready for them."

She swallowed and nodded. "Okay, okay. Let's do it. Yes, let's do it." She smiled and stood up, delicately smoothing her coat over her knees. Then she went into her act, with the bedroom eyes and the walk, all the trimmings. If I hadn't been so shit scared I'd have been turned on, for sure. I tossed a couple of notes to the garçon, who scowled at me. I led the way out of the bar. I followed hard on Jeanne's heels, as she led the way up to the bedroom. It was on the second floor and there wasn't a lift. We got to the room without any blasts of gunfire or anything like that, but then, I wasn't expecting there would be.

This time they wouldn't send any amateurs, they'd send a top pro. I just wondered when she was going to make her move.

Seventeen

Once the door of that bedroom closed behind me I knew that the cards were dealt. I wondered what it would be; a gun, a knife, the garrotte? Would she strangle the life from my body in just the way that she had disposed of Harry?

Oh, yes, I was on to her. It was too neat, like too many random chances coming together. Like the way that she'd just happened to turn up in the bar, had happened to get into conversation with me and the way that the very next night she'd been turned over and asked questions. Like the way that she'd arrived in the guise of a prostitute; knowing as she must have about Irene, she supposed I had a soft spot for working girls. I must have set her back by turning down her proposition the night before.

Jeanne let her fur coat drop from her shoulders and slung it onto the bed. Well, I thought, it won't be a gun; not unless it's in the handbag. She wasn't wearing so much under that coat that she could have hidden a piece. She set the handbag casually on the bedside table and stretched out on the bed. My, but she was a cool customer.

"Are we safe here?" she asked, her eyes searching.

I nodded. "For the time being, anyway." Christ, she was still sticking to it. Was it because she wanted to make me take off my coat, where she must have noted, with her trained eye, the ungainly bulk of the Luger? If that was the way she wanted to play, I was game. It was a small room and I was back on form after all those hours of practise at Irene's place. I reckoned that I could take her with my bare hands even if she did have a weapon.

"Aren't you going to lock the door?" she asked.

"No. What would be the point? It's through that door that they'll come in, isn't it?" I took the Luger from the coat pocket and placed it on the table. Then I got rid of the coat and my jacket. "And when they come, I'll be ready."

Her eyes widened. I almost found myself believing her. She was lying seductively on the bed. She was too calm, that was the only flaw. Everything else was perfect, from the floosie makeup to the department-store camisole and stocking set she was wearing. I remembered Harry, what they'd said about him being found in that God-awful car of his.

The thought crossed my mind that maybe she liked to make it with her victim before she killed him. An even nastier thought followed hard on the heels of that one; did she go both ways? Was that the reason for Julie letting her into our flat, letting herself be killed in her bed by someone she trusted, someone who was familiar with the house, someone whose presence was no surprise? Who would have been better placed than a lover?

That thought sickened me. I flashed an angry look at her. I wondered when she was going to end the charade.

"If you locked the door, then you could come over here with me," she went on. "Surely they won't come while the staff are still up and about."

"And what's the price for this one?" I tried, but I couldn't keep the snarl from my voice,

"No charge."

I could feel a terrible dryness in the back of my throat and a tingling sensation in my sinuses. There was a warning there, a memory of something unpleasant, but there wasn't time to worry about it. I glared at her. "Is that what you said to Harry?"

She looked at me and began to laugh, a horrible, smug, satisfied laugh. I blinked and tried to say the words again. Again they spilled out in a hopeless knot of syllables. My stomach did a cartwheel and I moved to the table to get the gun. I must have missed it by about a foot but my hands were not hands any more and my fingers not fingers, but worms or snakes, or something else nameless and awful over which I had no control. I grabbed the edge of the table for support.

I turned to stare at her. She'd turned from being a beautiful whore into a full blown demon of Hell.

"You bitch!" I screamed, but it came out like the terrified bellow of an ox dying.

She stood up and crossed the room towards me. She wasn't even being careful; why should she have been? I was as helpless as a day-old kitten. My hands slipped off the table as more and more my physiology surrendered to the drug. I measured my length on the floor. In slow motion the carpet came up to meet me, a carpet writhing as if it was alive, the sentient skin of some indescribable beast that might haunt the edge of nightmare.

The tiny part of my brain that was still mine shouted at me, "It's only the drug, it's only the drug!" but right then the hallucinations were more powerful than the truth. I rolled on my back, with a tremendous effort of will and watched the lizards and rattlesnakes run up the curtains, saw the gleaming, awful eyes in every dark corner of the room. Jeanne's merciless laugh ran throughout like some lunatic symphony of fear and evil. She pushed me with the point of her toe. I rolled over, feeling as though I'd been mortally wounded.

"You like it?" she asked, her voice echoing. "We've been working on it for quite some time. Makes LSD look like candy, doesn't it?" I noticed that she'd given up the Alsatian accent, or at least so it seemed, though I was no longer sure whether we were speaking in English or French; my brain was just too scrambled. "It's great for getting the truth out of people; though we'll have to wait until you come down a bit to recover the power of speech. But you'll be physically helpless for hours and, if you had the time, it would be days before you could add up two and two again. But you won't have the time, of course."

"When?" I gasped.

"When you went to look out of the window in the bar. That was your only mistake, you know. I have to hand it to you; you sure have been stirring up the shit until now."

"In the drink?"

"Mmm." She nodded. "That's a beautiful little drug, that one. See, when you mix it with alcohol, it slows up the effect. You stay normal for about twenty-five minutes and then, bang, it's blast-off time."

My body began to convulse, as if someone had plugged me into the mains.

"That's a side effect. It'll pass." She lit up one of her caporal and blew the smoke towards me. "Now, you and I are going to wait a while. Then you're going to tell me so much. Oh, don't think you can avoid it. The drug is quite unique, it behaves like a very powerful hallucinogen in the early stages and then like a hypnotic. You'll become totally governed by my suggestions. You'll tell me everything I want to know. And you will do everything I tell you to do." She laughed again. To me, it sounded like the laugh of a hyena, but it was probably only a little chuckle. Another spasm racked my body and I fought off the pain. I tried to muster what was left of my sane mind, but the madness was winning.

"You had three times the normal dose, you know," she went on. "I thought I'd be better safe than sorry. They told me so much about you when I was briefed. Like you were some kind of superman. But you're not, are you?" She sneered the words out. Through the whirling, kaleidoscopic vortex of the drug, I could hear a ring in her voice, a ring I didn't like.

"You're just like any other man," she continued, "A dead sucker for a piece of ass, a piece of tail. All you need is a few flutters of the eyelashes and your cock takes over."

The tiny voice that was me that still could be heard through the awful storm yelled out, "Psycho! She's crazy!" In that tiny part of me that was still mine I knew what the hooded eyes meant, the weird lights in those featureless pools of blue.

It happens sometimes to agents who kill a lot; they get to like it. Then they get sick and they play out their fantasies. Oh, the controllers don't mind, so long as things don't get out of hand; it makes the agent keener, a better killer, if they take pleasure in their work. Not at first, anyway, but in the end, they have to be terminated, put down like mad dogs. And the psychosis usually has something to do with sex; they begin to confuse the sex urge with the urge to kill; then you find, maybe, a couple of girls are raped and killed. Then the security services neatly kill the 'suspect' while they catch him, just in case ever the truth came out.

This was a bit different, the killer being a woman. I wondered what she had in mind for me.

There's a way to handle these drugs; we had to use hallucinogens as part of our training after the KGB began to use LSD as a truth drug. This was different, much, much more powerful, but it could be beaten, somehow. At least I could stop myself going right off the rails. You have to concentrate, find a centre and stick to it, like a refuge of normality while the storm rages all around you. I wondered when I'd recover the use of my body; that was the worst. There seemed to be no relation between the commands coming from my brain and what was actually happening at my fingers, or toes, or vocal chords.

"Who...who are you?" I grunted, the effort making the sweat spring from my brow.

"Well done! You've only been under for about half an hour, maybe forty minutes and you can almost speak already. Usually it takes much longer." I was surprised that so much time had elapsed, but that's an effect of the hallucinogens.

"My name is Zeigler," she went on. "Elizabeth Zeigler, but you can call me Betty, honey." She smiled at me, but I knew that there was no warmth in that smile. "I mean, you aren't going to be alive for that much longer, so you might as well be familiar."

"My...My...wife. You..."

"You shouldn't worry about her. I liked her, she was a nice woman. She was real unhappy, though, Johnny. And she was real dangerous. Still I'm going to enjoy killing you a whole lot more than I enjoyed killing her." She looked at her watch. "Well, pretty soon we can get down to business; you'll be able to answer my questions just as soon as you can speak a bit better." She returned to the bedside table and pulled my bottle of cognac out of the little cupboard. I was lying on my back, a position I could not move from, but I could see everything that was going on in the room.

I was thankful that the hallucinations were beginning to wear off, but I wondered what nightmare the next stage of the drug would plunge me into. I could guess a lot of her questions. Like where Irene was. What did she know? That sort of thing. And if what this woman, Zeigler, had said was true, then I'd tell her everything; I wouldn't be able to help myself. Whilst under the effect of the drug, I was completely susceptible to suggestion.

"I guess you won't want a drink, Mr Macfarlane," said Zeigler.

Damn right there. I watched the woman in deadly fascination as she sipped the cognac out of my tooth glass. I croaked. "CIA."

She just nodded. "Why naturally; who else but Uncle Sam's finest?" I suppose that was the final confirmation of all that I'd feared. "'So, okay, Johnny, let's get down to business. What are you doing in Paris?"

For a moment I was taken aback.

"I live here."

The woman's eyes flashed a deadly fire. "Don't give me that!"

"It's true...I've been dormant for a long tine...Out of service."

"Liar. No one retires. I'll say this for you, you're tough, but it doesn't matter. Now, where's the girl?"

My head swirled. I tried to bite back the words, but it wasn't my voice anymore, though it seemed to pass through my lips. "Joigny. At...A pension."

"We'll deal with her later, my friend. And anyone else who's been helping you." Zeigler seemed to relax a bit, as though she had what she'd come for. "You think you've been mighty smart, Macfarlane; wiping out my group was quite a job. Oh, yes, I was the Control for those guys. I organised the hit on your little love-nest at Versailles. I underestimated you. That's why I came in person this time. And this time you won't walk away. But just to cheer you up, let me tell you that those boys were only providing the covering fire: the real honey hasn't happened yet. But in three days time, it'll be all over." She glanced at her watch. "Time for me to go, Johnny."

She picked up her handbag and drew from it the gun she'd had there all along. It was Dad's old Webley .455, the one that had spelled the end of my family life. It was now going to do its work on me. I tried frantically to fight the drug, to make my body do as I willed it. I felt the perspiration bead on my brow and trickle down my cheek with the effort.

Zeigler, who was smiling in a distracted, lethally dangerous way, picked up a pillow from the bed. She slowly began to walk back across the room to where I lay, like a tethered animal awaiting the butcher's knife, knowing no hope of escape, knowing that I had blown my only chance to avenge the poor, innocent children who had died on Christmas Eve; and what of Julie, if it came down to that?

They say that the dying man sees his life before him; I don't know if that is true, but I can tell you that in the few brief moments it must have taken that harpy to get to me, moments that seemed an eternity to me, every one of the mistakes I'd made since the awful affair had begun, was written in neon letters in my brain. The cold, terrifyingly emotionless light which shone from Ziegler's eyes only made it worse. Oh, yes, she was a psycho, there was no mistake. I could see the anticipation there; even, perhaps, the excitement.

She kneeled down at my side and ran the muzzle of the revolver along my quivering cheek. She sucked in her breath and sighed. "Did you do it to him? The one you killed…You know? That was pretty wild, Macfarlane. I never thought you were into that. Or was it that little whore you like to hang around with? Don't worry, she'll get hers. You may have broken up my team, but there are others waiting to take over from them. You robbed me of promotion, though, I hope that comforts you."

"What…What?"

"Believe me, I could think of much more fun ways to terminate you; but the Control wants it to look like suicide. A fitting end to your career, shot yourself in a dingy hotel room, all alone, out of what… Shame? The papers will think of something, I'm sure you'll get front page attention."

With a last desperate effort of will, I threw out my arm to strike at her, but it was useless, she brushed my fist aside as if I'd been a kitten that had played too rough. Her face set, she lifted the pillow to cover my face and I knew that it was all over. "Bye bye, Johnny," she said, as sweetly as a mother kissing her baby to sleep.

And then the world exploded. I saw her head jerk up in an angry movement. The pale mad light died in her eyes as she tried to muster herself back into action. I saw her pull up the revolver to train it on the doorway. I'd been granted a reprieve, though by whom I had no idea.

Once again, I lashed out with my fist. This time my weakened blow was just enough to throw her off balance; for a fraction of a second she was unprepared. And in that fraction of a second I saw the door of the room fly open and there, unbelievably, but a more welcome sight I never saw, was Irene. She had the sawn off twelve-bore. I saw the hate and the fury on her face. Then she fired.

Zeigler's face disappeared before even she had the chance to recover her balance; she was half way to her feet when the first charge struck her. She crumpled backwards, her arms flailing, red bubbles escaping from the hole where her mouth had been. Irene fired again, her petite frame half-crouched behind the recoil of the weapon. The American agent was whirled like a rag-doll by the impact and thrown against the far wall of the room, where she fell like a heap of dirty laundry at the side of the wash-stand.

Irene threw down the gun and flung herself across the little room to my side, taking me in her arms and hugging me with a passion that was almost ferocious. I could feel the salt wetness of the tears on her cheeks and her whole body was quivering as if with an electric force.

I saw another shape loom above me; it was Joseph. He laid his hand on Irene's shoulder and murmured, "Come, come, we must get out of here!"

Irene turned to him. "They've, they've done something to him!"

I tried to speak, slowly. "Drug...Be all right. Joseph right, we have to go. Police." I tried to stand up, but that was less successful. "Help me," I whispered. I felt Irene and Joseph pull me to my feet. "My gun – the Luger. It's in her bag. And hers. But use towel...fingerprints..."

Irene nodded and fetched the things and then, as I hung suspended between the shoulders of my rescuers, we began to make our way down the stairs.

Soon we were at the foyer, where, to my surprise, the concierge was standing with his hands in the air, looking down the barrel of an Uzi, held by Françoise. She had succeeded in convincing him that she'd use it if she had to.

Eighteen

I became aware that Irene was trying to speak to me. I'd been too busy watching the lightshow of the streetlights passing as our car raced through Paris to pay that much attention until she began to shake me.

"What?" I gasped.

"Where are we going to go?" hissed Irene, desperately. "The concierge at the pension saw everything. I'm sure he took the number of the car. Where are we going to go? Come on, Johnny, pull yourself together!"

She was right. We were in big trouble. No way would the law see what had happened in that hotel room as anything but murder. And there were a few other items they wanted to speak to me about. An image flashed into my mind. "Delauney," I croaked.

"Delauney! Are you right out of your mind?" Irene's face was a picture of disbelief.

"He owes. For Harry. He has to look after us." She wasn't happy with this idea, but she obviously couldn't come up with a better one, or she wouldn't have asked me, with my brains still littered over the cosmos. I could hear her whispering directions to Françoise, who'd slowed to a less manic pace of driving. In fact we were lucky that Irene knew how to find Auguste Delauney: he wasn't the kind of guy who leaves a forwarding address. I'd have wondered about it if I'd been a little less spaced out.

Zeigler was right about that damned drug, whatever it had been; my brains were like scrambled egg.

Like many of his gangland pals, Delauney had a few legitimate business interests. It saves the tax man from getting too curious about the precise source and amount of his income. As well as that café in Clichy where this had all begun, he owned several others and a couple of very classy clubs, you know the sort of place, legal roulette wheel out front, good restaurant, swish furniture, gorgeous and scantily dressed girls. And, of course, for those who were in the know, out back there would always be a high-stakes poker game and a massage parlour where those intimate desires could be catered for.

It was at one of those that Irene told Françoise to pull over. Then she leapt out of the car and began to tap on the panel of a robust door. After a while, a man in a tux swung the door open and Irene quizzed him for a moment or two. Then the door closed. Irene returned to the car, clearly agitated.

"I think he's there," she said and lit up a caporal with shaking fingers. "The goon has gone to see if his lordship will see us. I really don't know about this, you know."

That last comment was directed at me. Suddenly there was a tap on the roof of the car and the door beside me swung open. I was still made of jelly and I slid out onto the wet tarmac at the feet of the man who stood there. I looked up at him. It was the same goon I'd met at the funeral. I managed a smile.

He just swore. "Merde! Hey, what did you bring this mess with you for? And who are these people? This is a classy joint, Irene. You know better."

"That'll do!" rang out another voice, instantly recognisable as that of the man himself, Delauney. I grinned, well I tried to. It probably looked like a manic leer, but it was meant in the best way.

Then it was Irene's voice. "Auguste? Is that you? Oh, thank God. You must help us, please!"

Delauney stepped out from the shadows of the alley and into the backwash of the streetlights. "Yeah? I wondered when..." Then he saw me. "Well, if it isn't our old friend Macfarlane." He turned to Irene. "And you know I don't like drunks!"

"He's not drunk, Auguste; he's been drugged!"

I nodded, from my recumbent position. "And you know what, Delauney?' She got Harry's killer for you. That's right, blew her right away."

Delauney looked back at Irene. "That true?" She nodded.

"I might be able to do something for you." He gave a filthy, lecherous chuckle that I didn't like one bit. It was pretty clear to me, even in my state, that he and Irene were more than passing acquaintances. "But you can't stay here. This car hot?"

"No, but I think we may have been seen."

"Jesus, Irene, you always were a bundle of fun. Okay. Raoul," he said, to a figure in the shadows, "Bring my car round here. And make it quick. Somebody get rid of this heap. What do you mean, where? Do I care? In the Seine, or better still, go and get that piss-ant down at the scrap-yard to switch on the crusher."

I noticed that all trace of the refined accent had disappeared as Delauney spouted the argot of the street. It was an impressive transformation. During all this time, Françoise and Joseph hadn't said a word. I guess they were thinking about what they'd got themselves into, now that the action was over. I didn't have time to feel sorry for them then; I knew I was going to feel bad about it later.

Delauney's goons manhandled me into the back of a black van parked in the alley and ushered Joseph and Françoise in too. Irene was about to step in with us, but the goon from the graveyard caught her by the arm. "Hey, Irene, the man wants you to travel in style. He wants to congratulate you."

Irene gave me a look that said, "I knew we shouldn't have come here," but there was nothing else for it. For good or for ill, we were in the power of these hoodlums for the time being; I could only hope that she'd be all right. I knew now who the 'boyfriend' who'd taught her how to shoot was.

I don't remember too much about the journey. My sense of time was right out of the window; I just remember Françoise cradling me and hushing me as the cramps began to bite into my muscles like iron teeth. Joseph just sat with his back against the side of the van and gazed out of the window in the rear door. Every time we passed a street-light, his face was illuminated in the harsh blue glare. I guessed he had a lot of questions to ask himself. And to ask me.

Françoise? She just looked at me with that sad look on her face, as if I were the prodigal son returned. I wondered if she'd thought about what she'd got involved in – what I'd got her involved in. I swore to myself that I'd make it up to her; I just hadn't a clue how I was going to do it.

We pulled up and the back door swung open. It was the goon again. He helped Joseph to get me out of the car, though, so I was prepared to forgive some of his transgressions.

We were caught in the glare of the lights from another car, which I guessed to be Delauney's limo. Sure enough, the man himself came out to meet us, followed by Irene, who was looking a bit dishevelled. It was some moments before I noticed the deepening red of a palm shaped weal on his cheek. Irene glowered at me. It was pretty clear who she thought was to blame. One of the goons stepped into the house and switched on the lights.

"This is one of my little pieces of real estate," announced Delauney, seemingly none the worse for his presumed rebuke at the hands of Irene. "No one will find us here." He led the way in and I began to follow, with Joseph's support, but we were stopped by a pair of powerful arms and held while the goon from the graveyard frisked us.

He got around to starting on Françoise, when she exploded. "Pig! Take your hands off me!"

"Okay, okay, lady, it's the rules."

"She's clean, honest," I blurted out. The man just looked at me, but he thought about it and decided against incurring Françoise' wrath; she can be pretty awe-inspiring when she's roused. We were led into a spacious room with a deep red pile carpet and fine plaster cornices. The light came from an enormous chandelier overhead.

"You like my little place?" asked Delauney. He was standing at the far end of the room, making expansive gestures. I noticed the return of the cultured accent. Irene was sitting on a chair not far from him, sulking. "It was built by an exiled member of the Russian royal house. I picked it up for very little. It is going to be the best club in the city." Poor Joseph could no longer support my weight unaided and he let me slip into a chair like the one Irene was sitting in. It was all red upholstery and gilded woodwork. Very fancy.

"Can't you do anything with him?" asked Delauney impatiently and the goon from the graveyard shrugged.

"Orange juice," I whispered to Joseph. "Vitamin C pills, anything like that."

"Get him whatever he needs," commanded Delauney to one of his minions and the man, a skinny type with dark hair and a scar down one side of his face disappeared. When he came back, a few moments later he had a large jug of orange juice and a glass.

"Pepe," said Delauney to the goon from the graveyard, "Go and get some vitamin C pills from the all-night chemist."

"She told me it was like LSD, only stronger," I explained, to Joseph. "Vitamin C might just be the antidote for it. Here goes." So saying, I began to drink the stuff. I hate orange juice and for it to have any effect against a hallucinogen, you have to drink pints. I was not a happy man. Pepe came back with the vitamin pills and I knocked back half the bottle. One thing was for sure, I wasn't going to catch any colds that night.

After about half an hour of this, I was beginning to feel quite myself. I still had the savage, searing cramps, but I could cope with pain. Joseph and Françoise were helping me as best they could, while Delauney drank cognac and tried to make conversation with Irene. Pepe and the guy with the scar stood by the door. I got up and tried a few steps. Aside of being so full of orange juice sloshing around inside of me, it went not at all badly. I tried a few more and soon was feeling quite confident that I could function more or less normally. Mind you, I had the devil's own hangover.

Nineteen

Irene was looking pretty good, all things considered; Joseph's leeches had indeed worked on that eye of hers. It was still a little puffy, but it wasn't obvious. I crossed the room to where she was sitting. Delauney was watching me with narrowed eyes, but I didn't give a damn. I put a hand on her shoulder and stood in silence for a moment before I spoke.

"Thanks," I said, simply. She took my hand and pressed it to her lips.

"I was so frightened," she said at last. "When I heard Françoise say that you were hoping to meet this woman again, I remembered at once; it was what I'd been trying to remember ever since.... She was seen, you see, with Harry...On the night, after we saw him. I didn't think anything of it at the time, I just thought he'd been up to his old tricks again. It's funny, you know, how a new girl in town always attracts comment."

"I knew it was her," I replied, "Almost as soon as she walked in that night. I don't really know how."

"Why did you take her to your room?"

I gazed into those brown orbs. "Because I hoped I could get her to tell me something that would lead me to the person who sent her."

Irene's eyes filled with concern. "Oh, no, Johnny, it's over now. Isn't it?"

I shook my head resignedly. "No. It's not over yet. She was just a pawn, an expendable pawn. She was like a symptom; we have to strike at the heart of the disease."

"Bravo!" put in Delauney, a trifle sarcastically. "And how do you propose to do that?" I looked at him. It was quite clear that he was jealous of the intimacy between Irene and me. I hoped that wasn't going to be a problem.

"And anyway," went on the big man, "Why should we care? If what you say is true and Irene killed whoever it was who put Harry away, then our business is finished. You're on your own."

"Am I? Harry died because he was seen talking to me. This organisation will stop at nothing to achieve its ends. What do you want, Delauney? Do you want to wait until they finger you and then they come after you? Because they will, you know. They already know about our last meeting; it's only a matter of time before they get the idea that you know more than is good for your health."

Delauney shrugged his shoulders as if to say 'So what?' But I could see that the idea worried him. And that was good. "So how are you going to stop these people, eh, clever boy? I mean, what can you do? Kill all of them? You haven't been doing very well so far." His voice was a sneer as Delauney spat the words at me. He had a very good point though.

But I had a better one. "The thing is, Delauney, you haven't been listening to me. We have to find a way to get these people to lay off. We don't have any choice. Now there's one thing that the CIA is supremely frightened of, one thing that they fear above all else."

"What's that?"

"Publicity. How many US Senators and Congressmen do you suppose know about this? What do you think they'd do if ever they found out? This is a White House back-door job, clandestine, undercover. Oh, sure, the Presidential office knows, it's behind it, but you can bet your last centime that as soon as the shit looks like hitting the fan they'll back-pedal like crazy."

"So?"

Delauney, Irene, Françoise, Joseph and even Pepe and Scarface were staring at me as if I had all the answers on the tip of my tongue. And the truth was that I was as much in the dark as they were.

I thought about it. "Look, Zeigler, the American agent, she said that something was going to happen which would let her go home. That could only mean that the company is planning a major coup; something so big that they'd have to get their heads down out of the way afterwards. So we have to find out what exactly they're planning to hit and then expose them in action. That's where you'll come in. Delauney, I want the whole of Paris to be on the look-out."

"Yeah, that's great. I really need this, Mac. Maybe I'll just hand you and your friends over to them right now and do a deal."

Irene broke in. "No, Auguste," she said, firmly. "You won't do that. You owe me. You know that."

The man sighed and stamped his foot. He wagged a finger at me.

"Are you involved with her? Well, let me tell you, you're getting into more than you can handle." He turned away. Irene just smiled. I was impressed.

"Okay, okay," said Delauney at length. "You win. I'll do what I can to help you. But what is it you're going to do?"

It was Joseph's voice, dreamy and distant, which answered his question. "I know. I know what they're going to attack. I follow the news. The Heads of State are meeting here, in Paris, at the Elysée Palace. It will be the biggest summit meeting Europe has ever seen; a milestone in its history."

"Christ, you're right, that has to be it!"

"Oh, come on," put in Delauney in a voice full of disbelief. "No one in their right mind is going to try to hit that! Do you know what precautions have been taken against an attack? There are three whole divisions of the French army on 'exercises' not five kilometres from the city; there have been mass reinforcements of the local police and gendarmerie from the provinces and the Sûreté is mounting the biggest security operation this country has seen since De Gaulle died. Who do you think you're kidding?"

"All the military protection in the world can't protect against that one stratagem, the terrorist's favourite. You see, they can defend against an attack by those who fear for their lives, like the rest of us, but no security agency in the world has ever been able to discount the threat of the suicide attack, the attack by a fanatic who is quite ready to lay down his life to achieve his goal. Remember Munich and the Iranian Embassy and countless others; no, Delauney, all the divisions of the French army can't be sure against this threat. And remember that our friends from Washington will have briefed the attackers and supplied them with the most sophisticated weapons and equipment. Joseph is right; that's the target. And we have less than seventy-two hours to find out how they're going to do it and spike their guns."

"And then?"

"Then the organisers are mine," I said, grimly. "They're responsible for all the killing. They're mine."

There was silence for a moment and then Joseph spoke again. "My friend, you must take care that the desire for revenge does not possess you entirely. You shouldn't go too close to that brink, or it may be that you can never step back." He looked at me with those eyes of his and he knew that his words had hit home.

I nodded and then turned again to Delauney. "First thing is, I want my friends here taken care of. They have to be safe until all this blows over. Françoise, Joseph and Irene. Will you do that?"

"Françoise and Joseph, yes; but not me," said Irene, as firmly as she'd spoken to Delauney some moments before, "You don't leave me behind this time, Johnny. Not now; not after what happened."

I looked into her eyes. "It's going to be dangerous. More dangerous than you know. But I don't think I can resist you. Only you promise me that if ever I have to give you a direct order, you'll do as I tell you."

Irene said not a damned thing. I sighed. "Okay, dammit, we'll work on that one later. But Joseph and Françoise."

Françoise left Joseph's side and came to me. "Are you quite sure that we cannot help?"

I shook my head. "You are more involved than you should be already. Delauney, can you ensure the silence of that concierge at my hotel?" He made a gesture with his hand that said it was already done. "Good. Joseph and Françoise are to go somewhere safe, out of the city and under guard. When all this is over, then they can go home. It will be safe for them then."

Delauney smiled. "I have the very place...A very long way away. In the Alps, I go there sometimes when I have had enough of the city." He summoned the man with the scar on his face from his station by the door and murmured to him in soft tones for few moments. The man nodded, again and again. "Very well," said Delauney at the last. "These people leave at once. Antoine will take them; there will be another guard too. Make your farewells."

The scar-faced man walked swiftly to the door and held it open. I stepped forward to bid farewell to my friends. I embraced first Françoise and then Joseph. There was little that I could say. Irene did the same, but when she came to embrace the doctor, she could no longer prevent the tears.

"Thank you, Joseph, for, for everything."

"Please be careful," he said. "And take care of that crazy man you're with. Don't let him play the hero." Then he turned and followed Antoine and Françoise from the room. I wondered how long it would be before we met again, or if ever we would. Irene dried her eyes and resumed her seat.

Twenty

There was silence in the room for many long moments and then Delauney spoke. "They will be safe with Antoine," he said, in a voice that was almost concerned. "But we have other fish to fry. What else do you have in mind?"

"Check this number for me," I replied and related the number of the Mercedes that had been parked in the alley opposite the pension. "You could check to see if it's still there." Delauney nodded and crossed to the telephone.

While he was making the call, I began to rummage through Zeigler's bag, which Irene had brought with her. Nothing much; a purse with some money in it, a couple of hundred francs, nothing that would look untoward, a powder compact, lipsticks and some keys, including a set of Mercedes car keys. I wondered. Irene watched while I ripped the lining out of the purse; nothing. Then I dismantled both the powder compact and the lipstick, but they were similarly innocent. I must have been watching too many movies.

The keys might tell a story, though. There were several of the old latchkey type, which are pretty well untraceable, but as well as those, a high-security lock key of modern design. I held it up. That was a break; copies have to be made by the original supplier, who keeps a record of the patterns. The lock which this key was for had been made in Sweden but the company had a French subsidiary.

I motioned to Delauney. "Your mole in the Sûreté; how pliable is he?"

"How pliable do you need?" I smiled. I had to admit, I liked the way that this man had his affairs sewn up. Hell, I've never been against corruption like that; at least you know where a man stands when he's after money. It's a damn sight nicer than idealists; you never can tell what they'll do next.

"Well, get him to find the lock this key fits. It shouldn't be too hard for him to arrange," Delauney nodded and took the key. "You'd better get him on to it right now," I added and then I checked my watch. The drug really had knocked my internal clock out of kilter; it was only just after five a.m.

Delauney smiled. "Don't worry. I pay him enough to get him out of bed at this time in the morning."

"Good. Chances are there's something there that we should know about. The rest of her stuff is clean. How long before we get something on the car?"

"One of my people has gone to see if it is still where you left it. He'll get in touch before he goes near it."

"He'd better; most likely it'll be booby trapped." I saw Delauney raise an eyebrow and allowed myself an instant's satisfaction. I wanted to stay one jump ahead of the man. Irene was beginning to look exhausted; I didn't blame her. I'd have liked the opportunity to talk to her in private, to say some of the things that had to be said, but the time would come later. I turned to Delauney, who had pulled out a chair at the long polished table in the centre of the room and had sat down. He looked tired too.

Personally, I felt as if I'd been shot full of amphetamine, but I guessed that that was a carry-over from the hallucinogen. When the tiredness did catch up with me, it would be like being hit by a sledgehammer, "This place have somewhere Irene can rest?" I asked.

Delauney smiled like a wolf. I wondered if I should set him straight with regard to Irene, but I decided against it: She didn't need me to fight her romantic battles and Delauney already knew that. There were a couple of questions I wouldn't have minded asking him, either, if ever there were a quiet enough moment. Irene nodded her appreciation and rubbed her tired eyes.

Delauney signalled to Pepe to lead her to a bedroom and then I pulled up a chair at the table opposite him.

Before she left, Irene kissed me, gently, a lover's kiss, on the lips, making sure Delauney was watching.

"Ciao," she said to him and followed Pepe out the door. The man opposite me watched her leave and then turned to me with an expression approaching frankness on his face.

"My friend," he said, "I hope you appreciate how much you owe to the girl who just left. It is only because of her that you and your friends are still alive, but I would not like you to get the impression that you can push me too far. Now. I want to know exactly what happened tonight."

"She didn't tell you?"

"Only that she had killed Harry's murderer and that you had been drugged. Now, since we are going to be partners, if reluctantly, you must explain all you can. You owe me this much."

I nodded. "Do you have any cognac in this place?" He nodded without smiling, rose, crossed to the far side of the room and returned a few moments later with two glasses. I smiled and drained mine. Then I told him everything I knew. Well, almost.

At ten to six the phone rang. Pepe answered it and then shook Delauney, who'd dropped off, by the shoulder. He grunted and began to talk into the receiver. Then he looked at me. "They found the car. It was still there. But so very like gendarmes. They thought the car had something to do with the dead woman." He grinned. "Unfortunately, no-one warned them that it might be unwise to try to pick the lock or force the door. Boom!" He rolled his eyes. "So sad. But what is one flic, or even two, more or less? It will teach them to go poking their noses in where they're not wanted."

He paused. "And I must congratulate you. You know your enemy."

The car had still been there? Then Zeigler had been alone after all. She must have been a highly rated agent. It was good, though, because it meant that our trail would be cool before the company got round to tracking us.

"Well," I said, "It looks like it's down to your friend at the Sûreté. Let's hope he comes up with an address. In the meantime, circulate her description to all of your people. I want to know where that woman's been and who she's been with. It would help if we had a photograph, but we might be able to get that when we find the lock for that key."

Delauney nodded. "Even my people would find it hard to trace her on the description you gave. Paris is full of part-time girls and they all look like her. We can account for the regulars, but she could have been any one of thousands of girls who supplement their income while their husbands are away from home, or something like that. But with a photograph, yes, then we can trace her."

"Good. It's just the time that worries me. We have so little."

"You better be patient. We will find her."

Delauney's mole at the Sûreté did, indeed, call back in the end. He was puzzled about what was going on, but I didn't want him to know anything until we'd traced Zeigler's movements.

The key turned out to be one made to fit a lock in a building in, guess what? Number four, Rue Michelet. And the key was for flat forty-two. Which was the flat directly above the one used by the gentlemen from Spain whose operational careers I'd put an end to some days before.

I had to smile. The terrorists had probably never seen their contact; everything would have been done by telephone, which was normal CIA practice. Yet all the time, the contact was literally above their heads. It was a certainty that that flat had been bugged rotten so that the CIA could keep constant tabs on their pawns.

"Well, I think we'd better go there and give the place the once-over," I said to Delauney when he'd put the phone down. He nodded thoughtfully. "What if there are others there?"

"There won't be. There must have been two teams, one active and the other dormant. I managed to scupper the first team, which was Zeigler's, so they must now activate the second team for their next action. Of course, it may have been their plan to do that all along, you never know. But they wouldn't double up. Not their style at all. No, if that was where Zeigler was holed up and everything points that way, then it'll be empty. Except for the booby-traps."

Delauney groaned. "Merde. I hate dynamite."

I chuckled. I knew what he meant.

"What about Irene?" he asked.

"Not this time. Let her sleep. Do you trust Pepe?"

He nodded.

"Then leave him here to look after her. Plus some of the other guys you have outside that door. Oh, come on, I've got ears: at least six cars have pulled up on the gravel outside since we arrived. This place must be like a fortress by now."

Delauney smiled, a bit sheepishly. "Okay. Raoul will come with us. He's the best driver I've got. Used to smuggle cannabis up through Spain from Morocco. You have to be good for that run. Another car will follow us."

"Yes and that will be plenty," I put in. "What do you want to do,

stage a street parade? Let's just try to do this a bit subtle."
He looked at me and nodded, slowly. Then we left.

Twenty One

We drew up around the corner from the depressing grey concrete edifice that was number four, Rue Michelet. From what
Delauney had told me, I reckoned that Raoul must be a pretty cool
customer. I decided to take him with me to the house. I noticed that the
big man didn't volunteer his own services. I told him to stay in the car
anyway. I had a feeling that he'd only clutter the place up.

I took two guys from the second car to cover us and set out for the
building.

I wasn't going to do anything heroic, so before we left, I held my
hand out to Delauney.

"Piece." I said.

He smiled and then withdrew my Luger from his coat pocket.
I was quite delighted. "I found that on Irene," he said, by way of an
explanation. "I thought I recognised it."

I smiled. The familiar weight or the gun felt good in my hand as I
hefted it and then slipped out the magazine, checked it and pushed it
home again. I drew back the receiver. There was one up the spout.

"Thanks," I said. We left one of the soldiers at the entrance to the
building and the rest of us went on inside. The hallway was depressing;
it smelled of piss and the walls were covered in graffiti in several
different languages. Like you'd expect in a run-down block, the lift
was out of action, so we took the stairs. It was safer that way, anyway. I
left the second soldier to guard the landing and Raoul and I made for
the door of the flat.

I took out the key and gingerly slid it into the lock. "Stand back,"
I said to Raoul. "No sense in two of us getting blown to bits." I turned
the key and it snicked precisely. I pushed the door open a quarter of
an inch; then I pulled it to again and retreated down the hall to where
Raoul was waiting, with an interested expression on his face.

I gave it five and then turned to him, "You got a knife?" He didn't
say a word, but his hand made a movement too swift for the untrained
eye to follow and the flick-knife in his palm snicked open. He smiled.
A big, ugly, simian smile, but sincere enough. I knew that if Delauney

ever said the word, then he'd stick me with that knife and not bat an eyelid.

I tested the blade. It was sharp, all right. I nodded my thanks and returned to the door of the flat. I pushed it open once again. Where was it? I was looking for the inevitable, almost invisible strand of fishing-line.

There were two; one near the floor, where they usually put them and one near the top, a back-up. I sliced through them and let the door swing wide open, at the same time crouching back behind the wall. There was no withering blast of gunfire.

My mouth was as dry as sun bleached bone. I motioned for Raoul to come up to cover me and snicked the safety off the Luger. Then I went into the lion's mouth.

I paused by the door long enough to point out to Raoul the bomb and the detonator which had been attached to the fishing lines. Raoul whistled and I didn't blame him; that little lot would have blown the whole wall out, in a hail of deadly shrapnel.

The flat itself was just the cheap, utilitarian house you'd expect in a building like that. There was a short hallway behind the front door, with several flimsy panelled doors giving way to who knows what traps. There could have been anything from bombs activated by tremblers under the carpets to something as simple as a door handle wired up to the mains. If you thought I wasn't enjoying myself, you'd have been right.

Raoul wasn't looking too keen on the situation either. I left him by the front door and ventured on. It was fortunate for my nerves that all the doors had keyholes in. them, so I didn't have to open any more than I had to.

In the far room, at the edge of my limited, field of vision, I caught sight of what I was looking for. I opened the door and checked for the fishing lines, but there weren't any. I sighed with relief and realised that my palms were slippery with sweat. I nosed inside the room. Nothing. No bangs, no flashing lights, not a thing but the serene ticking of the clock on the mantelpiece.

I swallowed and edged forward. In the corner of the room was a bank of electronic equipment, video machines and recorders, along with a couple of monitors. Not far away was a large bureau, with a roll-top lid. I tried the keys I'd found in Zeigler's bag; one of them opened the top and I rolled it back.

At first I couldn't find anything of any importance at all. Then, in one of the drawers, I found a passport in the name of Jeanne Dore. It had a decent picture of Ziegler and that might be helpful.

Then, as I was almost on the point of giving up, I found it. Under one of the shelves was a little catch; I pulled it and a package dropped into my hand. I pulled it back; it was a plain brown envelope. I stole a quick look inside. There were a number of black-and-white photographs and a notebook.

I wondered whether to take a closer look and I suppose that was why I glanced over at the clock. My heart froze and alarm bells started ringing crazily in my head. That clock was stopped.

"Time-bomb!" I roared as I passed Raoul. He didn't need any second telling and we both fled the place. The soldiers didn't hang about either and we didn't stop running until we emerged from the building. It was just beginning to cross my mind that all I'd heard was the kitchen clock when the fucker went off. And I mean a fucker. I'd have said about twenty-five pounds of plastic. Blew the God-damned side of the building clear off on the third floor and fourth floors and took off half the roof for good measure.

The pre-cast concrete supporting wall collapsed like a pack of cards and the whole building assumed a drunken list to one side. I felt the blast like a shove in the back and we were peppered with fragments of masonry. I got into the car quicker than a startled rabbit.

"Hit it!" I yelled to the driver and I felt myself pushed back into the soft upholstery of the seats as the car took off in a howl of protesting tyres. To his credit, Delauney didn't say a word; but I could tell he was impressed.

"Time-bomb," I sighed. "Probably activated by a trembler under the floor. They set it on a five-minute lapse; just time enough to let an intruder get comfortable. Bastards!"

Christ, it was like using a sledge-hammer to crack a nut. It wasn't until later that we found out how many innocent neighbours had been killed or injured by the blast, which was somehow explained away as the result of a gas leak; but at the time, as the limo sped towards the

Route Peripherique and I listened to the distant sound of sirens, I had other things on my mind.

At last, Delauney could contain himself no longer. "What did you get?" he demanded, clearly impatient.

"These." I opened the envelope and gave him Zeigler's false passport. "Think you can get that photograph onto the streets tonight?"

"I think so."

I looked at the bundle of black-and-whites that I'd found. There was something funny about them, something that gave me the eerie feeling that I should recognise them, but I couldn't see why at first. I leafed through them one by one. They were all clearly taken within minutes of each other.

The location was a street café, the kind which Paris is famous enough for; and this one was like any other I'd seen. There was something though; and then, as I leafed through the bundle, the something was pointed out to me by a ring, marked in black permanent marker, near the centre of one of the prints.

I squinted closer, but on that scale, it was difficult to make out the face of the person whose image was marked. He was reading a newspaper and the face was partially obscured. I leafed through the others quickly. And then I realised. The subject of interest was me. I swore.

"What?" asked Delauney, hearing my oath.

"Look," I jabbed a finger at the picture and held it up. "That's me."

"Hey, you're famous."

The humour was lost on me; I was trying to work out when the hell that photograph had been taken; but all I could tell was that it looked like late autumn. There's more to this...Perhaps it was just that the shots had been taken to identify me to Zeigler, but that was a little thin. These people would have had the right gear; a telephoto lens, had me filling the frame. No, it wasn't that. So why had they been taken at all? It was a mystery and there was no solving it unless I got larger copies of those prints.

I turned to Delauney. "You said you had a tame photographer?"

He just nodded and looked at the photographs. "You want him to make some copies of these?"

I was about to say yes and then I stopped myself and, reconsidered.

"No. I want you to take me to him," When you want something done in a hurry, the only way is to do it yourself.

Delauney raised an eyebrow. "Sure, sure. Anything you ask!"

"You don't have to stick around. Just leave me a car."

"Okay, okay, don't get upset. I'll leave you Raoul."

I smiled and settled back into the plush leather upholstery of the seat. Every inch of my body was aching.

Twenty-Two

The photographer was a small man, with a pronounced gut, grey hair and a beard. He didn't take too kindly to being dragged from his bed by Roual hammering on the door of his studio-flat with the butt of his Colt. I guess I might have been pissed off too.

He looked at me blankly as I stood in his hallway and sized him up. As well as being short and fat, he had no shoes or socks on, his hair was tousled and his shirt was buttoned up wrong and stuffed carelessly into the waistband of his leans. He was a mess. But then, I hadn't seen myself in a mirror lately.

A female voice, heavy with sleep, emanated from one of the rooms. The man gesticulated. "What do you want? I got company."

"Don't let us disturb your private life," I said. "Just point me in the direction of your darkroom. And make some coffee." Just at that the girl who'd called from the bedroom appeared. She was blonde, willowy, wrapped up in a sheet, had those limpid, seductive blue eyes and I'll be damned if she was a day over fifteen. "Your mama know where you are?" I asked. She pouted.

"Mama pissed off with an Italian."

"Such is life."

I turned to follow the photographer into the deep red gloom of his darkroom.

"I can look after myself in here. You go and catch up on your beauty sleep." If you ask me, he needed it. "But don't forget the coffee."

I took off my jacket, rolled up my sleeves and set to work. It was a fiddly task, blowing up the prints without the original negative; I had to contact-print an internegative and then enlarge that and I was beginning to feel like something the dog brought home.

After half an hour, the girl came in with the coffee: she was now wearing a pajama shirt several sizes too large and decent by all of half an inch. She leaned up against my shoulder; she had that musky scent of sex lingering to her all over and in the confined space of the darkroom it was overpowering. I gathered myself. "Thanks for the coffee. Now get lost. Don't you know not to fool around with older men?"

"I like older men, they teach me things. You know?" She stuck out her tongue and ran it round her lips. "And I learn real quick."

That I could believe. "Anyway, Marc says I'm gonna be real famous as a model. He's a great photographer, you know?"

I just gave her the most old-fashioned look I could manage and she pouted at me and left me alone.

Teach her things? Jesus. The coffee was made the way it should be, very strong and very black and it helped a lot; soon I was well into the swing of the work. I blew up the prints I'd found at Zeigler's by a factor of ten.

I examined them as they came through the print dryer, but nothing clicked into place. Mind you, by that time the images were swimming in front of my eyes.

I got hold of Raoul, who was being entertained by the girl. The owner of the flat was nowhere to be seen. "Don't like to spoil the party, Raoul, but we gotta go."

Raoul shot me one of those lopsided grins, heaved the girl off his lap and slapped her arse. She swore at us and then we left. Nice kid, I thought.

Irene was waiting for me when we got back to Delauney's place. I could tell she was mad, but when she saw me, she mellowed. I must admit, that if I was looking half as bad as I was feeling by then, she must have thought I was close to death. She looked me up and down, walked into the long room, picked up the cognac decanter and a couple of glasses and returnee to my side.

"Bed," she said and I was in no state to argue.

"Oh! I didn't mean to wake you!" I turned my eyes from the sliver of pale, late afternoon sun which passed through the gap between the heavy brocade curtains and looked across the room at Irene. She was sitting at the dresser making up her eyes. I was impressed. The world was collapsing all around her and this girl still had found the time to get her hands on some make-up and do her face. "It's all right, you didn't, wake me up, I mean. My God, I feel as if I've slept for days. What time is it?"

"A little after four."

I leapt out of bed like a scalded cat. "Jesus!"

"Calm down, Johnny, what could you do? You needed to rest. Auguste has put the picture of that woman on the streets, as you asked. It will be some time before he has any news. His people don't get up so early as a rule."

I sighed. She had a point. "Did you have bad dreams?" asked Irene. "Only you were restless for a while. You kept saying something, like a name, I don't know. Don't you remember?"

I frowned. "No. No, I don't remember anything. What was the name?"

She turned to look at me. "I don't know. It was not one that I know."

I crossed to where she was sitting and kissed her as she turned up her face to me. Suddenly I remembered a certain other time when I'd wakened up with her, when she'd sat at the dresser of her little flat, happily stark naked because the central heating had been jammed on full. She hadn't been so carefree since then and it had little to do with the inadequacies of central heating systems.

Someday, I promised myself, silently, if ever I survived the mess I was in, I'd try to make it up to her, if I could. And you know, the thing was, that just one look in her eyes told me that she had all she desired, as long as she could be with me. I didn't deserve her, that was for sure.

"The name," I said, when we had done talking with our eyes and it was time to get back to business. "What was it like?"

"Funny. An English name, at least, not French. It began with an 'M' like, like 'Maroon' or, 'Moran'."

"Moran!" I sat down on the bed with a thump.

"Yes, yes, like that, that's it!"

"Moran," I repeated. But why should he come into my dream, why should I have seen that spectre of the past? Christ, Dick Moran had been killed long before, in Chile; everyone knew that. He'd died when a bomb he'd been setting had gone off prematurely.

"Is there something special about this man?" asked Irene, knowing there must be.

"I knew him, once, years ago. I was on active service in Chile. Nothing official, I was just there to quietly keep an eye on our friends from Washington, see if they had any new tricks we might like to know about."

"I didn't know that the British spied on the Americans."

"Well, not to the extent that we spy on the Russians, or the East Germans. But the Firm always liked to know what the other companies were up to, just to stay one jump ahead. I suppose MI6 would have been horrified, but we just regarded it as part of the game. But Moran, now there's a name. I haven't thought about him for years."

"Was he a friend, Johnny?"

"Well, as far as our professional commitments would allow, yes, we were friends for a while. Then, after I was recalled, he died. Bomb accident."

"Oh, how awful!"

"Yes. Blown to bits. He was a pretty regular sort of guy, well, as far as anyone can be in the racket we were in. I mean, you could have a beer with Dick and feel you could relax. I was sorry to hear he'd been killed."

Then a thought hit me. There was something, someone in that series of pictures. There had been something, I didn't know at the time, like familiar and yet not so. I'd been so tired the last time I'd looked at the blow-ups that I could hardly trust my impressions. Ah, but no, it wasn't possible. Nevertheless I had to know for sure.

"Where are those photographs, Irene? The ones I brought back with me?"

"Over there, by the bed; with your gun."

I quickly sorted through the bundle of photographs. Yes; this man. Most of the time he'd had his back to the photographer and not until the last one, when I was leaving, did his face turn into profile. What seemed to be a coincidental turn of the head before, now seemed suspiciously as if the man had watched me leaving. I found the blow-ups from that print. There! That one. I took the enlarged print over to the window, where the soft daylight streamed in. "Oh, my God. No, it can't be. It's not possible."

"What's not possible?" said Irene and came over to me, treading as lightly as a cat and putting her hand up on my shoulder. "Let me see."

"That's him," I said in a whisper. "It's impossible, but it is."

Well, I'll be damned, so the old bastard wasn't killed after all. I looked at the silver halide ghost again. There was much that was different; like the tightness of the skin around the eyes and the shape of the mouth: but the eyes themselves and the line of that proud, craggy forehead, were unmistakable. I looked to see the hands, but they were gloved.

"He survived. It looks as if he was burned, see, here, look at that. That's a scar. My God, they must have put him back together, patched him up and put him under deep cover. So deep that everyone else thought he was dead. And so he should have been; it's a bloody miracle that he survived."

"Is that bad news, Johnny?"

I shook my head. I just couldn't figure it. "I don't know, Irene, I really don't know. One thing I do know, though, whatever he was before, he's an enemy now."

I took a shower. When I came back to the room and began to dress, I was still as sure that the phantom face in that series of prints was Dick Moran's, older, scarred, but he nonetheless. Somehow a tray with coffee had appeared.

"Auguste has brought in some staff to take care of the place while we're here," said Irene by way of explanation.

"What about the man himself? Is he here?"

"No, I think he's at his penthouse; but he may have gone on to one of the clubs. Pepe says he's coming here at six." I didn't like waiting around. I took a look at myself in the mirror. Not bad, not bad. Considering all that had happened, I thought I was bearing up well.

Irene saw me and chuckled. "You'll do," she said. "I understand that there's a cold buffet in the hall. Shall we go down?"

I suddenly realised just how hungry I was and followed her downstairs.

A man in a tux was standing by the door to the long room with the chandeliers. There were a couple more guys standing inside the front door and all three of them hard the same blank, heavy jowled expression and large bulges under their left armpits. I was glad they were all on our side.

A buffet had indeed been laid. I had to admit, Delauney knew how to look after his guests. I suppose that as the owner of three of the top five restaurants in the city, at least by some accounts, he had a reputation to live up to.

I went out into the hall and asked the guy standing there whether he'd seen Pepe recently. He didn't say a word, but shortly afterwards Pepe himself appeared. It was funny; he didn't look any less like an ape for being on my side.

"This picture," I said, showing him the profile shot of Moran. "I want it circulated in exactly the same way as the one of the woman. Right away. This one isn't dead." Pepe nodded; he was good at taking orders, he'd spent his life doing it.

"Okay. Right away," he said simply and withdrew, leaving me alone with Irene again. I took something to eat and poured another cup of coffee. I thought about Moran.

It was perfect. Moran had worked in South America for years; his command of Spanish and Portuguese was so excellent that he could pass for a native speaker. He could even do a variety of regional accents in either language. Who better to co-ordinate a campaign of violence using the Basque separatist group ETTA as a spearhead? And then there was his ability with explosives.

We'd all been shocked, those of us who knew him, when the news had come through that he'd been killed with one of his own devices. The man was a magician with gelignite.

He'd begun his career in Vietnam, like so many other CIA recruits. He'd been in the army's Special Ordnance section; basically that means all the fancy weapons of the day. But he'd had a flair for undercover work too and our friends from Washington had wasted no time in getting him onto the payroll. I flicked over what I knew of his service record in my mind as I sipped my coffee.

After 'Nam he'd been sent to South America. I'd been in Chile at that time to report on the CIA's methods and add to the Firm's profile.

I had to admit that I was pretty sickened by what I saw: I'm no bleeding heart liberal and I know a pro never gets involved emotionally, but it was a pretty dirty sort of war that the CIA waged. I mean, the Government there wasn't much further left than the Labour Party at home.

When I found corroborated reports of known CIA field men directing the right-wing death squads to their targets, standing in the shadows while union activists, local politicians and the like were dragged out into the street and murdered in cold blood, even I questioned the morals of the men behind it all.

Twenty Three

That was when I first met Moran; I remember it quite clearly. I was posing as a journalist for a British publication that the Firm just happened to have a controlling interest in; he was posing as a Political Attaché to the American Embassy in Santiago.

We met in a little town in the mountains called Vicuna, about two hundred miles north of the capital. The rainy season had begun and the place was damp with the chill moist air that the Humboldt Current brings to that land, locked between the Pacific and the high Andes. The road back south had been cut off; the local papers said it was due to a landslip, but I had a hunch that someone had started that slip with a lump of gelignite.

Finding Moran in a bar there just confirmed it.

Oh, yes, we knew about him, even then; he'd been one of the motivators behind Operation Tomahawk in Vietnam and he was pretty cut up when Washington suspended it.

The Yanks were fighting a dirty, bloody guerrilla war and the way to get ahead was obviously to weed out the communist sympathisers who were helping the VC. So they borrowed an idea from the French and started kidnapping suspects at gunpoint, taking them up a couple of hundred feet over the village square in a HUEY and then throwing them out. For a while it was pretty effective and VC attacks went right down.

Only the White House chickened out; it wasn't good publicity to murder civilians, at least not if it were discovered. And 'Nam was a media circus; there were no secrets there. But Chile wasn't on television in sixty million American homes every night, so nobody gave a fuck what the CIA was doing there.

So anyway, there was I and there was Moran, in that bar. From the way he sort of half smiled at me when I walked in I could tell that he knew who I was and who I was working for. I knew who he was and it was a dirty, depressing night in a dirty, depressing town, in the midst of a dirty, depressing war. I bought him a beer and sat down at his table.

It was one of those conversations, you know the kind, the 'I won't try to milk you if you won't try to milk me' kind. Professionals the world over have them every day. He was open about the subjects he was free to talk about and didn't try to feed me a line on the ones that were off limits.

We got pretty drunk together and talked about the things men far from home talk about, you know, the lousy food and the terrible phone service and the women; most of all the women, I suppose. I mean, the girls in Chile gave a man plenty to talk about.

Other things came up, as well, like that we'd been in Saigon at the same time. We compared notes like old travellers. Turned out we'd even had the same favourite whorehouse. And, as the evening wore on, we got drunker and drunker on cheap Chilean beer, until it was time for us to head off for our hotels.

We were stuck in Vicuna for four days before the authorities could repair the road; and of course there was no chance of a plane out, not in that soaking pea-soup mist.

Then one morning I woke up with my usual hangover and the radio news told me that the road was open again. I didn't have to ask whether or not Dick had already split. I took my battered old Ford back down the highway and I doubted if I'd ever see him again.

I was wrong, though. I did, just once again. It must only have been about a week before he was reportedly killed; I'd already been recalled. Things were out of control by then: the Government was in hiding and the military were butchering any who opposed them.

I'd been staying at a little hotel on the outskirts of town. Every night now there was gunfire in the streets of the capital and I was glad to be handing over to our regular man in the city and going home.

I went into town to check on a few items with a journalist and afterwards, when I sat alone thinking about the frightened little man who'd just left me in the bar, who wasn't leaving the nightmare on the first plane out in the morning, I suddenly became aware of a presence by my side.

It was Moran. Silent, enigmatic Moran. He bought me a beer this time and we talked for a while. I said it looked like he'd be going home soon, but he just chuckled and shook his head. I left it and we talked about the chaos outside. I can remember clearly how the fat little barman jumped every time there was another dull bang of a bomb going off, or the rattle of machine-gun fire as the military silenced another dissenting voice. Sure, I was glad to be getting the hell out of that mess.

That was the last I'd seen of Dick Moran; the next day I was on a flight home, leaving the country along with the thousands of others who fled the awful reality and about a month later, back at home, we began to get reports that the American agent we knew as Moran had been killed, apparently while setting a bomb.

And now he was in Paris. You know, I like to think I'm not easily surprised, but seeing that picture did.

Twenty Four

I racked my brains to try to remember the exact time when the pictures must have been taken. I could tell where the café was and I looked closely at the pictures to try to find a clue. I could just make out the headline on the newspaper. It was a reference to a strike at home. That jogged the memory back into position.

It had been taken before the Damascus job. I would still have been living on the earning of my previous trip and Julie and I would have been in the process of discovering that our attempt to salvage our marriage was turning into an unmitigated disaster.

Only a week later I'd been approached to do the run to Damascus. I remember that at the time I'd thought it was a bit odd, you know, because I didn't do that kind of work as a rule. But I'd said yes, because I needed the money and because I couldn't stand going home at night. I wondered.

I'd been completely involved with that contract from the time I struck the deal until I got paid in Damascus. It takes a bit of doing, organising routes and drivers, to get a dozen new limos from Paris to Syria without raising any eyebrows. I'd sort of enjoyed it.

The more I thought, the more I smelled a rat. I'd been snarled up for weeks and then the payment was delayed?

I clucked my tongue. What if the whole thing had been set up as a ruse to get me out of the city?

It was the little things again, like the way that Zeigler had said something about me not giving them enough time; like the way they'd sent a couple of amateurs after me on that first night home, Christmas Eve.

I thought and I thought and the more I thought, the more clear it became. I'd been set up all along, from beginning to end. It had only been the chance that I'd made a special effort to be home by Christmas that had thrown it all out of sync. They could have had me fooling around in Damascus for months if I hadn't decided to be a bit more than just firm.

That might account for their using those two goons in the café.

They hadn't been expecting me to return so soon and so they'd thrown a contingency plan into action. That had been Dick's only slip to date. He must have thought that I was onto something and that must mean that he thought I'd been listening to his conversation that day. And that meant that the conversation was very important indeed.

So who was the man he'd been talking to? For the very first time since the whole dirty affair began, I knew that I was no longer two steps behind, but just one and if we could get the breaks we needed, we might be in with a chance. I leafed through the pile of photographs until I found one that gave me a clear view of the strange man's face. Irene came over, looking curious. I glanced up.

"Did you ever see this guy before?" I pointed to the face.

Irene looked blank for a moment and then her face cleared and she gasped. "Yes, I have. I don't know who he is, though; I saw him in one of Auguste's places, one of his restaurants. He'll know who this man is."

My eyes narrowed. "Irene, you don't suppose that Auguste could be working with them, do you? I mean, that he's helping these people." Irene looked at me. "I mean, he's really laid it on thick here for us. Why? Why didn't he just get rid of us?"

"You are too paranoid, my friend," said a voice, quietly, from behind me. I spun round and there he stood, the man himself. "You know, under other circumstances you would not survive making such an allegation. You are very lucky that you are with her."

There was something in his voice I didn't like, but before I could say anything I felt the gentle touch of Irene's hand on my arm.

I turned to face her. She was shaking her head and her face was troubled.

"Johnny...Please," she said, quietly. "Don't press it. There are things it is better not to...But while you are with me, Auguste will protect you. He has given me his word."

I wanted to say that I didn't think a gangster like Delauney was someone whose word I'd like to stake my life on, but I decided to let discretion be the better part of valour. I nodded. "There's a lot here I don't know about. But for the moment we'll let it pass."

The haughty tone in my voice was just a gesture; I didn't like the thought of backing down, but I owed Irene too much to cross her.

Anyway, I was only recently recovered from the effects of the drug Zeigler had spiked me with and I wasn't quite sure how much of an effect it was still having on my thinking. Nasty thing about hallucinogens, that.

It was Delauney who broke the silence in the end. "Have you done anything with the photographs?" He came a step nearer to us.

I nodded. "Irene thinks you might know who this man is," I said.

I gave Delauney the print of the unknown stranger sitting next to Moran and awaited his response. I really didn't know what I expected him to say. His eyes narrowed as he looked at the picture and he looked up at me and then back at the print. "Take my advice, my friend," he said at last, "And get out of this while you can."

Now that surprised me. "Why? You know who that man is, don't you?" The big man nodded, slowly, as if admitting something he would rather not. "Then talk," I went on. I don't doubt that that's not the way one should address a gangland boss, but I was just sick of playing games. I could see a worried look cloud Irene's face, but I paid it no heed.

Delauney suddenly snapped and waved his finger at me. "I tell you, you will ruin us all! This is too big for you – too big for me! You are behaving like a madman. Is it not enough that you escaped with your life from that woman...the one who killed Harry?"

"And my wife and my two sons. The blood-debt hasn't been paid and you know that. Zeigler was a pawn, someone sent to do the dirty work by another. I doubt if she even realised the full significance of what she was doing. I will take my revenge, whether you help me or not."

"You are a pitiful little man. These people would eat you alive. Even I, with all my power and influence, could not stand against them!"

I could see that Irene was getting frightened and the atmosphere in the room was becoming charged, as with static electricity. At last she could stand no more and she burst out, "What? For Christ's sake, tell him, Auguste."

The man looked at her hard and once again I was given a demonstration of the peculiar hold that she seemed to have over him. He sighed, shrugged his shoulders and seemed to deflate. He waved his hand deprecatingly. "Yes, of course I know who this man is. In himself he is nothing, a message-boy for someone much more powerful. Perhaps indeed the most powerful man in all France."

I pricked up my ears at that. Whoever it was had the power to frighten Delauney and though I could see that he was trying not to show it, the fear was staring bright from his dark eyes at that very instant. I could feel those little hairs at the back of my neck begin to stand up again and it was as if a new and ominous presence had come into the room.

Delauney suddenly laughed, a harsh, unhumorous laugh and I started. "You still have no idea, do you, my friend? You who would walk through the doors of Hell to take on its master and you don't know who he is. My God you are quite unbelievable." He paused and then sighed again. "I will tell you who this man is; and I will tell you for whom he is the mouth. He himself, you understand, is unimportant; his name is Koestler."

I started because the name was known to me and I looked again at the photograph.

"Yes." he went on, "You have heard of him. He has achieved a certain degree of notoriety in the last year or so."

He was damn right there; Koestler was an outspoken supporter of the extremist right. I'd never seen his picture before, but then, he'd always shunned the photographers and the exposure he might have attracted. He had been making noises on the fringe of the lunatic right for years, but I'd never thought that he amounted to much. That tied in with Delauney's impression of the man, but it surprised me to see him involved with someone like Moran; I mean, Moran was strictly professional.

Still, Koestler could be an intermediary; he would have had the right contacts in the various terrorist groups on the right. But I could tell from the guarded tone of Delauney's voice that it was no bunch of gun-toting hooligans and psychopaths.

"So? Who is the great power behind all this?"

Delauney swore and looked to Irene, but she was siding with me, if reluctantly; there was no help for him there. At last he nodded. "Very well. Koestler is a fool...A mouthpiece, one whom the real powers of the world use to their own ends. It was the same with the Brownshirts in Nazi Germany, of course. It is Koestler's knowledge of people that makes him important; he knows so many."

Delauney turned away from us for a short moment and when he turned back, his face bore the expression of a new resolve. "There are many who regard the Government as dangerously Socialist. They are the same as those who resented the withdrawal from Algeria and the end of the French Imperial age; but allied to them are other interests, far more dangerous and modern ones, industrial, commercial and banking interests who will do all that is in their power to defeat the Socialists."

It did occur to me that those were interests pretty close to Delauney's own. Still, I refrained from saying anything about my fears or suspicions. "Who are the people behind Koestler?" I asked, again.

Delauney stared at me. "It does not mean anything to give you a list of the names of the people. What would you do, spend the rest of your life plotting to kill them all? But I will tell you who they all pay homage to and if that knowledge does not make you get on the first plane out of France, then I will know that you are quite mad. The chief among them is Charriet."

I was stunned into silence. The more I thought about the significance of that name, rattling through my shocked consciousness, the more horrible it seemed, the more frightening. Sure, Koestler was important, he was an ideologue who had the support of the Neo-Fascists and yet who was just respectable enough for the saner elements of the right to deal with, but Charriet? Now we were in with the big guns. The last of the great financiers, he liked to call himself, the one who'd risen from the gutter to become one of the richest men in Europe and the most powerful.

Like all of his kind, he still had that streak of pure greed and ruthless, soulless avarice painted along the length of his soul and it was mean and ugly in proportion to his fabulous wealth. No wonder Delauney had said that he couldn't stand against this man; in fact he would be blown away by his merest breath as if he were an autumn leaf caught in the first gale of winter. Charriet...Not just a man, but a legend.

He had been the diehard supporter of de Gaulle, with the one exception of the difference they'd had over the withdrawal from Algeria. At that time, Charriet had bought his way into the newspaper world to find a voice for his opinions. De Gaulle was lucky; his popularity at home was enough to carry the day and Charriet was for once defeated.

Well, he got over that, though there were those who thought that Charriet had more than a passing connection with a plot to assassinate the President. The public rift was healed, though; the next time that Charriet put his weight behind a cause was when he pressed De Gaulle to veto the acceptance of Great Britain into the Common Market.

Since de Gaulle's death, things had gone downhill for Charriet; the Community had been enlarged several times. The voice of France was diluted time and time again, though at every occasion he'd campaigned with all of his strength against the proposals. To no avail, though; France after nineteen-sixty eight was a changed nation and the old Chauvinist nationalism was unfashionable. Charriet became less and less influential on the political scene, to his great chagrin and even the parties of the right began to regard him as dangerously close to Fascist in his ideology.

I guess all that changed when the French elected their first socialist government. At the time you'd have thought that the end of the world was nigh, if you'd read any of the Charriet publications. But the Left got in anyway, with a majority that allowed them to push through sweeping changes. Ever since they'd been elected the main thrust of right-wing politics had been the destruction of their powerbase; the Right had vowed to prevent the Left from ever gaining power again. Charriet had come in from the cold; he was once again a respected figure in the ranks of the Right.

Where once his ruthlessness had been unfashionable, he'd come to be regarded as a potential saviour because of that very quality. Ever since that fateful election, he'd been pushing, striving, using all of his influence to discredit the Government, to the joy of the Right and yet without making any serious dent in the Government's standing. Could it be that at last he had decided, with the aid of the CIA, to take some drastic step that would guarantee his aims would be acheived? It was a horrible thought.

I could tell without asking Delauney that that was exactly what was going on. It didn't take a lot of working out to know something else, as well.

"You've known about this from the start," I said, quietly, to Delauney.

"Auguste, is that true?" Irene was clearly upset by that thought. For a moment I thought that he might do something drastic there and then, but he didn't.

"I knew," he said at last. "But I had nothing to do with any of it. Charriet has promised to clamp down on us. He talks as if he were going to be elected in person, such is the power he has over his puppets. I don't want to cross his path. I want to keep my nose clean..." His voice trailed off and he looked at Irene appealingly. The tough guy facade slipped a fraction as he shrunk under her hot gaze.

"And do you know what these people have done?" she hissed, at last.

"Irene, his fight is not our fight...It is not your fight, either. Leave it."

His attempt at conciliation fell on deaf ears. "And you know what they did to Harry? You would let them away with that? And do you know what they did to me, the filthy animals? Do you care? Have you forgotten once again who I am?"

Delauney had no power to stand against the deluge of vituperation.

"What...What have they done? Of course I didn't know about Harry, not until it was too late. That was why I let this guy have a go. I was working on it. But what have they done to you?"

Slowly and with great attention to detail, Irene told him of her encounter with the Basques at the house in Versailles. She spat the words out in a hail of cold rage, her arms akimbo, her eyes flashing.

Me, I was back to square one with their relationship. There was one thing sure: Irene's story had a devastating effect on the man before her. His face took on an expression of anguish and rage and he reached out her, but she jerked away.

"Don't touch me!" It was quite a picture. I felt like the proverbial fly on the wall, watching the scene unfold. Irene turned and came to my side. "Well?" she snapped.

"What can I do? I can't take on people like that. I'd be wiped out. These people aren't playing by the rules at all."

"You can help me," I put in.

"You? What are you going to do against them?"

"You let me worry about that. I'll look after my end, but I need back-up."

"And you expect me to give it to you?"

"Auguste." Irene didn't have to say much when she used that tone.

"For Christ's sake, these people are going to get what they want whatever happens," he protested. "You know how people feel...The socialists are bound to lose. So what will happen to all those who helped them? Charriet will have a free hand; he'll make sure we're castrated."

"Give it a rest, Delauney," I said. "Do you think I give a damn which bunch of liars is elected? Do you think it matters? All I care about is what they've done to me. And I'm going to see to it that somebody pays the bill. In full."

"You're mad."

"Auguste, just do as he asks, will you," put in Irene. "There's been enough talking."

Twenty Five

After Irene made her revelation to Delauney, he became sulky and morose. He started to drink, though he hadn't been entirely sober since we'd arrived at the nightclub. To make matters worse, it seemed that we had a breakdown in communications between ourselves and Delauney's sources and as the evening wore on, the atmosphere in the house became more and more strained. The place was like a tinderbox, with the abrasive Delauney as the flint.

I was pretty well wired up, too; the realisation that Charriet was on the other side put an even greater strain on me. If it hadn't been for the fact that I was determined to kill Moran, I'd gladly have left the country until whatever it was that these people were planning was all over. I couldn't, though. As soon as Moran had done his job he'd disappear like a puff of smoke and then I'd never catch up with him. I couldn't let that happen; I couldn't let him awaywith what he'd done to Julie and Paul and Sam.

No. Whatever the consequences, I had to carry the business through.

Then, at about eight-thirty, Delauney's mood changed. He seemed to snap, as if he'd finally decided to do something about a problem that had been niggling at him. Without saying a word to me he got up from his seat by the fire, walked out of the long room with the red carpet and the chandelier into the echoing hallway and called for Raoul.

I perked up; Raoul was his regular driver. I didn't follow him, though, even though I still didn't trust him not to deliver us to the enemy. I was too well aware that at a word from him, I would have been gunned down where I stood by his soldiers.

Irene had been upstairs, resting; she was still feeling weak. But when she heard Delauney's voice echoing through the marble corridors of the house, she came down to see what was going on. From my position by the side of the polished table, I could see into the hall where he was standing, as Raoul assisted him in putting on his overcoat. I watched, fascinated, as Irene came quickly down the steps and stood before him, the apprehension clear in her eyes.

"What are you going to do? Auguste, you must tell me."

Delauney looked long at her and suddenly, from I know not where in the recesses of that dark soul of his, an expression of real kindness and affection came over his face. He lifted his big hand and gently caressed Irene's chin, tenderly, like a lover and yet not so; she looked long into his eyes and then looked down, took the hand and kissed it before he drew back.

He looked again at her; her eyes were still cast down and then he spoke; and though it seemed incredible, I was sure, quite sure, that the word that came echoing along the floor and walls to where I sat.

The echo of a whisper, "I told you I was sorry."

I watched, fascinated. This was a mystery greater than I had ever imagined. I crossed the room and pulled back the curtain, to see the lights of Delauney's car flicker on and the growl of its motor starting up. Then he was gone. Did I see the pale and ghostly image of his face watching me as I looked out, or was it just a trick of the light?

I turned back to the cocktail cabinet, poured myself a cognac and drank it slowly, thoughtfully. I was just on the point of wondering what I'd do to Delauney if it turned out that he'd gone out to betray me, when Pepe walked into the room. I glanced up.

"Has there been any word yet?"

He shook his head. "Non." The best that you could say for Pepe, when it came to conversation, was that it was sparse. He, too, crossed to the cocktail cabinet and poured himself a drink, a stiff shot of Calvados. He didn't bat an eyelid as he downed the clear, fiery liquid in one.

He eyed me. "The man told me to make sure you had anything you need while he was away."

"Thanks. That was big of him. By the way, where has he gone?"

Pepe eyed me again and poured himself another shot. "That, he did not tell me." He swirled the drink in his glass and then knocked it back. "Why don't you get some rest, friend?" He didn't say another word, but put his glass back down on the cabinet, sat down in a chair and lit a cigarette.

I left the room and slowly climbed the stairs to the upper floor, where the bedrooms were. The whole house was full of Delauney's soldiers; faceless, forgettable men, all of imposing bulk, all with bulges beneath their left armpits.

I opened the bedroom door to find Irene standing at the window, gazing out into the night. It was as if she too, had watched Delauney leave, but had never left her station, still watching, still waiting.

She turned as she heard me enter and. managed a smile, but it wasn't going to convince anyone. Her face was stained from the dark lines where her tears had smudged her mascara and there were red rings round her eyes.

I crossed to her arid placed my hands on her shoulders. She reached up and covered one of them with her cool fingers. "Is there anything you want to tell me?" I asked, gently.

She shook her head. "No," she whispered. I remained silent for a long moment and then suddenly she turned to me. "Do you accuse me, now?" There was real anger in her voice and I was taken aback.

"No," I replied, honestly. She was the last person I could think of... She was practically the only one I had left. I must have looked, hurt, because she bit her knuckle and then stumbled, forward, so that her head was pressed onto ray chest. Her left hand thumped onto my ribs, weakly, desperately. "I didn't mean too...Oh, Johnny, you must realise..."

"Ssh," I said and took her wrists. "What is it? Don't you see that whatever it is, you must tell someone. Why not me?"

"But I am afraid."

"So am I."

"No...Not like that. Of course, I am afraid of what might become of us. But not that."

"Then what?"

"You know, Johnny, I should never have told him. Never. It was cruel and spiteful of me."

"About Versailles?" We still could only talk about the rape at a distance.

"Oh, God, I think I'm going mad! Yes, of course, about that. I should never have told him."

She fell silent and. turned away from me again. Nervously she fretted with the heavy velvet of the curtain. "You know I vowed I'd never spend the night under the same roof as that man again. For...I don't know how long, two years, three, since before I first net you, I nursed my rage and my anger but now, now that he's gone..."

"Gone where, Irene?"

"He has gone to do something, something stupid, chivalrous, I know that. I know. And I didn't lift a finger to stop him." She swayed slightly and I thought she was going to faint, but she steadied herself. "I should have known, I should have known what he'd do."

"Irene, I..." It was an awkward moment; I had the impression that perhaps I was treading where I should not.

But Irene turned to me again. "Oh, Johnny, I'm so sorry...You must be so confused."

"It night help if you told me something. I mean, I know that you and Delauney must have been...involved, once, but you say it was a long time ago. Why should he be so concerned now? Why should you be so concerned? "

"Involved? Yes. Let's speak the truth. We were lovers, Auguste and I. You knew that, didn't you?"

"Yes, of course."

This thought seemed to occupy her for a few long moments and then she picked up the packet of caporal that lay on the sideboard by her and lit one up. She folded her arms and leaned again against the window frame. "I wish I could say that I behaved properly.".

She turned to face me again. Her eyes were far away, "Did you know that I was an orphan? Or, at least, I was abandoned. I heard that perhaps there was someone, somewhere…When I was a child. But no-one ever came. I was brought up in a home, you know the sort of place." She drew hungrily on her cigarette.

"I was never very good...As a child. I was always getting into trouble and when I was old enough to leave, the sisters were glad to see me go. But before I left, I was taken before the Mother Superior who looked after the place and she told me...For the first time, ever, mind you, that I was not orphaned...That my mother had been a very young girl; too young, you understand? And that my father was still alive and living in the city. It seemed that he had provided the money to keep me at the home. But the Mother would not tell me who he was, this man.

"So I determined to find him myself. I came to Paris and pretty soon I found out how hard it was to live without money. I had just turned seventeen. I tried to get jobs, but I was too young. Then I met a boy and he introduced me to a man." Irene smiled, without any mirth.

"That was my first trick. I took to it...Men have always liked me.

"Then I met Auguste. It was very strange...At the time he seemed to be looking for me. Anyway, he was bold and he was very rich and powerful and he gave me things and...and I fell in love with him. We became lovers."

"So? That's nothing to be ashamed about," I put in as she began to cry again.

She looked at me with an indescribable look on her face, shaking her head quickly. "Oh, you don't understand! I...I still wanted to find out who my real father was. I was determined. Auguste told me I was a fool, to forget it, to enjoy life. I very nearly did."

"Go on."

"Then, one day, I was out walking in the park. Auguste and I had been together for eighteen months and I was happy...I had something to tell him; something that I was sure would please him. I had been to the doctor and knew I was pregnant. He'd said how he'd like to have a child, often; he'd given me so much...I wanted to give him this gift. Anyway, I was in the park and who should I meet but the old Mother Superior from the hostel.

"I was embarrassed...I didn't want to speak to her, but she caught my arm, made me talk; and she asked me why I was so happy and I told her. Instead of being happy too, she crossed herself and said a prayer! I was shocked. And then she told me. The man who had paid for my upbringing...The man who was my father, was my lover, whose child I was carrying!"

There was a stunned and shocked silence in the room for several moments after that. I looked at the girl and her eyes met mine. "I tried to kill myself. I didn't succeed. But...but I killed the baby. Then I left him and. went back to the street. You see...He knew all along. He knew all along."

I put my arms round her and guided her back to the bed. I didn't say anything.

She was silent for a long time and then she spoke. "And that is why I should not have told him, because now he will go and get himself killed."

"He's too smart."

Irene just shook her head and sighed. "Johnny?" She looked at me.

"Yes?"

"Make love to me."

"Now?"

"You are always so very gentle. I need you to love me now. I need you." She slipped out of the clothes she was wearing and stood before me naked. I took off mine and we held each other; then we began to kiss and to embrace and our passion was lit...It seemed so long since we had had the delight of each other's sex.

The air in the bedroom was still musky with the scent of our combined orgasms as I lay beside the sleeping Irene. The soft light of the bedside lamp lit the room softly. I couldn't sleep; my body-clock didn't even know what day it was any more. I got up and crossed to the window to look out. It was a clear night and I could see the oily sheen of the frost on the ground outside.

Somewhere out there was Dick Moran, the man who had been responsible for all the hurt, all the butchery. I wondered for a moment what I'd say, when the time came to kill him. Would it be in a fight, a shoot-out? Or would we have the few minutes together when he might, just might tell me why? I was sure that he was the only one who could tell me that.

Would it be that old-fashioned, gentlemanly way, like you read about, where I give him a pistol with one bullet and leave him alone for five minutes? I smiled involuntarily at the thought. Not Dick. He'd have used the bullet on me and taken his chances. After all, that was what I'd do if the situation were reversed. And there was the thought that he might get me first; he'd come close already, too close.

Moran. I heard his voice, I saw his face. My eyes narrowed. He was out there and I was going to have my revenge upon him; no matter what the cost. Suddenly I heard, behind me, the crackle of a match being struck. I turned, quickly; Irene's face was still lit by the flare of the dying match, her finely shaped, angular features thrown into high relief. She was thin and she looked tired.

She tossed the match into the ashtray. Her face was in the shadow now, but I knew that her gaze was questioning. Ah, yes and then there was Irene; was she to be hurt again or even die in my search for revenge; was that to be the cost?

"You should try to get some rest." I said, quietly.

She nodded. "I should rest. And you, you pace the floor like a caged animal, a wild beast that cannot lie down. Johnny, your energy was all used up long ago. What are you living on now?"

I turned to face her. "I don't really know. I don't know. I just know that until all this is over, I can't rest. Not until I find him." I sighed. "I wonder if he's changed, over the years? Is he still so convinced, so dedicated as he was then – as I was then? Hasn't the passing time done anything? It may seem odd to say this...But I couldn't have done what he's done to me. Not now."

"Come here." I crossed the room and sat on the edge of the bed, while she stubbed out her cigarette and then, with her strong, slender fingers, began to message away the tension in the knotted muscles in the back of my neck.

"That feels good," I whispered, closing my eyes for a moment and succumbing to the pleasure. "That feels so good. She pushed me down onto the bed and began to work her magic all along my spine, so that I felt I was being washed with waves of deeply sensuous pleasure; then she turned me onto my back and set to work again. The feel of her skin, the scent of her body, the slight rasp of her breath as she pounded my resisting muscles was overpowering. She stopped and in the faint light I saw her raise her head to look at me.

"I love you, Johnny," she whispered. "Promise me you won't go and get yourself killed."

I bit my lip and she gave a sudden, fey little laugh. "I shouldn't worry about the future; I should just take pleasure in the moment we have." I felt her take my erect manhood in her hands then and caress me there and the blood began to pound in my ears; and then I felt the impossible ecstasy as her hot breath swept over it and the delicious warm wetness of her lips and tongue, doing something she knew how to do so well that I soon had forgotten all about Moran and killing and everything more than the touch of a body away.

Then she pulled her head away and guided me to her as she rolled onto her back, guiding my urgent penis into her, as we came together passionately, yet unhurriedly. We made love until we shared the explosion of each other's orgasm and then again after that and then we slept.

Twenty Six

I woke up to the early grey of the dawn light sluggishly penetrating the gloom of winter, telling me that it was time to rejoin the hunt. I slipped out of bed. Irene smiled in her sleep and moved, but did not wake. I dressed and went downstairs to see what was on the go.

At first sight, the house seemed deserted, but then, as I descended the stairs, I. saw, in the shadows of the vestibule, one of the soldiers, watching me with a blank expression devoid of curiosity on his face.

I went into the main room and helped myself to some coffee. It was some moments before I noticed Pepe, who had fallen asleep by the fire, fully dressed, crumpled in one of the gilded chairs. The fire had long since gone out. I woke him up.

"What the? Oh, it's you."

"That's right; your early morning call. Where's Delauney?"

He just shrugged and yawned. "Dunno."

"Has there been any news? About Zeigler, about anything?"

"Nope."

I left him. It occurred to me that his boss might have got cold feet, put me on hold and disappeared for the duration and that thought did not help my mood. I went back upstairs to see if Irene was awake and on the way, I thought, Koestler. If I could get my hands on him, then I wouldn't be long making him talk.

Irene was awake when I got to the room and she agreed. "It's all we can do. I have no idea where Auguste is...Though I have a bad feeling about it. I think he's in trouble."

I looked at her. There was no doubting the concern in her voice but I still thought he'd done a bunk.

"I'll get ready," said Irene.

I was about to say something along the lilies of "No you won't," but she cut me dead with an icy look.

"I'm coming with you, Johnny. We'll take Pepe too."

"Pepe? Are you kidding?"

"You don't understand. Pepe used to be my bodyguard. He has a special feeling for me. And you must not underestimate him; he may seem rough, but he's reliable and loyal. He will be very valuable if there's trouble."

I thought about it and shrugged my shoulders. If Irene could keep him in line, then he might be useful yet.

Finding Koestler was the problem. He wasn't the kind of guy who advertises his whereabouts. I thought over the things I knew about him.

He'd been pretty vocal on a wide variety of issues over the previous five years or so. You know the sort of thing these people like to shout about, immigration, the loss of France's national character, as they saw it, to the American influence and the rest of Europe. That certainly made Koestler's jumping into bed with the CIA look like confused ideology, but I knew enough about the extreme right to know that it was not so peculiar.

These people will go anything just to be listened to. They're like all fanatics, of whatever persuasion, if they think they've got an audience, then they're in heaven.

Anyway, the simple fact of France having a government they didn't like the colour of was enough to unite the disparate elements of the right. To tell you the truth, it was a dung-heap I didn't want to go turning over too many stones on.

Delauney had had one thing right and that was that there was precious little chance of the Socialists being returned at the next election in any case and who knows how many so-called "legitimate" politicians might be standing in the wings of this mess, behind even Charriet?

If they were put into power, they would be sure to make life hot for any of their enemies. Me, I liked France: I always have and I wanted to go on living there if I could. All I wanted to do was to kill Moran and call it a day, but the more I found out, the more difficult that looked.

As they say, you can't make an omelette without breaking a few eggs.

The first place to look for Koestler was the office of a certain political newspaper. The paper itself was hardly more than a scandal-sheet, no different from any other of its ilk, but I did know that Koestler regularly contributed.

I got hold of Pepe again. "I need a car. Now."

Pepe frowned, his beetling eyebrows knitting together. "No way. The boss didn't say anything…"

He didn't get a chance to finish the sentence, as Irene broke in. "Never mind what Auguste said, Pepe. Just give me the keys. And get your coat on, you're coming along for the ride." That seemed to cheer him up and he nodded, uncertainly.

Irene stamped her foot impatiently and he got into gear. I was impressed. I turned to her. "Have you got a piece?"

She shook her head and turned down her eyes.

"Get her one," I said to Pepe, who withdrew once more to the long room and from the drawer of a desk, produced a nice little chrome-plated .25 Beretta, with a mother-of-pearl grip. A real lady's gun. You know the funny thing was, that as Irene looked at it with a certain distaste and then slipped it into her bag with a sigh, I could have sworn that she'd handled it before.

Irene gave me the keys as we followed Pepe out of the house into the chill morning air. He led the way across the gravelled surface of the driveway outside the house towards a black Audi coupe. All the cars were black.

I was just on the point of wondering why that should be when I heard the growl of a powerful engine coming along the street outside the gate. I don't know what it was, what sixth sense, that made me leap forward and fling open the door of the Audi, throwing Irene bodily before me across into the passenger seat. "Pepe, get down!" I yelled, I heard the scrunch as the tyres of a big Citroën hit the gravel, the car see-sawing from side to side as the driver broadsided the corner under power.

I fumbled to find the ignition switch and as I glanced into the mirror I saw Pepe, behind the car, unship his Colt .45 auto. I cursed him silently for being a fool but there wasn't time to do anything.

The Citroën, gravel chippings flying from its wheels, came surging towards us like a hungry shark. I swore and suddenly the keys slipped home into their slot. I twisted the switch viciously, cursing the timeless agony of the moment as the cold engine tried to fire but missed and missed again. I looked up. The Citroën was almost upon us. I saw the snout of an Uzi poke through the passenger side window.

"Irene, for Christ's sake, get down!" The nose of the Citroën suddenly dipped, like a speedboat with the power cut off, as the driver hit the anchors, to let the gunman get a good shot. Just at that instant the Audi's engine burst into life with a snarl. I didn't wait.

It was too late to do anything for Pepe, who had come out from behind the cover of the car as he heard the engine catch. I saw that goddamn cannon of his come up and the recoil kicking at his body, his lips drawn back into an animal snarl, his legs straddled for the best balance.

I slammed the protesting car into gear and floored the throttle. Not a second too soon. I heard the first bullets smash in, but we were already moving and they caught the rear quarter. I hoped they hadn't got one of the tyres. Pepe just stood there, pumping round after round into the oncoming vehicle and then, incredibly, as his magazine emptied, he threw the gun at the driver. Then he went down.

Me, I had other things on my mind, like doing a u-turn on that gravel. I was furious and I booted the throttle as the car came round. The Citroën was zigzagging wildly, still under power; looked like Pepe had hit the mark. Over to my left, by the steps up to the main door of the house, a suspicious-looking bundle had fetched up against the kerb. The rear door of the Citroën was still swinging open and there was no doubt that it was where the bundle had come from.

The front door of the house itself had been flung open and I could clearly see one body there. From the cover of the doorway there were puffs of smoke as one of the soldiers opened up in return fire. That Citroën was doomed, though. The driver's foot must have jammed the throttle down. The car had swerved off the drive and smashed into the wall. The passenger in front had been flung clear and was trying to pick himself up, dazed, from the gravel.

He got to his feet. There was blood all over his face; he couldn't see. He heard the howl of the Audi's motor and managed to wipe the blood from his eyes in time to see me, only feet away. I saw the terror in his face in the instant before the car struck him. Almost in slow motion, like a broken marionette, he crumpled at the knees, crashed onto the bonnet of the speeding car and then flew up and over the roof.

I slammed on the brakes and watched as the rag-doll figure came to earth, a mass of broken bones. I stopped the car and backed up. I don't know what stopped me running over the bastard again, just for good measure.

I looked over at where Pepe lay. His body had lost that compact sense of balance, like a bull terrier, that he'd had in life; the pool of blood around him told me that his final hand had been dealt. At least, I thought, he had died well. I was dimly aware of the sound of Irene calling his name as my mind raced.

It was such a coincidence, wasn't it, that they'd made their attack just as we'd come out of the house and were away from cover, at our most vulnerable? Too much of a coincidence, in fact.

And then...I heard the sound of a motor-cycle being started. It came from behind a clump of rhododendrons in the lawn. I'm no great admirer of fine lawns and the car had four-wheel drive, so before I'd really thought about it, I had wrenched the wheel round and was venting the engine wide across the grass.

Then he broke cover. A man on a moto-cross machine. Lord knows how long he'd been watching the house.

As the Audi slewed across the lawn, cutting furrows in the grass, I felt a sudden pressure, as if a giant hand had pushed the car from behind. In the same instant the world seemed to light up in orange flare. I glanced into my mirror in time to see the debris from the explosion, pieces of mangled black Citroën, fall to the earth and the billowing pall of black smoke mushroom upwards. Jesus! Booby-trapped.

That was going to bring every flic in Paris down on us.

Not before I'd had a chance to talk to the biker, though. There was a hedge at the bottom of the lawn, where the boundary with the street was. At first I thought that it must block the path of the speeding machine in front of me; but no, I'd underestimated my man as he powered onto a low hummock and the whole plot took off, clearing the hedge by inches. He'd done his homework on the geography.

I wasn't too worried; I have as little regard for fancy hedges as I do for fine lawns and I pointed the car straight at it.

"Oh!" gasped Irene, her eyes wide with horror as we crashed through the greenery in a hail of splintered twigs and branches. I broadsided the car onto the main road and screamed the engine. I could see the biker, up ahead, with the front wheel of his machine pawing the air as he applied all the power he'd got to shake me off. I set my teeth.

Not this time, laddie, I thought.

The pressure of the G-force pushed us deep into our seats and then from side to side as we powered round corners. I was glad that we were in a nice, quiet area of the city. Still it was hard going keeping up with the biker; he really knew the area, whereas I hadn't a clue where we were headed. All I could tell was that we were roughly aiming towards the centre of the city.

That was it, of course; the rider wanted to meet some of the morning traffic, at its worst at that hour, where he'd have no trouble losing me. I had to get to him first. I drove the car harder, but every time I got close enough to knock him flying, he jinked right or left and managed to give me the slip.

We surged onto the last straight before we had to join a major thoroughfare up ahead. It had to be now; I could see the traffic bottled up ahead and I knew that once he got amongst that, I'd lost him.

He knew it too. He turned round in his seat long enough to make a rude sign of victory in my direction.

I doubt that he'd have seen it, anyway, in time to stop, or swerve.

The milk-float, silent, whirring, its driver near the end of his round and not concentrating, sailed into the road we were bearing down, right into the path of the motorcycle. It was classic. The driver turned, saw and his jaw dropped. He paled as the motorcycle charged towards him.

The rider grabbed the biggest handful of brake that he could, the tyre smoking on the tarmac, the rear end shimmying from side to side, but he was far, far too late.

The bike cannoned into the float with almost enough force to knock it over; but the rider just kept on going, smashing through crates of empty milk bottles. A blizzard of shards of glass accompanied him as he crashed onto the tarmac and slid.

I had no desire either to hit the stricken milk float or to rip out my tyres on the cascade of deadly shattered glass. I swerved hard, braking all the time and mounted the pavement. Well, there was nowhere else to go. Two ladies watched, awe-stricken, as the Audi ploughed into a pavement litter-bin, hurling paper, rotting fruit and Coke cans into the bizarre melange on the street, before coming to rest only feet away from the semi-conscious motorcyclist.

I think they got an even bigger surprise when I leapt out, gun in hand and, instead of ministering tender care to the injured man, grabbed him by the scruff of the neck and dragged him to the car without a word, opened the door and bundled him into the back seat. I had a few questions to ask him before we got to the subject of first aid.

Twenty Seven

Ipulled up in a quiet side street not far from the scene of the crash and listened to the sirens echoing through the city. I chuckled – it's often like that when the tension relaxes – and thought of the amount of work we'd given the emergency services.

Irene wasn't saying a lot. I think she'd probably stopped praying by that time, but hadn't quite got round to trusting herself to speak.

I left her to it and turned my attention to the mess in the back seat. That biker was lucky; he was wearing full leathers, so he hadn't been sliced to ribbons by the glass. He groaned. At least he was still alive. I t leaned over and flipped up the visor of his helmet. He opened his eyes. I was surprised at how young he looked: I doubt if he was a day over nineteen.

I sat him up in the back seat; he moaned a bit, so I knew he was hurting. I could see from the crazy angle his right arm had adopted that it was broken.

"Who sent you?" I asked. Nicely. The kid just sneered. I sighed. "Look. I'm going to give you a break. You tell me what I want to know and I might just take you somewhere where you can be fixed up. You keep shtum and I'm going to hurt you. You follow? And then I'll take you back to that house. The one you were watching. There are some people there who'd like to unravel your intestines and I won't try to stop them."

"Bullshit, man. I don't tell you nothing." I swung the Luger round and stuck the muzzle of it between his eyes. That made him sweat, but he didn't say anything. Then I got hold of his right arm, the broken one. I saw his eyes widen with the pain and his face screwed up as I grated the two ends of the broken bone against each other. Sweat beaded large on his forehead and he whimpered.

"No!" The boy tried to twist away from me, but that only made it worse for him. His face was blue with pain and contorted. I felt Irene grab my arm to restrain me and I turned to her.

"You want to find Delauney? This is the only way." I turned back to the boy and twisted the bones in his mangled arm again. I wasn't getting any more pleasure out of this than Irene was, but I wasn't going to show that to the kid. He knew some answers.

"Oh, sweet Jesus, stop, please stop!" He blurted out. He'd developed a severe nose-bleed and he was choking on his own blood.

"So okay. What are you going to tell me?"

"What do you want to know?"

"The American. The one with the scar down the right side of his face. You know who I mean, don't you?" I could see that he did, but he shut his trap. I sighed and reached for that arm of his again. Once again there was the sickening crunch of the ragged ends of the bones grating across each other, but this time he'd had enough. He began to blubber. "Okay, okay, mister, I'll tell you. The American...Yes! Yes! I know him! Please God don't hurt me any more!"

"Where is he now?"

"I don't know...I swear, I swear!" His eyes widened: in terror as he saw my face set grim. "I only seen him once or twice. Maybe a bit more, yes maybe a bit more."

"Where did you see him?"

"At the garage...Where I work."

"Garage? What garage? Where?"

"Rue de Thionville...By the Canal de L'Oreal, where it joins the Canal St. Denis. I work there."

Right in the North-East of the city, Rue de Thionville was in an industrial zone; quite an old, well established one. There was some working-class housing, but by and large the area was depopulated. A good location for a terrorist squad to set up.

I turned back to Irene. She was looking out the window, chewing her knuckle and looking distinctly sick. I guess all this cold-blooded stuff wasn't her cup of tea.

"You got any cigarettes?" I asked her. She looked at me with questioning eyes, as if she thought..."Light one and give it to him, would you?" I was just naturally misunderstood.

Irene, visibly relieved, took out a couple of caporal from her packet with shaking hands stuck them both in her mouth, lighting them off the same match. She passed one back to the kid and smiled for him. Then she shot me a dirty look.

Once he'd taken a couple of good, puffs, I returned to the job in hand.

"Now," I said, all sweetness and light, "You tell me the whole sorry tale, right from the beginning and we'll go on being friends."

"They'll kill me."

"I'll kill you if you don't. And I've got you." The kid thought about that and then he began to talk. I did a lot of work on interrogation technique when I was with the Firm; not so much for our own use, but more so that we could train our people to cope with the worst. Believe me, if you think I was hard on the kid, you should see what the IRA do to people they want to talk to. Or the KGB. Iron fist, then the velvet glove.

Once they begin to talk, the less they want to stop. The more they feel the relief of the pain subside just by saying things, quietly, calmly, the more they can't stand the thought of it starting up again. So I just let him sing.

"I been working there for two years now. Yeah. Then, about six weeks ago, the boss let the house next to the garage out to some new people. I never seen any of them before."

I reached into my pocket and pulled out the wad of photographs. I showed him one of Koestler. "Sure...I seen him. And the American, the one with the scar. They came first. It was all kind of hush-hush, I dunno."

"How'd you know he was an American?"

The kid smiled as best he could. "He knew about cars...American cars. We got to talking. I knew he had an accent."

"Go on."

"So anyway, this American guy, he moves into the house next door. It's a big place and pretty soon there seem to be other guys there too. Only they don't look like Americans. This guy...The other guy," he tapped the picture of Koestler, "He's there all the time. And sometimes there's a girl...Looks like a tart. But I ain't seen her for a few days."

"She's dead."

"You kill her?" His eyes widened.

Irene smiled grimly. "No. I did." The kid's eyes widened more. Irene was getting the hang of this.

"How'd you find all this out?" I put in. "You just watch the place?"

"Yeah...Well, you see, the garage used to be pretty busy. Then, after the house was let to those people, the boss began to lay off the mechanics, one by one, till they were all gone. I was the only one left. Then there were other cars corning in. Not from the regular customers. I was pretty sure that they belonged to the guys in that house and I got kinda curious. So I stayed back after work once when the boss went away early.

"Sure enough, there was this old door from the house into the garage. I thought it had been nailed up, but no, it opens and these guys come through and they start to work on the cars there. I couldn't see what they were doing, so I moved to get a better view. That was when they found me. I slipped off the oil-drum I was standing on and fell onto the ground.

"Well, these guys were mad. They jumped me and dragged me into the house. They beat me up and they threw me into a room with the lights out. I thought I'd had it. I just lay there, waiting for them.

"The door opens and one of the guys comes in, with the American. Course, I'd met him before...They seemed to be arguing about something, but I couldn't understand the language. I figured it was probably about what to do with me.

"Anyway, the American must have been on my side, because the next thing I know, the other guy storms out and leaves me with him. And he says, 'Can a kid like you keep a secret?' Man, I said yes. Then he tells me that I can earn a little extra dough on the side, that they could use a smart kid to do little jobs for them, run around here and there, watch things. He'd seen me on the bike; he knew I was pretty good."

"So what did he tell you they were doing there?"

"Drugs. Honest, Mister, I swear. I never knew about bombs, or guns, I swear!"

"Okay. Tell me about today."

"Yesterday the boss comes in. I hardly ever see him these days. Says that the guys next door want to see me. So I meet this guy," he said, pointing to Koestler's image once more, "And he says there's job for me. Says there's a thousand francs in it for me if I do right. So I say yes to that.

"He tells me they want to make a drop...Says I have to wait outside a certain house, with a radio and call them when you and the girl come out of the house, because they want to meet. Then I was supposed to get the hell out."

"How did you know us?"

"He gave me a picture." With some effort, the kid managed to get his left hand into his pocket and pulled out a battered photograph. It was a blow up of one of the café shots, like I'd found at Zeigler's.

I nodded. "But you didn't get out when you saw us coming? You stayed around to see what was going to happen, didn't you?"

The kid nodded. "Honest, I didn't know there was going to be any shooting. I didn't."

I thought about the things he had said for a while, then I looked up at Irene. "How much influence do you have over Delauney's people?"

She shrugged. "I don't know. Pepe...Pepe was sweet, under that skin of his and with Raoul, he was Auguste's top man. He'd have helped.

"Then there's Raoul. God knows where he is; but I could probably win him over. The only other lieutenant with any real power over the boys is Antoine; but he's taken Françoise and Joseph to the chalet."

She sighed. "I don't know, Johnny. If we can persuade them that the only way to get Auguste returned safely is to get them to do as we say, then, maybe there's a chance."

I thought about it. I didn't like trusting my luck that much, but I couldn't see what else was to be done.

"Well. I'm going to have to find a PTT. I'm going to send all the stuff from Zeigler's flat to...let's just say an old friend. And I need to make a phone call."

Irene looked at me quizzically but there wasn't time to explain and anyway the less she knew about certain things, the better.

We got back to the house about an hour later. The bomb had done a lot of damage to the elegant frontage. There was broken glass everywhere. The police had gone; there were no cars or officers in sight. That seemed uncommonly decent of them, but I soon found out why.

From the recesses of the interior appeared the tall, wiry figure of Antoine. He didn't look to be in a very good mood. He was accompanied by a couple of soldiers. He'd arrived in the thick of it, with police and firemen all over the place. Fortunately the Inspector of Police who'd come to the scene was a 'friend' of Delauney's. That was just another way of saying that he was on the payroll and he'd recognised Antoine's authority as Delauney's lieutenant.

Twenty Eight

Were all in the long room with the chandeliers, where I'd wakened Pepe from his sleep before the long-dead fire. "Let me show you something," said Antoine as he closed the door behind us, in a tone I didn't like. "This." He lifted a packet from the table. It was an envelope, a rather ordinary envelope. It was covered in already browning bloodstains and there was a small hole in the centre of it.

I turned it over. "Where'd you get this?"

"It was nailed to Raoul's body. With a six inch nail through the heart," snapped Antoine.

Irene gasped and I nodded grimly "He was that bundle they threw from the Citroën, huh?"

Antoine answered by ignoring the question. I didn't like the look of this. He didn't seem to object to me opening the envelope, so I drew out the folded sheet of paper within. It answered the question that I didn't need to ask; Delauney was in big trouble.

So was I.

"You realise, of course, that even if you do as they ask, there's no chance of getting your boss back in one piece?" I folded the letter into its original creases without showing it to Irene. "Not unless you do something positive."

"Like what, Mr. Smartass?"

"We know where they are. They'll have Delauney under wraps there as a kind of hostage; we can go and get him out."

Antoine just leered a scar-faced, vicious leer. "I don't think so. You know what? I think we're going to play it just the way they say." He made a movement with his head and one of the soldiers who'd been hovering close by moved in quickly. "Take his gun." I felt rough hands grab me from behind and quickly remove the Luger from the waistband of my trousers.

I saw Irene jump forward, but Antoine himself restrained her. There was something in the way that he touched her that sickened me, something in the filthy leer on his face, but I didn't have time to worry about it, because Antoine nodded and the lights went out.

A smell of petrol. That was the first thing that penetrated my consciousness, even before the pain reminded me of the blow on the head that had laid me out. No fancy drugs for these guys, just the simple, old fashioned butt end of a pistol.

It was dark, pitch black and I thought that maybe that blow had knocked out my vision centres. Then, slowly, I became aware of a dim sliver of light, not far away from my face. I tried to focus and it came sharp. I tried to move, but I was bound hand and foot. The thin bindings cut into my flesh and I could hardly feel my hands.

I swore and then lay still. Wherever I was, it was cold and hard and cramped. I wriggled some and the whole world seemed to move a little with me; that wasn't just an effect of concussion, I realised. I was locked in the boot of a car and the whole vehicle was moving on its suspension.

I stopped moving and listened. There was no sound from outside my metallic prison.

There was a pressure on my back, a soft pressure. I felt the touch of leather; it was the kid who'd been watching the house. I found his face, but there was no gentle sigh of breath, not even the slightest. He was dead.

Disorientation is a very frightening thing; much more frightening than real danger. I fought back the panic that I felt rising in my gut, imprisoned as I was in that black hell hole, bound and trussed, sharing my bed with a dead man. What if we'd been abandoned, left to die? How long before the chill made a corpse out of me, too?

I had to survive, I told myself and that depended on keeping a cool head. There had to be some way out, there always has to be a way out. I remembered the leer in Antoine's eyes as he had laid hands on Irene and I became more determined.

I began to grope along the floor of the boot. It was difficult, because of the tightness of the bindings. I had to keep resting to allow the blood to flow back to my fingers. All the time the minutes were ticking by inexorably. It seemed that I searched for hours, but there was nothing, not even a sharp edge of metal, that I could find to cut my bindings.

Nothing, nothing, nothing. I tried not to let myself get desperate and turned over onto my face again to let the feeling return to my hands, numbed by the restricted circulation. For the hundredth time I brushed against the dead boy's leathers.

Leather, I thought, leather. The image of the boy in life flashed up in my brain. Leathers...and zippers! That kid's jacket had them all over it. Christ it was a long shot, but it was time for one of those. I twisted my body back to the corpse. It was sticky with blood.

When the kid had ploughed through that milk-float, the zip on his jacket had been damaged; there was a sharp edge somewhere along it, and I prayed that I could reach it. My muscles screaming with the contortion, my fingers going numb, I managed to find the edge I was after.

It was horrible work, slow, painful and macabre, as I worried away at my bindings in the dark, in pain, not knowing whether it would work at all. The still-warm corpse of the boy was sticking and oozing beneath my weight. At any time the boot lid might lift and my struggle end with another blow, or worse.

Then the tension on my wrists began to give, almost imperceptibly at first. I sawed away with renewed vigour and began to feel my bindings part. All at once my hands were free.

There was no time to enjoy freedom before the agony of returning circulation hit. I writhed and cursed and waited for the pain to go away. I winced as the cuts I'd made in the flesh of my wrists began to sting.

When I could move my hands again, I swore. Someone had taken the knife I always kept tucked up my sleeve.

I could only just reach my ankles. I swore again and slumped back into a resting position. It might have been cold in the boot of that car before, but by then I was bathed in sweat.

This wa a problem; as my body heated up, the circulation to my extremities would increase, effectively making the bindings on my ankles tighter. This was no joke.

There was simply no way that I could turn round enough to use the ragged metal of the broken zipper on my ankles, not in that tiny space. In the end I decided that I would have to chance it and try to get out with my ankles still trussed. I didn't relish the prospect; if I ran into trouble, I'd have no chance.

I felt for the catch to the boot. It was really a question of what kind of design I was up against. Some locks are activated by an exposed metal bar and others are completely encased in metal. If it was one of the latter then my luck was right out. Fortunately it wasn't and I began to twist the bar to release the lock.

I was hampered because the bar was partially hidden behind a metal bulkhead and also by the fact that it was so dark. In the end, though, I heard the snick of the catch releasing and I hastily caught hold of the boot lid lest it should fly open.

Slowly, very slowly, I let it up, fraction by fraction, until I could see out. The cooling breeze was wonderful after the stale air in the boot, heavy with the stench of death and blood and sweat. I drank in the air. If only I could get my ankles free, I'd have some chance. I missed my old flick-knife.

I had no idea where I was, but I could see that the car was in a lock-up or garage. I wondered if I'd been abandoned. I'd never seen the garage before, it wasn't the one that the dead kid had spoken of; this was too small, more like a domestic one. However, even these humble places usually have a few interesting items lying around. Letting go my hold on the boot lid so that it swung open, I rolled out and landed heavily on the dirty concrete floor.

My feet were numb from the tightness of my bonds and they would not support my weight. I couldn't even crawl properly and had to move like a caterpillar, dragging my knees behind me.

In the dim corner of the building, I saw a hacksaw, hanging up on a nail in the wall. If only I could reach it! It took me a sweating age to manoeuvre myself into position underneath the nail where it hung. But could I reach up to it? It wasn't that high up, but my legs were almost useless and the nail was just out of my reach from a sitting position.

I braced myself against the wall, all the time my heart pounding with the exertion and the fear that at any moment the door might open and someone would come in. Pushing as hard as my enfeebled legs could, I squirmed inch by inch up the rough surface of the concrete wall. When I thought I could reach it, I threw out my hand towards the saw, but I was just short. The sudden movement made me pitch over sideways onto the floor.

I got mad. My blood up, I made another attempt. I wasn't going to be beaten; I would not allow myself to be beaten. I inched and wormed and struggled up again, braced against the wall, eyed my target with as much accuracy as I could and then threw myself towards the saw.

Once again I tumbled painfully into the dust of the garage floor. I sobbed, but not with anger or frustration, for my hands had closed on the hacksaw and had brought it crashing down with me. I was triumphant. I unscrewed the blade from the saw and set to work on the binding round my ankles. Within a few moments I was free.

I wanted a weapon now and that hacksaw blade was going to be it. I crossed to the car, brought down the boot-lid on the blade to hold it and snapped off the free end. It was a crude weapon, a sharp blade of saw steel with a jagged point where it had been snapped off, about nine inches long in all. That would do.

I heard the sound of footsteps coming towards the garage. There were several people on their way. Amongst the heavier footsteps of the men, I could make out the lighter, neater step of a woman. What to do? I decided not to make a fight of it unless I had to. I threw myself back into the boot of the car and pulled down the lid again.

I didn't stretch out beside the dead body but remained coiled and ready to pounce. I would give those bastards something to think about if they decided to open the boot to see how I was doing. They didn't and I breathed a silent sigh of relief. There were five of them and I knew as soon as I smelled her perfume who the woman was. I clenched my teeth.

The car started up and then we were moving, out into the open. It was now completely dark. The light that I'd seen was from a nearby streetlamp.

From time to tine I glanced out of the boot to get my bearings. We were travelling across the city from west to east. The lock-up must have been hidden in the grounds of the house we'd been staying at.

I knew where we were going. I was being taken to the lion's den and I had no back up. It wasn't a comforting thought.

After about twenty five minutes driving, the buildings became less fashionable and residential and more run down and industrial. We were approaching the canals, where the enemy had set up camp.

The car turned a corner and slowed. I braced myself. I heard the sound of a sliding door being run back on well greased rails and the car passed into deeper gloom. The engine cut and I heard the occupants begin to get out. Would it be now? I braced myself, listening as hard as

I could for the sound of a hand grasping the catch of the boot lock, but it didn't come.

Instead, I heard a scuffle and Irene's voice, raised sharply in anger and the grunt of a man experiencing pain. There was more scuffling and the sounds moved away; they must have decided to get Irene inside before they came back for me. I kicked off my shoes, opened the boot as quietly as I could and rolled onto the floor. I brought down the boot lid again with no sound.

My eyes were already adapted to the darkness. I was in a large, old fashioned commercial garage. On each side were high, whitewashed walls and overhead, a slight indigo light came through the skylights set in the roof.

On my left as I stood behind the car was the faint outline of a door, with a window beside it. Further along the wall, towards the back of the building, I could make out a rickety wooden staircase. I made for it. I stopped there and watched and waited. I was sure that I was not alone in the garage, that there was some other presence there, but I couldn't place it.

It was as silent as the grave and as still. There wasn't even a breeze to ruffle the feathers of the pigeons roosting in the rafters. Yet I was sure, quite sure, that I was not alone. I moved along the wall towards the door and there, suddenly, I saw.

. It was an eerie, unpleasant movement, though the shape that made it was unquestionably that of a man. I'd seen that movement before and I tried to remember where; that slow, side to side, swinging movement that is at once so relaxed and so ghastly.

Then I remembered and moved close to the silent hanged man swaying almost imperceptibly, his feet a good nine inches clear of the ground, his head forced over to one side by the pressure of the hangman's noose.

It was Koestler. His eyes seemed to glint, as with life, but it was only a trick of the light. .

What had happened, I wondered? What argument had they had, what unrest amongst the villains, had brought this on? And hanged, too. Not just shot, or strangled, or stabbed, but hanged. Why?

There was no time to savour the delicate intrigue, for at any moment, the terrorists, or perhaps even Moran himself might return to take care of me.

As well as the Cadillac I'd arrived in, there were three other cars in the garage. I could see that two were black Mercedes, similar to the ones the government used for State occasions. I decided to come back and take a closer look later, if the opportunity arose. In the meantime, I planned to recce the house.

It was a fair bet that the rickety wooden staircase which the body was hanging from would give me access to the house next to the garage at first floor level. With any luck, the terrorists would not be so alert up there as they were bound to be by the front door.

Gingerly I began to ascend. The treads of the old stairway were rotten and cracked and at any moment I thought they might give way and send me plummeting onto the concrete floor below.

I finally came to a wooden landing. I felt around. It was black as pitch. Before me was solid wall, but to my left and right were doorways. The faintest glimmer of light showed through the open one to my right.

I stepped forward and without warning, the floor gave way beneath my weight. Only just in time I leapt back onto the landing and cursed as pieces of rotten wood clattered onto the floor below.

My nerves ragged, I turned to the door on my left. Feeling all over it, up and down, I realised that it was secured by a bolt from my side. It was rusted with years of disuse, but nevertheless I had to persuade it to move, silently. I braced my knee against the jamb and began to heave at the bolt, working it up and down to ease the rust. At first nothing seemed to be happening, but then, slowly, it began to move.

At last it cleared far enough to allow the door to spring slightly and I pulled it open. It was stiff and the hinges squeaked. I cursed, waiting for the burst of machine-gun fire I was sure the noise must bring, holding my breath. Miraculously no bullets came, nor pounding feet.

I slipped, ghost-like, through the door and found myself out in the open air. I breathed it in deeply.

Overhead, the sky was clear and there was a moon, but there were patches of broken cloud, so that every few minutes, the world around me was plunged into darkness. The doorway I'd just come through was on the unlit side of the building behind me and before me was the brick rear view of a house.

Between the doorway where I stood and the house was a flat roof about ten yards across. The house was fairly large; I was already one floor up and there was another floor above the level I was on. There were lights on in several of the rooms, but heavy curtains obscured the view both in and out.

I waited for the next cloud and hurled myself across the intervening space towards the house. I held my breath; there was no sound. My friends had not yet decided to take a look in the boot of the Cadillac. Well, I thought, the last place they're going to look for me is in their own den, so I might as well go on. There was a door into the house on this level; the flat roof was obviously used as a sundeck. It was secluded from the outside world.

The doorframe was in a similarly rotten condition to the woodwork of the stairway, but to force it would have been to risk too much. I examined the lock in the light of the moon.

You need the right tools to pick locks but if the key was in it I might be in business. It was. I cut out a piece of the roofing felt with the saw blade and slipped it under the door. The step had rotted away so that it was easy.

Then I pressed the saw blade into the keyhole and gently began to work at the key. Even if the person who locks up leaves the key turned to one side so that it can't be pushed out, if you shake it around enough, gravity will always pull the business part down and then you can push it through. Five minutes of that and the key fell onto the scrap of felt. I pulled it back, unlocked the door and stepped inside.

I locked the door behind me and slipped the key into my pocket. Every nerve ending in my body was tingling with apprehension as I moved through the dark, silent room on the other side. I crept along the wall, my bare feet making no sound on the uncarpeted boards, the snapped-off hacksaw blade at the ready. It would have been suicidal to switch on a light to try to get my bearings, so everything had to be done by touch.

There was another sense that helped me in that moment: smell. Everywhere around me there was the sickly aroma of sweet almonds. It was so strong that it was at once overpowering and unmistakeable.

Gelignite. I must have stumbled into their bomb factory.

The stench made me want to throw up but at least it meant that there would be no other person in the room. And of course, it made sense: one of the prime requirements in any room where explosives are to be handled is that there should be good ventilation. This room, safe from the prying eyes of the world, yet with a door into the open air, was ideal.

I shuddered. I wouldn't like to think what would have happened if anyone had started shooting in there. I could see, outlined by a square of light through its frame, a door at the far end of the room.

There was just enough light to see that there was a long table down the middle of the room. I decided it would be in my best interest not to bump into it and made my way towards the door. I pressed against it to listen. I could hear voices, but couldn't make out what they were saying; the speakers were too far away.

The question was, were they somewhere in the corridor, where they could see the door I stood behind, or were they in one of the rooms, out of sight? There was a Yale type lock in the door, which I could open from my side; whoever made the bombs evidently liked to be in peace.

Opening the door a fraction, I peeped out into the well lit stairwell beyond. It sounded as if the speakers were above me, on the top-floor landing. Before me I could see a polished wooden balustrade, not a very fancy one and the stairs themselves, going up on my right and down on my left. On my landing there were two other doors. What lay behind them? And where had they put Irene? And Delauney?

Twenty Nine

Just at that, all hell broke loose as someone came running into the house, shouting. There was a thunder of footfalls as the two speakers ran down the stairs past me. From the door on my left, more men issued. They were all armed, mostly with Uzi sub-machine guns. My absence had been noted.

Then, from below, I heard a voice that sent a tingle of satisfaction running through me. It was a voice I'd have known anywhere, just because I'd listened, to it over and over in my head in the sleepless hours after I found out who was behind all this.

It was Dick Moran. And he was no fool.

As everyone else went running out into the garage to find me, Moran started to make his way up the stairs. I froze. I doubt if he really thought that I was up there, inside his precious workshop, but he was going to make sure. I couldn't let him catch me there; I wasn't ready. I saw his shadow lengthen on the wall as he climbed the stairs.

There was only one way to go and that was up. I had no choice. I closed the door and flitted up the stairs to the attic floor just in time.

I rolled out onto the floor of the landing. From beneath the door of each of the rooms came a glow of light. I could hear Moran, only feet below me, slipping his key into the lock of the door I'd so recently closed.

I went for the room to the back of the house, I tried the door, it was locked. I rapped on it. "Qui?" demanded a voice from within. "C'est moi...Antoine," I chanced, hoping my luck would hold. "Ca va." I glanced behind me; Moran and a companion, whom I was sure was the real Antoine, had entered the bomb-workshop and switched on the light.

The occupant of the attic room was fumbling with the lock. He opened the door. When he saw me he tried to cry out but my hand was already over his mouth. I pushed him back into the room within. The terror was bright in his eyes as I dealt with his carotid with a slashing stroke of the saw-blade, slicing his windpipe too. . I made a good job of it and he made no sound as he fell to the floor. I pushed him aside and prepared to fight off another attack. But none came.

Before me, looking on with horror mixed with relief on their faces, were the trussed figures of Joseph and Françoise. I closed and locked the door and I stepped over the twitching body of the guard, whose blood had spread all over the cheap carpet. The prisoers were n a bed, their ankles and hands bound and a strip of tape across their mouths.

I swore. Whoever had tied them up had beaten Joseph up for good measure. I dreaded to think what they might have done to Françoise. I moved across to her and cut her bindings. She gasped and breathed heavily and then turned to help Joseph.

I returned to the door. Françoise spoke softly to her man as she cut him free. His face was swollen and bleeding from many hurts that hadn't properly healed. He looked over at me and managed something that might have been a smile.

I raised my hand in recognition and pressed my ear to the door. There was someone moving outside.

"Everything okay?" a voice called out, in French.

"Sure," I replied, keeping my voice as gruff as I could. "You hear anything?"

"Keep on your toes. Those creeps let that interfering bastard loose." The footsteps moved away and I allowed myself to breathe a sigh of relief.

Françoise was watching me from the bed. "Oh, Johnny, thank God. I thought..."

"Ssh. We're, not out of this yet. Antoine brought you here?"

"That's right: it was a nightmare. They wouldn't believe us when we said we knew nothing...They beat poor Joseph so."

"Yeah. That's their style. I found out about Antoine today, too. I think he probably betrayed Delauney as well."

"I thought I heard them, last night, with someone else, in the room next door. And earlier this evening I was sure I heard Irene. She was close by, too."

"They took her when they took me." I wondered what Moran had promised Antoine in return for his treachery.

The guard was dead. He was dressed in green combat fatigues, with a khaki field jacket over the top. I checked each pocket in turn and made a pile of the contents on the bed.

"What do you know about the operation here?" I asked Françoise.

"Nothing: only that they are not French, these people."

I thought about that as I looked through the pile on the bed. A pack of Marlboro, some coins, French, spare clips of ammo for the Uzi. There was a photograph of an elderly couple whom I took to be the man's mother and father. And a standard American Zippo lighter, but on it was an inscription, a design of a dragon breathing fire and round it the words 'The Golden Church of the Christian Sword'.

I looked at that long and hard and the more I looked, the odder it seemed. I leaned over to the body and rolled up the left sleeve of the jacket. There it was all right. His name and his blood group. I let the arm fall from my grasp.

"Well I'll be damned!" I turned to Françoise. "How many are there of them?"

"A dozen, maybe."

"Okay," I said. "I'm pretty sure that whatever they're going to do, they're going to do it tonight. There's little time left. And they have Delauney and Irene. I don't know whose side Delauney's on any more, but I have to get Irene out."

Françoise nodded.

"And then I want Moran." Very quietly I opened the door of the room. The coast was clear and from downstairs I could hear the echoes of an argument. Moran was doing most of the talking and, I guessed, Antoine was taking the dressing-down.

"I warned you about him! I told you he was once the best operative the British had. You left him unguarded and you didn't check to see if he was still there...He could be anywhere."

"He probably got out back at the house." It was Antoine, all right.

"You're sure you weren't followed? I mean, really sure? You know, Macfarlane's a pro."

"I'm sure."

"Okay. But I'm bringing the operation forward. The teams are to move into position immediately."

"But what about...You know that Charriet..."

"Shut it, or you'll end up like that weasel Koestler. Do you think I care what a corrupt French businessman wants? I have a mission here!"

"You would go ahead on your own? You're crazy! I wash my hands of you and this whole insane scheme!"

"Really? Is that the way you guys do business? You wait until I get your boss out of the way so that you can take over and then you welch on the deal?" There were two loud bangs, silence for a moment and then the sound of something heavy tumbling to the wooden floor. "Goddamn shit-for-brains hoodlum!"

I softly closed the door and turned back to Françoise. "Okay. You'll have to come with me. How fit are you?"

Sooner or later someone was going to try to get into that room and I didn't want to be there. I opened the window. The room faced the rear of the house and with any luck we should be able to get down onto the flat roof one floor below.

Both Joseph and Françoise were stiff from being tied up for so long, so it was slow, but before too long we were all standing out on the ledge outside. The window was of the dormer type and below us was a gutter; if we could find the down pipe, then all we would have to do would be to slither down it. So long as it didn't come right away from the wall. Slowly, inch by inch we made our way out along the roof until we reached the down pipe.

I went down first, to try it out: it held. Then came Françoise and finally Joseph.

"Come on, quickly!" I hissed and led the way to the door I'd used on my way in, the one that led onto the wooden staircase. But instead of going down, I held my friends back and gingerly felt my way into the room on the other side, where the floor was rotten.

"It s okay," I whispered. "Stay right next to the wall. But if anyone comes in and steps in the middle, there, down they go." I'd brought with me the Uzi that I'd taken from the guard. I pressed it into Françoise' hands. She was helping Joseph to remain upright against the wall and I could see her eyes flash in the gloom.

"You know how to use this, don't you?" I asked and took off the safety.

She nodded.

I was half-crazed with worry about Irene. She was still somewhere in that house, if she was alive at all. I had to get her out. I crossed the flat roof and shinned my way up the guttering pipe once more. As I came to the top, I dropped the broken saw blade that had been my weapon, but I did not return for it. Time was too pressing. I regained the room that had been my friends' prison, quickly crossed to the door and opened it.

The whole of the house was bustling with activity now; Moran had meant it when he'd said that there would be no further delay. These men were well trained troops going into action. I could hear orders being rapped out and responses given, the drumming of rapid footsteps and the deadly snapping of well-oiled gun-bolts being shut home.

I waited. I had a hunch that Moran himself would not accompany his teams out on their mission. His job would be over as soon as they launched themselves into action. If I wanted him, I had to pay attention. The sounds of activity died down and I heard, from the distance, the sounds of car engines being started and the deep rumble of the great garage door being slid back; and then, with a roar, they were gone.

I no longer cared much what the terrorists were about to do; all I thought of as I heard them growl off into the night was that the odds had been shortened in my favour.

I went into action. As I stepped out into the landing, I heard a voice I did not recognise and from inside the door to my left, as if in response, came the unmistakeable sound of a gun being cocked. I gave the door a splintering kick that burst lock and hinge.

The guard, a thick set man in fatigues, spin round to face me, but in two long, low strides I was on him, shoulder-charging him back. He reeled against the wall, holding onto his Uzi, though he had no time to aim. I followed up, moving in, sweeping his weapon to the side with my left forearm and then delivering a full power punch from the hip into his body.

He choked and winced and tried, to draw back and my foot struck a sledge-hammer blow to his knee, tearing his patella from its ligaments and sending him crashing to the floor. His gun clattered under the bed away from his grasp. In a last blind panic he leapt after it, but he never reached it, for as he stretched out along the floor, I brought down the edge of my foot on the side of his neck and had the grin satisfaction of hearing the ripe crack of the vertebral column parting.

All that preparation had been worthwhile, well worthwhile.

But it was not Irene who was lying on the bed, badly beaten; it was Delauney. They hadn't bothered to bind him, when they'd done. He looked at me with eyes that were puffed and swollen and his lips began to move.

"Not now, Delauney," I said, quickly. "They've got Irene."

"I know, I know," he nodded.

"I'm going after them."

"Did she...Did she tell you?" he croaked. "Yes, I can see from the way that you look at me. He...the American, has her with him. He knows how you feel about her and he intends to use that against you."

I thought as much.

He coughed and a trickle of blood escaped his mouth. They must have ripped him up inside when they beat him. His voice was a whisper and he coughed again. "Help me up."

I looked at him in surprise. "You must be joking, you're too badly hurt."

Delauney flashed his eyes at me angrily. "You can have Moran. You can have him. You crazy bastard, if you'd just got out in the first place, maybe none of this would ever have happened. So you owe me now." The sweat was pouring off his brow and his lip was set. "But I want a word with that shit Antoine!"

"You're too late. Didn't you hear the shots? "

"You mean? Oh my, that's funny! I told him they were crazy, there was no chance...but he went behind my back! He decided to take up with them, to betray me...me! Auguste Delauney, who brought him up from the gutter, from nothing, from being a little message-boy soldier, made him my friend, my lieutenant...that was how he was going to pay me back, by handing me over, trussed like a turkey, to these savages! And then they killed him. Poor little Antoine! I tell you it's what I'd have done to him."

"He brought you straight here?"

"Well, no...When I left you last night, I went to see a lady friend; she always helps when I feel bad. And the things Irene told me...I felt really bad. Then, while I was there, in the middle of the night, there was a phone call. It was Antoine.

"I was pretty surprised. I thought he was at the chalet, but he said no, that he had to see me straight away, in the city. I was to tell no-one, except Raoul." Delauney sighed. "If I had not been so angry, I would not have. But in any case, someone at the house must have tipped them off. They would not believe me when I told them you were alone. Then they began asking questions about Irene; but I told them nothing."

"Your loyalty is touching," I said. "You'd better stay here while..."

"I can still use a piece," he hissed between clenched teeth. "Give me his gun."

I stooped, picked up the Uzi and handed it to him.

"What are we waiting for?" His eyes glittered and I could see that though injured, he had fight left in him. We left the room together, in time to see two men coming up the stairs. There was no way we could avoid them. Their eyes widened in astonishment and they went for their guns. I felt a large hand shove me to one side and the cacophony of Delauney's Uzi discharging assaulted my ears.

I suppose that you could say that that was when the shit really hit the fan. The men went tumbling downwards like dummies and the house was alive with shouting before they even hit the landing below.

"Come on!" I hissed to Delauney and launched myself down the stairs. A man came out of the room on the landing, beside the bomb workshop, but he didn't even get the chance to find out what was happening before a punch smashed his throat to pulp. He fell, choking, to the ground. Before it hit the deck I'd caught his gun, kicked open the door of the room he'd come out of and fired the whole contents of the magazine. The men in there had no chance; they were dead before they comprehended what had happened.

Thirty

There was silence in the house, now, save for groans from those who had not yet expired. I turned and ran down the stairs to the ground floor. I could hear the laboured breath of Delauney following me.

All the lights were on in the hallway and the front door, which led into the garage, was open. I swore and ran out, throwing myself through the aperture and rolling, paratrooper fashion, lest Moran was ahead of me and waiting. But there was silence in the echoing space beyond.

A little along the wall from the door I'd come through, there was a bank of switches and I made for them, flooding the whole place with neon light as I threw myself into the cover of the Cadillac.

I began to move along the wall towards the old wooden stairway, slowly, slowly, expecting at any moment to see Moran leap into the open and start shooting. I put down the Uzi. The magazine was empty anyway.

I was about half way across the space between the door and the far rail when it happened. Two of them. And they had me well covered. They were, like the others, dressed in fatigues.

"Well, if it isn't the interfering British agent," said one, in a deep Southern States drawl. "I think your game is up, don't you?"

I was wondering what to do when I heard two shots from the direction of the house. The man who had spoken looked to the side, only for an instant, but it was long enough. I took him with a kick and then I threw myself onto his companion with all my strength. He made the fatal mistake of trying to turn and run, but I caught him from behind and then, with my arm round his neck, jerked his back over my knee. His spinal column snapped like a sapling.

"Hold it right there," came the voice of the other, who'd recovered both his wind and his weapon. "That was pretty fancy stuff. Let's see how you like this little number." He raised his gun, his knuckles whitened on the trigger; desperately I flung myself sideways to try to escape the inevitable hail of lead. I saw the first puffs of smoke from the ugly black snout of his gun and then, amidst the echoing rattle of fire, I saw his expression change to shock. He collapsed backwards, a barrage of fire making his body twitch as if it were still alive.

I just lay still for a moment; I couldn't believe that I bought my ticket yet. I rolled over, looked up and there was Françoise, standing half way up the wooden staircase, with the still-smoking Uzi in her hands.

"Thanks. Are you all right?"

She nodded, but didn't say anything: she just let the gun drop. She turned to Joseph, who was at her side and began to help him down the stairs.

"Both of you get out of here. There are people coming. Tell them who you are, that you're with me."

"What about you?"

I got to my feet and began to make my way back to the house. There was silence now, absolute silence. I edged my way in through the door; at first I could see nothing and. then, I saw a foot sticking out through one of the doors of the hallway. It moved, slowly and I moved forward. I knew who it was; no-one else wore socks like that.

Delauney was still alive when I got to him, but it was not going to last. He'd taken two in the chest and was lying in a pool of his own blood.

"Moran?"

"Yes. He got away. I tried to stop him, I swear. He has her! You must get to him; kill him. He has her!"

"Where did they go?"

"Upstairs again. He heard the shooting outside." He closed his eyes, his face screwed up with the pain. "I thought they'd got you, Johnny. When I heard the shooting I thought it was all over. You are... You are a lucky bastard." He groaned. "Shot me like a dog. In cold blood. Johnny? Kill him for me."

I hardly noticed as the baron of the underworld known as Auguste Delauney went limp in my arms; my thoughts were elsewhere.

Not far from Delauney was Antoine's body. I could see, poking out from his trouser waistband, the butt of my Luger. I took it: it was like meeting an old friend again. Moran had gone back to his bomb-factory, for good reason, I had no doubt. The house was probably rotten with booby traps and he'd gone to activate them before he finally baled out.

I was half-way up the stairs when I heard his voice. "Is that you, Johnny? Yes, it is, isn't it? Come on in, I'm waiting for you. And no fancy stuff, because I've got the girl here and we don't want her to get hurt, do we?"

I straightened from the crouch I'd instinctively adopted. "Moran? Dick? Listen, we can trade. Let the girl go."

"What do I get? What could you possibly have that I'd want?"

"I'll let you go. I won't kill you; you can go back, to the American Embassy, or whatever."

"The American Embassy? That would do me a lot of good!" I could, hear him laughing. "No, Johnny, that won't do. But I tell you what; you come on up here, then you and the girl can have the pleasure of dying together."

I hesitated, wondering what to do and then I heard a squeal of pain in a voice that was unmistakeable. "Aah! Salaud!"

"Leave her alone!" I made the intervening space to the door of the room in three strides.

"Put down the gun, Johnny," he said as I entered the room. He was standing with his arm round Irene's neck. She was nearly choking. With his other hand he held a pistol to her temple. "Long time no see, huh?"

"That's right, Dick," I said and gently put the Luger on the floor. "Long time. We all thought you were killed, long ago."

"All part of the plan, pal."

"Just like hitting Julie and the boys, Dick?" I looked into the eyes of the man who stood there, the face that I'd hunted for so long, the face I hadn't seen since that evening, so long ago so far away. "Let her go, Dick."

"What for? Old times sake? No. I think I'll hang on to the little lady a while longer, if you don't mind." Irene wasn't even struggling and I guessed that Moran was holding her so tightly that she could hardly breathe.

"Then what?" I asked, simply. "Why don't you shoot? Finish me?"

He just shook his head again, "No, no that's not what I have in mind." He laughed, an icy, deadly laugh, that sent a shiver down my spine. "You know, Macfarlane, you've screwed up a lot of what I'd planned. You've kept in touch when I thought you'd lose me. You've been lucky, too."

"Luckier than my two kids were, eh, Dick?"

"Oh, come on, now. That was unavoidable; when you came back to Paris, we had no choice but to take you out."

"Yes: of course, you really had no idea at all who I was working for."

"That's right; we just didn't know."

"You never even stopped to think that perhaps, just maybe, I'd be out of the game entirely."

He shook his head. "I guess that was a mistake...no, missing you was our mistake, but there won't be any more. I'm through here and you're just where I want you."

I smiled. "I guess you're right. Come on. You can tell me now. When did you go private?"

"Well, you took your time, Johnny my boy, but you got there in the end. I never rejoined the Service after Chile. I wanted to, but they wouldn't let me. Can you believe that? New administration, my methods were unsound, just like they said when they put an end to Tomahawk in 'Nam. Goddammit, it was the only thing we did in that whole fucken tragedy that actually worked!"

"You wanted to go further than the CIA – even the CIA – thought was viable, so you set up your own little party?" I made the mistake of stepping forward,

"That's far enough!" screamed Moran and I could see Irene wince.

But he calmed down. He wanted to talk, you see, he wanted to justify himself, to clear his name with someone he knew would understand, who had worked for one of the companies. "You know," he went on, "We just couldn't be sure about you: we might even have asked you in. We could have used an operator like you."

I shook my head. "No, Dick. There was never any chance that I'd have joined in."

"No. Well, then we did the right thing."

"Charriet pays for all this?" I wanted to keep him talking. I reasoned that the longer I could, the less chance there was of him doing anything drastic and the more chance there was of my thinking of something.

"Charriet? Not on your life. I wasn't going to trust that goddamn Frenchman. I never wanted him involved. But he's connected with one of our backers in the States and we were forced to."

"So even as a freelance you don't get it your own way."

"Yeah, well at least I'm not muzzled by a bunch of namby-pamby, bleeding-heart liberals. At least the people behind me now know when something has to be done!"

His face contorted. "Europe! Shit. Europe! This place is a stinking mess, man. I mean, the Commies are in everywhere, you've got Soviet-backed so-called peace movements all over the continent, even attacking our boys and your fucken Governments won't do a damned thing to stop it! Then they even have the nerve to suggest that the Russkis are just the big ol' friendly bear in the East; who the hell do you people think you are? You owe the fact that your countries exist at all to us and you ain't even grateful. It's well past time to teach you a lesson, pal."

"All part of your Holy Mission, I suppose," I said, sarcastically.

"Don't worry about that," snarled Moran. "God makes a good cover, but we know what has to be done. And it's going to be; it was a good try, pal, but it wasn't good enough. By lunchtime tomorrow this country is going to be plunged into confusion and the precious European project dead in the water. You were just too late."

"Just let the girl go," I said. "Take me as your hostage."

"You're kidding, aren't you? I'd rather stuff a rattlesnake in my pocket."

"You won't get out, you know," I said, quietly.

"You're not going to stop me."

I just smiled and shrugged my shoulders. Maybe Moran didn't have the acute hearing I had, or maybe it was because he wasn't expecting to hear what I'd been waiting to hear, but in the end it penetrated. The sound of vehicles, drawing up outside the building.

For the very first time, a trace of uncertainty crossed his face. "What the hell is that?"

"Glover, I should imagine, with all the help he thinks he'll need. He probably asked along the Bureau and the Squadron Bleu for company. Plus enough CRS to handle any of the hired help you have left."

"What do you mean?"

"Dick, your mind is slipping; I knew where this place was before I was brought here. Your spy told me, before you killed him. As soon as I knew, I called in the cavalry. You're not going to get away. Not this time."

Moran's face contorted into a snarl of rage.

"Let the girl go," I repeated. "She's no use as a hostage against the people outside."

He shook his head. "I'm not finished yet!" He circled round the table. It was still covered with oddments of electrical bits and pieces, the makings of timers and pressure-switches. He got to the door I'd first entered through.

Of course, I had the key in my pocket. He didn't have the time to argue the niceties of the situation with me.

I held up the key. "This what you're looking for?"

"Give me that!"

"Give me the girl."

"I could kill you both!"

"And get away? Face it, Dick; our people are coming up the stairs." Moran hesitated an instant and then threw Irene to one side; she gasped and fell to her knees by the window. I threw the key to him and, as he stooped to pick it up, I hit the light switch and rolled for cover under the table. Moran's gun spat twice and the bullets slammed into the plaster of the far wall of the room. My grasping fingers felt the comforting cool of the butt of the Luger, as I scrambled for Irene's side. By the time I got there, I could see the door onto the roof swinging wide. "Irene! Are you okay? Can you walk?"

"Yes, sure."

"We have to get out of here; this place is booby-trapped!" I helped Irene to her feet and began to make for the stairs, when we were knocked back by a blast, followed by searing heat; there was no escape that way. The only way out was to follow Moran.

I pushed Irene through the still-open door. She stumbled and we both fell, which was as well, because the deadly crack of Moran's pistol sounded. He was over by the door into the garage. I aimed for his muzzle flash and returned fire, then rolled out of the door and to the side. At that moment, the moon came out from behind a screen of clouds and showed him.

He was in the corner of the flat roof by the rotten old door, climbing down a ladder leaning against the railings on the far edge of the roof. We saw each other in the same instant; but he was holding on to the ladder and I was ready to fire. Before he could bring his gun up, I gave him three rounds and he jerked backwards and fell heavily into the alley below, crashing down amongst the dustbins and pulling the ladder down on top.

I grabbed Irene's hand and led her over the roof. We paused and looked down' Moran's spread-eagled body lay in a pile of garbage, slowly leaking a stain of blood that showed black in the moonlight. "So long, Dick," I muttered, to no one in particular.

Suddenly there was another dexplosion within the house and then several more around the garage. I looked back; the windows were already glowing with the light of the fire inside. I smelled the stench of petrol and I swore. "Fire bombs."

"Johnny...I..." I was just in time to catch Irene as she slumped, in a faint, at my side. She had reached the end of her strength. I pushed open the rickety rotten door before me and made my way down the wooden stairs as quickly as I could, trying not to let her head hit the walls as we went.

Down below the garage was itself ablaze and I couldn't see the door for the swirling clouds of smoke; but there was no other way, because my route back upstairs was blocked. The inferno had taken hold of the tarred wooden timbers of the roof. I put Irene's body over my shoulder and headed forwhere I knew the sliding doors must be.

I ran head down into the smoke and blistering heat, through the stink of bodies being roasted where they lay. I was blind and the fumes wereso thick that I could hardly breathe. It seemed that I had been running for eternity when I ran slap into the door.

I tried to haul it open, but the heat of the fire in the roof overhead had so buckled the runners that it was jammed solid. Pieces of burning debris were falling all around me now. I hammered on the door but I knew there was no hope of the sound being heard over the roar of the inferno and the pistol-shot cracking of old, dry timber bursting into flames. I staggered back.

My throat was on fire and I coughed and spluttered. The only other way out was through the house; that was how Joseph and Françoise must have escaped. But then the house hadn't been ablaze.

I staggered again and fetched up against something hard. My hand fell on it. The Cadillac! It was our only hope. I managed to get Irene into the back seat and then I got in. It wasn't happy to start, but it did and through the streams of tears that the smoke was wringing from my eyes, I found the selector for the slush-box and gave the vast beast full throttle.

The last thing I remember seeing was the wooden door, blazing already, appear momentarily in the glare of the headlamps, before we crashed into it and my head hit the steering wheel of the car.

Thirty One

There was a figure, dressed all in white, hovering near the perimeter of my vision. It came towards me and I was overwhelmed by the whiteness; and then all went black again.

The next I remember was waking up more fully. This time the nurse came over and spoke in gentle tones. She had a bright, pretty face, with freckles. She soothed my brow and then took my pulse. I felt strength begin to return to my limbs and I tried to speak; but my voice was only a whisper and my throat burned.

"Ssh...You must rest now," said the nurse.

"Where am I?" I managed.

"All Saints Military Hospital. You're safe here."

"Safe? What happened to me? How did I get here?"

"You do not remember? You were in a fire. They brought you in two nights ago; you were burned, but you will be all right."

Then it all came flooding back to me; the house, Moran, the fire; and Irene. With a sudden gasp at the pain of recall, I tried to raise myself, but I hadn't the strength.

"Ssh," scolded the pretty nurse. "You must rest!"

"I must know...Was there anyone else brought in with me? A girl? Her name is Irene."

The nurse stopped fretting with my pillow and smiled. "If you mean the young lady who has been waiting all morning to see you..." She stepped over to the door and then, another, familiar shape moved into my field of vision, a sight more welcome than I have words to relate.

Irene only hesitated in her headlong rush towards me to check herself so that she didn't hurt me, before pressing the sweet tenderness of her lips onto mine. "Oh, Johnny, thank Christ! We were so worried about you!"

"We?" I croaked.

"Yes. Joseph and Françoise are here too. They're okay. Oh, Johnny!" she cried again and kissed me; then she brought up a chair and sat by the bed and we just murmured quiet words to each other for a while.

It turned out that the shock of the heavy Cadillac bursting through the door of the garage had brought her round and she'd gathered the situation pretty quickly. The car was only halfway out into the street and had already caught fire. She managed, somehow and with God knows what reserves of strength, to drag me out from behind the wheel before I was trapped. Then she had found herself being helped by two men in military uniform. They got us both away seconds before the fuel tank in the car had blown.

She didn't remember too much more, after that, because we had both been bundled into a military ambulance and the medic had given her a sedative. Then she woke up in the hospital and had ever since been making everyone's life hell, until they let her sit outside my ward door until I came round. She had suffered minor burns to her hands, from dragging me from the wreckage of the car; but her spirit was intact.

I drifted off again.

Irene was still at my side, when I woke. The curtains had been drawn closed. She was still dressed in the light dressing-gown but from somewhere or another she'd managed to get hold of some make up. I smiled at her and she kissed me. "There is someone to see you...Do you feel well enough?" she asked and I nodded.

Moments later Rear-Admiral Sir James Glover KBE walked in. "Hello, Macfarlane. Lie still." He drew up a chair and set it alongside the bed. I looked at him. Who would have thought that this gentle-looking old man would have been the brain behind the Firm's operational activities since he'd resigned from the Navy in nineteen fifty-eight? He was the one who'd recruited me all those years ago, at that quiet meeting in the Service Club.

I smiled. It was good to see him. "I killed Moran, sir," I said.

He nodded. "Yes. We got to his body the next day. Bit difficult to identify, of course, but the dental records proved it. Well done, lad."

"Thank you," I went on, "For acting so quickly."

"Yes. I'm sorry about Julie and the boys. Wish you'd called in sooner."

"I couldn't, sir. I had to be sure the Firm wasn't involved."

"One of those misapprehensions, laddie. We weren't sure about you, either. We did have our disagreements and we knew that you knew Moran. It was a tricky situation. By the way, just out of curiosity, what was it that made you sure we were in the clear?"

"When I found out about Charriet. He was too high profile, too ambitious; and he has a reputation for changing sides with the wind. I knew he wasn't the kind of runner you'd back, so as soon as that kid told me where their base was, I got in touch."

"Wise move, Macfarlane. Mind, you seem to have done pretty well without us."

"Sir? Can you tell me anything? I mean, what was it all for?"

Glover sighed and looked at me for a long moment. Then he nodded. "Very well, Macfarlane, I think you've earned this much. To start with, you were right about Zeigler; she was genuine CIA. I'm surprised that you never came across her before, in fact. But she was also working for Moran. She wrote down the details of the work she did for Moran, dates, names, who paid the bills, all that and transferred it to a computer disk." Glover rocked back and forth in his chair, resting his gloved hands on his umbrella and watching me with the amused delight of a conjurer pulling off a successful trick.

"And do you know where she hid the disk? Well, I'll tell you; she pasted it into the cover of that notebook you recovered from her flat. We found it where you said it would be; a priceless document indeed!

"Anyway, I'm getting ahead of myself," Glover went on. "We became aware that Dick Moran had not, indeed, perished in the field, soon after you parted company with us. He'd been injured, but not killed. Our Washington mole was able to tell us that he'd been brought back to the States and patched up. But the CIA wouldn't have him back.

"Somewhere along the line, he'd become unbalanced, perhaps as a result of the concussion, perhaps something else and just at the time they were taking a lot of flak over their tactics in Chile. Moran was, I suppose, a scapegoat. He disappeared from view entirely for a while and then, of all places, he turned up in South Carolina, with a survivalist group."

"The Golden Church of the Christian Sword."

"That's right. The Church is a sort of Bible-thumping Falangist organisation. The Southern States are infested with these groups at the moment. Most of them are harmless noisemakers, but some constitute an effective paramilitary force. It seems that the Church was one of these. Moran had been recruiting a lot of Vietnam veterans into the ranks...Trained men, able to take orders; and with their help he turned a forgotten chapter of an obscure cult into the force they are – or were."

"Yes, sir. I knew they were military. It was obvious."

"Moran had been keeping up clandestine contacts with the CIA and of course, as always in politics, a change of Administration means a change of outlook. All of a sudden Moran's methods were right back in vogue and our American friends became decidedly tight-lipped about him. I don't think they trusted our Government.

"We did know he'd been given financial backing, but we didn't know for what. But we were on high alert. Then, Zeigler turned up on our radar again. In Paris. Now, we knew that she was connected with Moran; we think they might have been lovers.

"Whether they were or not – and Zeigler used sex as a weapon – she had a habit of being near him, so we wondered if he might show up. We knew that you knew Moran, but we didn't know if you were involved or not. It seemed unlikely but we couldn't take chances. You and Moran together would have been very dangerous. So we arranged that job in Damascus to get you out of the way till we worked it out."

"You did that? Well done – I hadn't a clue."

"Yes. Anyway, you were in such hurry to get back that we were very suspicious. I mean, you usually like to hang about and sample the local low-life."

"It was Christmas."

"Yes and with hindsight I see that. Still, we all make mistakes. But our usual Washington sources either didn't know anything or weren't telling and MI6 were very twitchy. You know what they're like. Having two of the best black-ops men in the world, both allegedly retired, working together, would have been a major security issue. So, since you were our responsibility, we put your flat under surveillance.

"We were even more suspicious to find that Julie seemed to have struck up a friendship with Zeigler. That really had MI6 in a tizzy. They wanted to terminate you immediately as a precaution, but they couldn't find you." He looked at me gravely. "We were under a lot of pressure from those fops and I couldn't have blocked them forever. They might even have been rash enough to use their own agents. So sending you on a wild-goose-chase to Damascus did have some benefits." He paused.

"Zeigler was a regular visitor to your apartment, you know, even before you left."

"Julie was...She was a very unhappy woman."

"I know; I am sorry. Deeply. Anyway, on Christmas Eve Zeigler visited the flat; then she left. She'd been visiting several times a week, so our man thought nothing of it. He didn't even know that you had returned to Paris that evening. So I'm afraid he stood there, watching, while it all happened. Then you arrived, injured and came out later, with a girl. Something was obviously up, so our man called in and tailed you.

"You were followed to the young lady's flat, but then I'm rather afraid we seem to have lost you."

I smiled.

"Then we got the tip that Moran had turned up, much as we feared he would and shortly after that we lost our best mole in Paris." He looked steadily at me. "Harry Jonsun."

"Harry was your man?" I hadn't expected that.

"Well, Harry was many people's man. But we did have a good working relationship with him. When he turned up dead after you met him, MI6 threw a hissy fit. They went above our heads. There was nothing we could do except take a back seat and wait for something to happen. I mean, if we couldn't find you there was no chance that lot would. And then, you brought matters to a head."

"I see."

"For what it's worth, I always had full confidence in you, Macfarlane. But I answer to the Cabinet and at the end of the day I have to take orders like everyone else. And MI6 had a point."

"Thank you, sir."

"Moran had come over with his group, while Zeigler was here preparing the ground for him. But we couldn't see their end-game. It was far too much effort just to embarrass the French."

Glover looked at me long and hard. "We only found out when we finally cracked the code in that computer disk. The White House briefed Moran to impede unification between the European states, particularly on currency and defence. He had been given full discretion. Of course, Moran was a freelance and the only connection was through Zeigler. Which makes that disk very valuable to us.

"The planned attack on the Summit was part of Moran's strategy. Marc Joubert was to address the meeting at the inaugural session. As you know, he is the single most respected voice on the subject of European integration. We have no doubt that he would have died in the attack. It would have set the project back years, perhaps decades. And at the same time would have deeply embarrassed our security services."

"So what are we – you – going to do about it?"

"Do about it? Nothing, my boy. The White House knows we have Zeigler's disk. They don't know everything that's on it, which may be very useful. That should be enough. We don't want to rock the boat too much. The Americans, for all the many faults they may have, are still our allies; it wouldn't do to cause a scene. And there's no need to; thanks to you, the attack never happened, Zeigler and Moran are both terminated and we know everything.

"By any standard it was a disaster for the CIA. It will be some time before Washington gets enough nerve to try anything like that again."

"What about Charriet, sir?"

"It turned out that his major funder was Intercontinental Enterprises – the CIA. All the details were on Zeigler's disk. Our friends at the Sûreté can be less than subtle, but very useful, you know. We shared the information with them and they called Charriet in for a chat, as we knew they would. They let him know he had no more secrets. His career was over, his reputation ruined.

"There would have been the most shocking outcry – the champion of the French Right accepting American money to help organise bombing attacks on French soil?

"Charriet shot himself; probably the best under the circumstances. Moran was setting him up to carry the can anyway."

He rose to go, arid then checked himself. "By the way, I've lodged some funds in your Swiss account. Out of the contingency budget, you understand. I think it would be as well if you were to take a holiday. You know what I mean."

"Yes, sir. Thank you."

He rose and stretched out his hand to shake mine. "Nice to see you again, Macfarlane. I noticed that there was a rather pretty young lady with you earlier. Why don't you take her somewhere she'd like?

I understand she's had something of a rough time. Oh and, laddie, I don't know how you'd feel, but we could use you, again. Call me when you get back, hmm?"

He smiled roguishly. "Something brewing in Argentina, you know. The last lot in the FO left a most hellish can of worms. And there's plenty of work at home, too."

Three days later we bade farewell to Joseph and Françoise at Charles de Gaulle airport. It was a more cheerful event than the last time we'd taken leave of each other. Glover had been generous to them too and they were planning a holiday of their own; also his idea. He didn't want the Bureau putting the screws on them.

Irene and I were going to the Philippines, partly because it's a nice place and partly because I didn't think anyone would look for us there. After that? We hadn't decided. We thought we'd play it by ear. We were in no hurry.

Delauney came up with the goods in the end too: it turned out he'd willed all he had to Irene. Like I say, we were in no hurry.

"What did you say we were going to do?" asked Irene as the plane taxied down the runway ready to take off.

"I told you; we're going to a tropical paradise and we're going to live like kings for a while."

"I hope this paradise has a good bed," she went on, nodding thoughtfully. "Maybe you'd better cable ahead." She finished buckling her seat belt and turned her face up to me. I reached over and brushed a stray strand of hair away from her eye.

"There's something I want right now, Johnny," intoned Irene, in that voice I knew meant she was serious. "Something I've been waiting for."

"What?"

Suddenly she grinned and it was as if the sun had come out.

"A kiss. For Christmas."

THE END

About Me

Picture: Charis Fleming

I am a Scottish photographer, multimedia artist and writer, with a long career as a freelance journalist and photographer.

I write books on a variety of topics in both fiction and non-fiction. I remain active as a writer, photographer, printmaker and publisher.

I graduated with Bachelor of Art with Honours from Edinburgh College of Art in 1983, majoring in sculpture and also pursuing life-drawing, printmaking and film-making.

After graduation I worked in film-making before returning to photography. During this time I also pursued Journalism Studies through Napier University in Edinburgh.

For decades, both as a photographer and Picture Editor, I presented the readers of the newspapers and magazines I worked for, as well as many disparate clients, with the very best of photographic imagery.

After publishing news and feature articles for many years, I began to write more intensely in the 1990s. My first book, *Poaching the River,* was published in 2006.

In 2009 I published my second full-length book, *The Warm Pink Jelly Express Train.*

I fulfilled an ambition I had held for many years and graduated with a Master of Fine Art degree from Dundee University in 2011, where my practical area was photography and printmaking, especially photogravure, and my Dissertation was on Goddess culture.

At the end of 2011 I returned to France and began to focus more on writing.

Books by Rod Fleming

French Onion Soup! ISBN: 978-0-9565007-3-1

The first book in this series, *French Onion Soup!* tells you about about arriving in France, wine, food, the *affouage*—a unique way of gathering winter fuel—French lawyers, renegade mules and many other areas of Burgundian life, in a quirky and hilariously funny style.

A Little Shop of Horors. ISBN: 978-0-9565007-8-6

Creeps and chills from a selection of modern horror stories guaranteed to make you think twise about turning out the light. Most are set in Scotland with authentic background details and tap into the rich folklore of the country. Just right for a winter evening!

Why Men Made God. ISBN: 978-0-9572612-2-8

The Egyptians, Greeks, Romans, Celts and northern Europeans all had pantheons of gods and goddesses. What changed and led to the idea of just one, all-powerful God? Why was the original Goddess abandoned in favour of a sequence of sky-fathers? Who wrote the Bible and why? What impact does that have on us today?

Why Men Made God answers these questions, in a pacy and easy-to-read manner, backed up with science. With Karis Burkowski.

The Warm Pink Jelly Express Train. ISBN: 978-0-9572612-3-5

Brian Macmaster is a journalist licking the wounds of a divorce in Paris. He meets a transsexual prostitute who leads him into a spider's-web of intrigue, deception and extortion. *The Warm Pink Jelly Express Train* is a sexy, powerful, relentlessly paced novel that is not only a page-turner but also explores one of the most fascinating taboos of contemporary culture.

Croutons and Cheese! ISBN: 978-0-9572612-4-2

The ongoing adventures of the Fleming family in France. This hilarious book has bulls in the back passage, throat holder-uppers, green poo, flaming Daimlers, flying cats and much more to keep you amused from cover to cover. Pour youself a nice glass of Burgaundy and enjoy!

The Children of Aldebaran. ISBN: 978-0-9572612-1-1

The time of the Big People is past and the world is ruled by the Animals. Silas Farsight, a young otter who looks forward to a life as a lawyer in the forest village, is horrified when his cousin is kidnapped by a gang of ferocious cats. With his indentured clerk Stoatwise Cuttleworth, he sets off in pursuit.

His cousin, Magda, is being taken to the Dark City, where an evil beast known as the Great Cat is plotting imperial domination of the Free Animals. Silas must rescue her. His adventures lead him to the Sea Otters, a wild and mysterious people, of whom he knows only myth and legend. Yet it is with them that he will find his own true destiny. A fast-paced and exciting fantasy adventure.

Poaching the River. ISBN: 978-0-9554535-0-2

It's a typical sleepy afternoon in Auchpinkie, a tiny fishing village on the east coast of Scotland. But all that's about to change. The action races to its riotous climax, as local hero Big Sandy poaches the River Pinkie in a daring adventure, the public convenience is destroyed by a freak explosion, and the minister is baffled by the sudden religious conversion of two formerly heathenish young lads. *Poaching the River* will make you laugh and cry out loud.

The Spring Run. ISBN: 978-0-9572612-5-9

Spring is coming to the village of Auchpinkie on the east coast of Scotland. With it, women's minds turn to romance and men's to something else — poaching. But it turns out these are actually very closely related. *The Spring Run* is a hilarious and charming romantic comedy set in a world full of larger-than life characters. (This is a standard-English translation of *Poaching the River.*)

Buying

You can buy my books as paperbacks or as e-books from any good retailer in most of the world, including Amazon, Barnes & Noble, Waterstones and all major e-book retailers.

Alternatively, please navigate to my site at http://rodfleming.com/ where you will find direct links to purchase them online or by digital download.

Visit my Amazon author page!

https://www.amazon.com/author/rodfleming